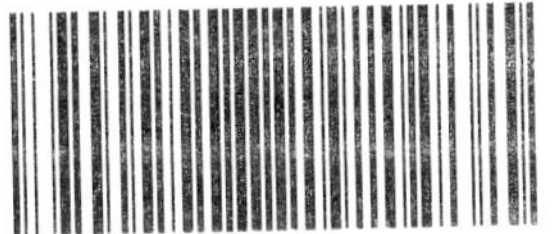

MURDER
on the
FRENCH RIVIERA

BOOKS BY HELENA DIXON

Miss Underhay Mystery series

Murder at the Dolphin Hotel

Murder at Enderley Hall

Murder at the Playhouse

Murder on the Dance Floor

Murder in the Belltower

Murder at Elm House

Murder at the Wedding

Murder in First Class

Murder at the Country Club

Murder on Board

Murder at the Charity Ball

Murder at the Beauty Pageant

Murder at the Village Fair

Murder at the Highland Castle

Murder at the Island Hotel

HELENA DIXON

MURDER
on the
FRENCH RIVIERA

bookouture

Published by Bookouture in 2024

An imprint of Storyfire Ltd.
Carmelite House
50 Victoria Embankment
London EC4Y 0DZ

www.bookouture.com

ISBN: 978-1-83790-060-2
eBook ISBN: 978-1-83790-059-6

For Lynn Forth, my fabulous friend, who gave me so much information about Nice. Much loved and missed by all her friends.

PROLOGUE

Torbay Herald 7th May 1936

Foreign Affairs from Around the World.

In France, the Front Populaire have taken 386 seats out of 608 and have been announced as the winners in the election held on 3rd May. Andre Leon Blum has been declared Prime Minister. A cabinet has now been formed, which for the first time, includes three women.

In Ethiopia, Italian forces are reported to have captured Addis Ababa, entering the capital on 5th May following victory at the battle of Lake Ashangi. Emperor Haile Selassie is reported to have left the country. It is now thought that Mussolini will appoint King Victor Emmanuel III as Emperor of Ethiopia, with General Pietro Badoglio as viceroy.

CHAPTER ONE

Kitty Bryant listened carefully as her husband Matt read the brief newspaper articles aloud to her. They were seated outside on the terrace of her aunt and uncle's home, Enderley Hall, near Exeter. The afternoon sun was warming the stone flags beneath their feet and Bertie, their roan cocker spaniel, snoozed peacefully at her side.

Kitty's aunt and uncle were inside the Hall with her cousin Lucy and her husband Rupert. The roses in the gardens were beginning to open, the sky was blue, and the only other sound was that of a fat bumble bee buzzing around the mossy stone balustrade. It was hard to believe that so much change was happening in the world.

'I take it that you do not think any of these developments are a good thing?' Kitty asked.

She knew her husband had been increasingly concerned, as had her uncle, at the changes taking place abroad. The reoccupation of the Rhineland by Germany in March had seen Matt being called to London. His former government employers had since engaged him on various small errands. Something which worried Kitty since they often carried an element of risk.

'No, I'm afraid not. There are so many signs that things are afoot. The Emperor of Ethiopia and his government have been displaced. And you know that the elections in Spain in February were also another cause for concern with all the civil unrest.' Matt folded the newspaper and dropped it down on the rattan table in front of him. A worried frown creased his forehead.

'Grams says the world has turned upside down since the king passed away in January,' Kitty said. She could see her grandmother's point of view. It had not been so long ago that they had been celebrating King George V's and Queen Mary's Silver Jubilee. Now it seemed that everything was in flux, with the world they had known crumbling away.

Matt smiled at her, a dimple flashing in his cheek. 'That's very true. We shall just have to hope that things settle down again soon.'

Kitty knew that he was trying to reassure her. Matt was a veteran of the Great War and he, like many others, feared that history might repeat itself and another conflict was building. There seemed so much change and unrest in Europe and beyond at present.

Bertie's ears twitched and his paws moved as he chased a rabbit in his dreams. Everything seemed so peaceful, and these changes felt very far away. Kitty could only hope that Matt and her uncle were mistaken about the ominous signs from abroad. Another war after so many had died and there had been so much suffering seemed unthinkable.

This short stay at Enderley with her aunt and uncle was a nice respite from their hectic lives. Matt had been busy running back and forth between London and Devon, while Kitty had managed their private investigative business.

It was also nice to spend time with her cousin Lucy again. Since Lucy's marriage to Rupert and her move to Thurscomb Castle in Yorkshire they had not seen much of one another.

Letters and telephone calls were all well and good, but it was still very pleasant to be able to go for walks and play croquet on Enderley's sweeping lawns.

Kitty's aunt opened the French doors and came out onto the terrace, a large flat-bottomed wicker basket over one arm and her secateurs in her other hand.

'Isn't it a glorious afternoon? I'm just going to do a spot of pruning. Tea will be served at four in the drawing room.'

Kitty smiled as her aunt carried on down the stone steps into her beloved rose garden. Aunt Hortense was an avid gardener, and nothing made her happier than to be outside amongst her roses. She was relieved to see her aunt doing normal things and tried to pull herself fully back to the present, and away from the worrying news.

Lucy's little dog, Muffy, came bounding outside, her tail wagging happily as she sniffed around hopefully for any titbits that Kitty or Matt might have concealed about their persons. Bertie lifted his head briefly to acknowledge her before resuming his snooze. Lucy and Rupert also came to join them. Rupert pulled out a chair from the table for Lucy to take a seat before sitting down himself.

'I take it Mother has gone off into the garden?' Lucy asked, her lips curving up in a smile.

'Of course.' Kitty smiled back.

Rupert and Matt immediately started a conversation about the articles in the newspaper and the possible implications that might follow. Lucy gave Kitty a wan smile.

Kitty thought her cousin looked a little pale, her usual delicate glow missing from her cheeks. Where Kitty was petite with short blonde curls, Lucy was dark haired and this made her new pallor more noticeable.

'Are you well, Lucy?' Kitty asked in a low voice. She knew her cousin had suffered a miscarriage in the autumn, and she was concerned that she might not have fully recovered.

Lucy leaned forward and took hold of Kitty's hand. She glanced at her husband who was engrossed in conversation with Matt, before saying quietly, 'I haven't said anything yet to Rupert so please don't breathe a word, but I suspect I may be pregnant again.'

Kitty squeezed Lucy's hand in delight. 'Oh, darling, that would be marvellous. Of course, I shall say nothing.'

She and Matt had held their own conversations over the last few weeks about if or when they might have a family. Matt's first wife and child had both been killed during the last war and it had taken him a long time to recover from their deaths.

Since Kitty had married Matt at Christmas in 1934, they had not, as her grandmother would have said, fallen for a child. Kitty was unsure if she particularly wished for a baby and Matt had not said anything until recently about his thoughts on the matter. The child he had lost with his first wife, unbeknown to anyone other than Kitty, had been fathered by a fellow married officer.

Matt had met his first wife while she had been pregnant, marrying her to save her from disgrace. They had fallen in love afterwards and Matt had loved little Betty as his own, grieving deeply when she died. It had taken him a long time to get over their deaths. No one except Kitty and Matt knew the truth behind her parentage and his first marriage. Now, though, the issue of having a baby of their own had raised its thorny head.

Matt had asked Kitty to think about what she would like, but the more she thought about it, the less certain she felt. Sometimes she thought it might be quite jolly, other times she could think of nothing worse. There was also the bigger, unspoken question of if it would even be possible since nothing had yet happened.

None of this, however, affected how she felt about Lucy, and she was delighted at the prospect of a baby for her cousin. Lucy and Rupert were the custodians of Thurscomb Castle, and the baby would be the titled heir to the estate. Something that was important for the continuation of the family lineage and to Lucy herself.

Lucy leaned back in her seat, her eyes sparkling now she had shared her secret. She cast a loving glance at her husband and changed the subject. 'Father is in his office. I suspect he would like to disappear down to his laboratory, but Mother has insisted he not do any work while you and Matt are here. She says he needs a break.'

Kitty laughed. Her uncle was notorious for vanishing into the highly secure workshop he had built in the grounds of Enderley. He would work there for hours developing all kinds of materials for the Ministry of Defence.

'Is he worried too about the events abroad?' Kitty asked.

The smile faded from Lucy's lips. 'I think so. He was talking about Mussolini only the other day and the Italian invasion of Ethiopia.'

A prickle of unease crossed the nape of Kitty's neck. It was as if a dark shadow was forming just out of sight. She hoped that Matt and her uncle were wrong about all these events. She knew her uncle was well-connected politically so if he was concerned, then the risk must be real. And yet the idea of another conflict was too terrible to contemplate.

Kitty changed the subject, and they spent the next hour happily talking on the terrace, before returning to the drawing room ready for tea. Muffy and Bertie accompanied them inside, ever ready to take advantage of any cake or biscuit crumbs that might come their way.

The maids wheeled in a trolley laden with delicate china tea things and a glorious multi-tiered stand containing all kinds of delicious pastries and cakes. Kitty's aunt came to join them, massaging rose-scented lotion into her hands.

'Where is your father?' she asked Lucy as the maids withdrew. 'Honestly, that man would forget his own head if he has become embroiled in his work. He had better not have gone to his workshop.'

Rupert had just offered to go and find him when the drawing room door opened once more, and Lucy's father appeared. Lord Medford was a jolly, plump man who always reminded Kitty of a genial grocer. He was accompanied by another man of a similar age and a more military bearing.

Matt immediately sprang to his feet, a look of surprise on his face. 'Brigadier, I wasn't aware that you were visiting.' He extended his hand to the other man.

Kitty sat up straighter in her seat. This must be Brigadier Remmington-Blythe, Matt's employer at Whitehall. She was still rather unclear about what the brigadier's department actually did, but she knew the work was covered by the Official Secrets Act. She had signed the act herself having been involved in the past with various cases for the department, but she had never met the brigadier himself.

Her uncle had many government contacts and she suspected he had the ear not only to most of the cabinet but also to the prime minister himself. Lord Medford knew the brigadier well from his work during the Great War. Quite why the brigadier was now at Enderley though was a very different matter. One that she suspected involved more work for Matt, and possibly for her too.

'Matthew, my boy. Just the person I hoped to find.' The brigadier shook Matt's hand.

'Sir, may I present my wife, Kitty. I know you have spoken on the phone, but I don't believe you've met in person.'

Kitty immediately stood and her hand was enveloped in a large male one and shaken vigorously. 'Mrs Bryant, I am delighted to meet you in person at last.'

'Likewise, I'm sure,' Kitty said and smiled. Privately, she wondered what was coming. The brigadier would not have made the long journey from London all the way to Devon just for a social visit. His arrival at Enderley appeared to be a surprise to Matt too.

Her aunt busied herself serving tea to her husband and his guest, while they helped themselves to cakes from the stand. The brigadier took a seat on one of the overstuffed chenille-covered armchairs. He spread a linen napkin across his knee and smoothed his bushy silver moustache with a finger.

'May I ask what brings you to Enderley, sir?' Kitty asked, before biting into a strawberry jam and clotted-cream topped scone. She decided she might as well take the bull by the horns and try to discover the purpose of the visit. She was quite certain that this meeting had been planned by her uncle and the brigadier.

'Oh, this and that, my dear. A word with your uncle about various matters and, after tea, perhaps I could speak privately to you and your husband?' He raised an enquiring eyebrow as he gazed keenly at her.

'Yes, of course, sir,' Matt responded before Kitty could swallow her bite of scone in time to reply.

The conversation switched to her aunt's rose garden and more general matters until the last drop of tea had been drunk and only crumbs remained on the cake stand. Muffy and Bertie having assisted in the disposal of the last two small pastries.

'Perhaps we should adjourn to my study, Humphrey. Kitty, Matthew, please come and join us.' Kitty's uncle looked at them both.

Kitty dutifully accompanied her husband as they followed the two older men from the room. It reminded her of having been summoned to the headmaster's office when she had been at school, and she had to stifle an irrational urge to giggle.

Her uncle's study was large and airy and surprisingly tidy. This was, in part, because he did most of his work in his office at the workshop. His study at the house was mainly used for correspondence and estate matters. Or to hide from her aunt.

'Kitty, Matthew, do sit down.' Her uncle indicated a small leather chesterfield sofa opposite the desk. The brigadier stood in front of the Portland stone fireplace, while her uncle seated himself behind his desk.

'I'm sure you are both wondering why I'm actually here and why we have asked to see you away from the others.' The brigadier looked keenly first at Matt and then at Kitty.

'I assume you wish to engage our services, sir,' Matt said.

Kitty's pulse quickened. She could see from the serious expression on her uncle's face that they were about to be tasked with something more than the usual smaller errands they performed for the brigadier.

'You would be correct in your assumption.' The brigadier reached into the inside breast pocket of his green Harris Tweed jacket and took out a sheet of paper which he handed to Matt.

Kitty could see from its size and colour that it was obviously a telegram.

Matt read the contents aloud.

'Dear Pa, On way to Nice. Spot of rough weather on way but Mother's present safe and sound. Home soon, Fred.'

'Federico Benedetto, also known as Fred Bennet, is one of our half-Italian and half-English lads. He was sent to Italy to retrieve some documents of great importance to His Majesty's Government. The papers are a briefing document prepared for the Italian cabinet and would be extremely helpful in terms of our understanding of their military strength and future plans.' The brigadier took the telegram back from Matt.

'The "rough weather" he refers to means that someone is onto him?' Matt asked.

The brigadier nodded. 'I fear there is a mole in our department. Clearly, that is what Fred thinks. Several countries would like to know the Italians' intentions: the French, the Germans and possibly others. Fred needs someone in Nice to hand those papers too. It can't be anyone there who could be linked back to us. Politically, things are rather sensitive at the moment.' He paused to look appraisingly at Kitty.

'You want Kitty and I to go to Nice, meet Fred, retrieve the papers and bring them back?' Matt asked.

'Will you?' The brigadier seemed to be asking Kitty more than Matt.

'How dangerous is this mission?' Kitty asked, pleased her voice sounded quite calm even though her stomach was turning somersaults.

'There is an element of risk, naturally. However, as a married couple enjoying a holiday, it's quite low. Whoever is after Fred won't be expecting you to be there. They will be expecting someone from the department. However, I must warn you both that the government cannot be seen to be involved in any way with this. In other words, if there is a problem, you would be on your own,' the brigadier said.

'And when would we be expected to leave for Nice?' Matt asked.

'First thing in the morning. The hotel is booked, and flights arranged.' The brigadier seemed to have already decided that they would accept the mission.

'Bertie can stay here at Enderley. Lucy and Rupert will take good care of him,' her uncle said, looking at Kitty as if anticipating her protest.

'This is the chappie you need to meet.' The brigadier produced a photograph of a dark-haired, good-looking young man for them both to study. 'Our intelligence in Nice has suggested there are some people at the hotel to be wary of. Unfortunately, I have no details other than they are foreign nationals of some influence.'

Matt looked at Kitty, one eyebrow raised questioningly at her.

'A few days in the sunshine of southern France at the Le

Negresco in Nice at the department's expense,' the brigadier added by way of inducement.

Kitty met Matt's gaze and gave a barely perceptible nod. There was no way they could refuse. It seemed they were off to France in the morning.

CHAPTER TWO

The evening passed in a whirl of packing, with Lucy insisting that Kitty take several of her evening gowns and some new holiday clothes she had recently purchased in London.

'It's terribly fashionable over there and you may need these,' Lucy insisted as she got her maid to pack her white fur stole in Kitty's trunk.

'It's very kind of you. I promise I shall take great care of your lovely things,' Kitty said as the maid left the room.

'Well, I may not fit in them for much longer.' Lucy smiled as she spoke.

Kitty picked at the satin coverlet of the bed she had been sitting on whilst supervising her packing. 'Lucy, darling, I wonder if you could do one more favour for me while we're away.' She looked at her cousin.

'Of course, anything. What is it?' Lucy sat herself down on one of the armchairs beside the fireplace in the bedroom.

'It's rather delicate. It concerns a mutual friend of ours.' Kitty bit her lip.

'Alice?' Lucy asked.

Kitty knew her cousin was as fond of Alice as Kitty herself

was. 'You know how proud and stubborn she can be?' Kitty began.

Alice worked as a chambermaid at the Dolphin Hotel in Dartmouth which belonged to Kitty and her grandmother. While Kitty and Alice were best friends, Alice was very conscious of her standing in society. She had refused to be a bridesmaid when Kitty had married Matt because she had felt it would be wrong to take her place beside Lucy, who was a titled lady.

Lucy nodded understandingly.

'Well, Alice was walking out with Robert Potter,' Kitty said.

'The taxi driver's son?' Lucy nodded once more.

'Things have ended between them and Alice really could do with getting away from Dartmouth for a while.'

'Why didn't she come with you here?' Lucy asked. 'Oh, let me guess, that pride you mentioned?'

Now it was Kitty's turn to nod. 'Exactly. Could you try to persuade her to come while we're away as a favour to you? She'll only agree if she feels she is doing something to help. You know what she's like,' Kitty said.

'Leave it with me.' Lucy grinned. 'I can be most persuasive.'

Kitty had to admit the brigadier's arrangements were most efficient. An early breakfast at Enderley Hall the next morning was swiftly followed by a quick lunch on arrival in France. Now they were already at their hotel and taking tea outside.

'This is all very nice.' She gazed approvingly around at the quiet bustle of the terrace where many others of all nationalities appeared to be enjoying the afternoon sunshine. The terrace was surrounded by palms swaying gently in the soft breeze. There was a low buzz of conversation and a tinkling of teaspoons on delicate china saucers. Across the road lay golden sands and bright-blue sea. If it were not for the fact that they were embroiled in some kind of espionage, Kitty would have quite enjoyed the experience.

Matt stirred his tea and smiled at her. 'They do seem to have done us proud.'

Their room, which they had seen on their arrival, was clearly one of the best in the hotel, and Kitty suspected it had cost the brigadier's department a pretty penny. Overlooking the sea with a wrought-iron balustrade, the room was enormous. A French carved and painted ornate bed dominated the space and every luxury she could imagine had appeared to be on tap.

'When do you think we might hear from our friend?' Kitty asked. She was careful about her phrasing of the question in case anyone might be listening in to their conversation.

Matt took a sip of tea and swallowed before replying. 'I don't know. Our London friends are arranging things so presumably they will let us know when we are to expect him. I don't know how the message will get through, as they clearly cannot use any of the regular channels.'

Kitty was forced to be content with her husband's response. He was much more experienced in this field. She finished eating the tiny strawberry-topped pastry she had selected from the gilt and china tiered stand.

'Shall we take a stroll around the town?' Matt suggested as she patted the crumbs away from the corners of her mouth with the crisp white-linen napkin. 'We can get our bearings and see something of Nice.'

'Excellent idea,' Kitty agreed as Matt caught the waiter's attention to add the tea to their account before they set off along the Promenade des Anglais.

The promenade offered a fine view of the sea and of the town itself. Kitty rested her hand on the crook of Matt's arm as they strolled along. Everyone appeared very elegant with the ladies wearing smart hats and the gentlemen in linen jackets, cravats and panama hats. Kitty couldn't help feeling a trifle crumpled and underdressed from their travels.

'I can see why they call ours the English Riviera. The layout with the sea and the hills is a lot like Torquay,' Kitty remarked, looking at the palm trees. She stopped at a small kiosk to buy a guidebook. It might prove helpful if they had to make a rendezvous with the man they had been sent to meet.

'Good thinking. That one seems to have some useful maps included,' Matt said, approving her purchase.

They continued their stroll after studying the map inside the book to gain a sense of direction.

'Is that Le Vieux Fort, the old fort, do you think?' Kitty asked, looking to the east. 'It seems quite high. I expect there is a marvellous view over the bay.'

'Rather like the one from the castle in Dartmouth?' Matt smiled at her.

'Exactly,' Kitty agreed. 'Although perhaps we should save that excursion for another time. It looks like quite a distance to walk at this time of day.'

'I think so. Shall we take a quick look at the town and then we can return to the hotel to rest before dinner,' Matt suggested.

Kitty slipped her guidebook away inside her white leather handbag and they turned inland to look at the shops.

'There are so many things to see.' Kitty had already spotted a number of items in the elegant shop windows that she would like to purchase; a silk scarf for Lucy and a charming coral bracelet for Alice, to lift her spirits.

For now, though, she contented herself with the purchase of several postcards and stamps from the tobacconists. They meandered along in a pleasant fashion for some time, turning off the main streets into narrow alleyways that offered tantalising glimpses of small cafés and tiny boutiques.

'Oh dear, we seem to have gone much further than we

intended,' Kitty said as they halted near a small bakery that was just closing its blue painted shutters for the day.

'Yes, I fear we have. Let's see that map again. Perhaps we can take a shortcut back to the hotel,' Matt suggested.

Kitty took the book back out and handed it to Matt.

'I think if we continue in this direction, there is a passageway there which we can take.' He indicated the route with his forefinger.

Once the book was stowed away once more, they set off again. Many of the shops were closing now and the streets were quieter. Kitty's shoes were starting to rub on her heels and she hoped they would be back at the hotel soon.

The part of town they were now in appeared shabbier and less salubrious than before. Kitty's grip tightened slightly on Matt's arm.

'This is the place. It should take us down to the main street and then we can rejoin the promenade.' Matt indicated a narrow shadowy passage between two tall buildings.

The street was now deserted and the warmth of the sun fading as Kitty followed Matt into the alley. The air was fetid with a faint odour of old fish and cabbage. Kitty decided she would feel much happier once they were back on one of the wider, more commercial streets.

She picked her way carefully over the cobbles, following Matt's broad back as he walked ahead of her in the narrow space.

'Kitty, wait!' The urgent note in Matt's voice halted her in her tracks.

'What is it?' She tried to see around him as he moved on a few more steps into a wider area of the alley.

All she could see was her husband bending over something, or someone. 'Matt?' She continued on to discover the body of a man sprawled in a doorway, half hidden from view behind a small stack of wooden crates.

Whoever the man was, he appeared to have been stabbed. A dark, sticky pool of red blood had pooled from the knife wound in his back. The victim was around Kitty's age, unshaven and dirty in a tattered dark-brown suit.

'Dead?' Kitty wasn't sure why she was asking, it was obvious from seeing him that all life was extinct.

Matt nodded, a frown furrowing his brow. 'A tramp?'

Kitty shivered. There was something about the corpse that worried her. 'His shoes are expensive, and his fingernails look remarkably clean and tidy.' She could see no callouses or signs of manual labour on the man's hands.

Her husband nodded. 'I noticed that too.'

Matt felt inside the man's pockets. The only contents appeared to be that of a small book of matches bearing the legend, Casino Plessy. Matt delved deeper into the man's jacket pocket.

'There's something else, seems to have slipped through a hole into the lining of his coat.'

He searched deeper and pulled out a small metal key with a wooden tag labelled 2 Vue Bleu. He gave the key and the matchbook to Kitty before straightening up. 'We need to get the police.'

'Of course.' She dropped the items inside her bag. Kitty looked down at the dead man once more, her stomach rolling afresh at the sight of the blood. 'Are you thinking what I'm thinking?' she asked.

Matt's mouth was set in a grim line as he moved the man's head slightly so they could see his face more clearly. 'I'm afraid so, old thing. I believe this may have been our contact. Despite the stubble and dirt, he does look like the man in the photograph the brigadier showed us before we left.'

His words confirmed her thoughts. No tramp would have such good shoes or such remarkably well-kept hands. What were the odds too that such a man would be randomly killed in

Nice at the time they were expecting to be contacted by a government agent? A man with no money or identification.

They left the man in the alley and hurried down to the main street anxious to find some help.

'*Au secours! Meurtre!*' Matt called out into the street, attracting the attention of some of the men in a nearby café who came over to discover what the commotion was about. Soon they were surrounded by a gaggle of people all babbling away. Matt indicated the alley and, in a few moments, a blue-uniformed gendarme bustled importantly along the street.

Kitty was swept up by a kindly looking elderly lady who promptly sat her down on one of the chairs recently vacated by the men outside the café. Matt disappeared back into the alley with the gendarme and some of the crowd. The rest remained at the bottom of the passageway talking amongst themselves and gesturing at the space.

'Madame, *anglais*?' Kitty's new companion asked.

Kitty nodded. '*Oui*, madame.'

The shock of their unexpected discovery was now starting to sink in. She felt surprisingly shaky and a little tearful. This was from both the sight of the victim and a sense of having failed their mission before they had even begun.

Her companion bustled off inside the dark interior of the café and re-emerged with a tiny cup of strong black coffee and a tumbler of brandy. She placed them in front of Kitty with a kindly smile. 'Madame, *pour vous*.'

'*Merci beaucoup*.' Kitty fell back on her vague remnants of schoolgirl French to try and thank the woman.

She took a sip of coffee and followed it with a sip of the brandy. The gendarme emerged from the alleyway, along with Matt, and the group of onlookers surrounded them. Kitty wished her understanding of French was better so that she might discover what was being said. A young lad was dispatched from the group and took off at a run along the street.

Kitty could only surmise that he had been sent to fetch more assistance from the police station. The gendarme positioned himself at the entrance to the passage and began to disperse the onlookers. Several of them returned to the café, glancing curiously at Kitty as they went inside to get more drinks.

Matt crossed the street and came to join her. 'Are you all right, darling? The gendarme has sent for his superior and more assistance.'

Kitty nodded and indicated the French lady sitting on the other chair. 'I have been very well looked after. This lady has been most kind.'

Matt shook hands with the woman and they exchanged a rapid conversation in French. The older woman blushed and beamed before disappearing back inside the café, only to return with more brandy and coffee for Matt.

Matt thanked her once more as she waved away his attempt to pay her for the drinks. She returned back inside after patting Kitty reassuringly on her shoulder.

'Madame Bouttier is the owner of this café. She is most distressed that visitors to Nice have witnessed such a terrible thing,' Matt explained, before taking a sip of coffee.

'She was very kind.' Kitty was feeling more herself now that Matt was with her.

'The gendarme has requested that we wait here until his superior arrives, in case he has questions for us,' Matt explained before finishing his coffee.

'What did he say in the alley? Was he surprised by what he saw?' Kitty had been wondering how often Nice saw such things as murder and violent crime. Like her hometown of Dartmouth, it was after all a harbour town and as such must attract an element of ne'er-do-wells.

'I'm not certain. Hopefully the inspector will be here in a moment, and we will be permitted to go back to the hotel.' Matt reached across the top of the small cane table and squeezed her hand.

He had scarcely finished speaking when a group of men came down the street. Two uniformed gendarmes and at their head a tall, thin older man in a well-cut suit.

'I rather think this might be the inspector,' Kitty said.

CHAPTER THREE

Matt watched as the gendarme at the entrance to the alley greeted the party of three. He indicated to the man in the dark-grey suit where Matt and Kitty were waiting at the café. One gendarme took the place of the original policeman while the rest then entered the alley.

A short time later, the man in the suit re-emerged and crossed the street to their table.

Matt stood and extended his hand. 'Monsieur, *l'inspecteur*?' he asked and introduced himself and Kitty. He and Kitty had both entered their occupations in the hotel register as hoteliers with their address as the Dolphin Hotel at Dartmouth. The brigadier had been very keen to ensure that no suspicion be roused by their trip to Nice. All arrangements had been completed via Kitty's uncle for the trip.

'Thank you, Captain Bryant, Madame Bryant. I am Inspector Villier.' The inspector pulled up a chair and took a seat.

Matt could see from Kitty's expression that she was relieved the inspector spoke good English.

'You are recovering from this discovery, Madame Bryant? It

must have been a most terrible shock?' the inspector asked, looking at Kitty.

'Yes, thank you. The café owner has been most kind. I was dreadfully shaken. One doesn't expect to see such things in such a lovely place,' Kitty said.

The inspector nodded and took down their details, his eyebrows lifting slightly when they gave the hotel name. '*Bien sur*. You told the gendarme that you only arrived today?'

'Yes, that's right, monsieur. We had tea at the hotel and decided to take a short stroll. We got a little lost following the map in our guidebook and the alley seemed a good shortcut to get us back,' Kitty explained, showing him the book she had purchased only an hour or so ago.

The inspector added to his notes. 'You had not previously encountered this man? The man who has been killed?'

Matt shook his head. 'No, sir, as my wife said we only arrived a short time ago and we have never visited Nice before.'

The inspector closed his book and returned it to his jacket pocket. 'I would have assumed this murder to be one of rivalry between a few undesirables. Nice is a very safe place, you understand, for visitors, but such things are not unusual between certain factions. However, this man has nothing to identify him and there are, well, there are aspects to his appearance which are strange.' He surveyed them both keenly.

'I assumed he must have been robbed, poor fellow, and a tramp such as that didn't look as if he would be carrying anything of value.' Kitty's blue-grey eyes were wide as she bestowed an innocent look on the inspector.

Matt had to take his hat off to Kitty, she really was most convincing. However, it seemed to him that the policeman suspected that all was not as it seemed on the surface with this death.

'We shall, of course, do everything we can to identify this man and to bring his murderer to justice. However, I fear it may not be easy. You did not see or hear anything at all which might assist us in this task?' the inspector asked.

'I'm afraid not, sir. The alley was quite deserted when we walked down, and it seemed to me that the unfortunate man had been there for some little time before we stumbled upon him,' Matt said.

'Very well. Thank you both for your assistance with this unfortunate affair. I sincerely hope it does not spoil your holiday.' The inspector rose from his seat and shook hands once more with both Matt and Kitty.

'I hope so too. If you do discover more or catch the person who did this, please could you tell us?' Kitty asked. 'I would feel so much safer knowing there wasn't a murderer loose in the town.' She shivered as she spoke.

'Of course, Madame Bryant. I assure you, however, this is a very unusual occurrence, and I am sure you will be most safe, especially at the Negresco.' The inspector bowed over her hand and went to join his gendarme.

A portly man in a checked suit sauntered into view smoking a pipe and carrying a large leather bag.

'That will be the doctor, I assume,' Kitty said as another younger man in a brown suit scurried along the street behind him. A camera in a leather case around his neck.

'So, it would seem. We should leave them to it and get back to the hotel,' Matt agreed and extended his hand to assist her from her seat.

'Yes, please, I rather think I've seen enough of Nice for now,' Kitty replied as she retook his arm and they set off towards the hotel.

* * *

After a soak in the bath and a change of clothes, Kitty began to feel much better. She fastened the gold necklace with the ruby and diamond dropper that Matt had given her for Christmas around her neck. The dark-red satin gown with its low back and bias-cut skirt had seemed the height of fashion in Devon. She wondered how it would stand up amongst the chic clientele of the Negresco.

Matt, as usual, was debonair in his evening attire. She always thought the formality of a tailcoat set off his raffish good looks.

'You look as lovely as ever, Mrs Bryant. Shall we go to dinner?' He stood behind her, his gaze meeting hers in the mirror.

Kitty was aware that they needed to keep up the illusion that they were simply a couple on holiday. There would be time later to work out how they could inform the brigadier of what had happened. They also needed to go to the address on the key they had found in the dead man's pockets. If the documents had not been taken from Federico when he was killed, they might still be in his lodgings.

'Of course, Captain Bryant.' Kitty smiled back at her husband and collected the white fur stole Lucy had loaned her for the trip, before heading out to the hotel restaurant.

The maître d'hôtel showed them to a table and presented them with menus. Kitty looked around her with interest. The dining room was a splendid affair. It seemed that everything glittered and sparkled; the huge crystal chandeliers, the glasses and silverware on the tables, and the multitude of diamonds adorning the female guests.

'I feel a trifle underdressed,' Kitty murmured to Matt as she studied the gold and black embossed menu.

'I see what you mean.' His blue eyes twinkled with amusement, and she knew that he too had been taking in their surroundings. 'Even the lights appear to be wearing jewels.'

A wine waiter came to take their drinks order, swiftly followed by the head waiter for their food order.

'The service here is very good,' Kitty observed after they had chosen a shrimp cocktail to start, followed by fillets of sole in a butter sauce with spring vegetables and dauphinoise potatoes, ending with a champagne and strawberry mousse.

'Indeed,' Matt agreed as their wine arrived in a silver bucket and was proffered to Matt for his approval.

Another party arrived to be seated at a nearby table, attracting attention from other diners as they did so. Kitty sipped her drink and watched as the maître d' and his staff all fawned over the group, which consisted of an older woman, a girl of around Kitty's age, and two men slightly younger than the older woman.

She decided they weren't a family, although she supposed the woman and the girl could be mother and daughter. They were clearly well heeled and regulars at the hotel. She wondered if these might be the people the brigadier had warned them about before they left Enderley. He had said his intelligence agents had told him of just such a group.

The older woman was obviously the queen bee, ordering both of her male companions and the hotel staff around. Kitty couldn't make out all the woman was saying but she thought she detected an American accent. The girl, despite her lovely lilac shantung-silk frock, seemed unhappy and distracted, Kitty thought. She appeared to be rebuffing the attempts of one of the men to engage her in conversation.

The arrival of their dinner caused Kitty to temporarily lose interest in the other table and she tucked into her food with relish.

Matt smiled at her. 'I'm glad stumbling across a dead body hasn't put you off your dinner, old thing.'

Kitty finished her shrimp and grinned back as she rested her cutlery on her empty plate. 'Never.'

They were just finishing their second course when the maître d' came towards their table. He was accompanied by a distinguished-looking man with silver hair dressed impeccably in evening attire.

'My dear Captain Bryant, Mrs Bryant, I have just been made aware of the terrible events of this afternoon. I am Monsieur Corot, manager of this establishment. On behalf of myself and my staff we wish to assure you that such tragic events are very unusual in Nice. I sincerely hope this unfortunate event has not distressed you too much and that you will permit me to make a small gift to you both.' He clicked his fingers and one of the waiters scurried forward with a bottle of champagne.

'Thank you very much, Monsieur Corot, but really, Kitty and I are both now recovered from the shock.' Matt's attempt to dissuade the hotel manager was drowned out by the pop of the champagne cork.

'No, please. It is a matter of civic pride, Captain Bryant. You must allow me to make amends for this ordeal,' Monsieur Corot insisted.

Kitty wondered how he had learned about the murder and that they were the ones who had discovered the victim. It seemed that Nice was not unlike Dartmouth when it came to the speed of news travelling through the town.

She noticed the palaver appeared to have attracted the attention of the group dining at the other table. The older woman had raised a gold lorgnette to her eyes to study them, making no attempt to look away when she realised Kitty had seen her.

After more apologies and protestations, Monsieur Corot was persuaded to allow them to continue with their meal.

'I rather fear that our attempts to keep a low profile have been thwarted,' Matt said once the hotel staff had gone back about their business.

'Quite. Still, it was nice of him to give us the champagne.' Kitty picked up her glass and took an appreciative sip.

'Very kind,' Matt agreed and chinked his glass against hers. 'It is quite amazing how news travels.'

Kitty smiled.

'Would we look very unfeeling if we were to go dancing?' she asked after the dessert dishes had been cleared and tiny delicate china cups of coffee had been deposited before them.

'I suppose that a few turns about the floor would not go amiss. We are supposed to be on holiday,' Matt said.

The ballroom was next to the dining room and strains of music drifted through the open doorway, mingling with the scent of tobacco and the lilies which adorned the tabletops.

The party who had been seated near them had also finished their dinner and were taking coffee. Kitty noticed the younger woman surreptitiously peeking at her elegant gold wristwatch. The man seated beside her appeared to be oblivious to her actions, apparently absorbed in some monologue.

The older woman was flirting outrageously with the other gentleman at the table. Behind an ornate fan, she made slightly ridiculous affected giggles and pouts. Kitty's attention was momentarily diverted by a slight kerfuffle at the entrance to the dining room.

A man of around her own age wearing a somewhat tired evening suit appeared to be conducting a heated discussion with the maître d'. There seemed to be much gallic waving of hands and pointing before the man managed to get past the staff and headed into the restaurant. Something about the man's appearance was familiar and she wondered where she had seen him before. Kitty placed a warning hand on Matt's arm as the man headed straight towards their table.

'Captain and Mrs Bryant?' the man asked, looking eagerly at them.

'Yes? Who's asking?' Matt replied.

'Roland Fetherington, I'm a freelance reporter and wondered if I might have a word with you about the incident you witnessed earlier today?' The man glanced over his shoulder at the waiting staff who appeared to be coming towards him.

Kitty was instantly on the alert. The man had an English accent. The brigadier had warned them that they could not be certain who they might encounter and who would prove friend or foe. Was this man a contact from the department? Or one of the people they needed to be wary of?

'I'm sorry, Mr Fetherington. I'm really not sure my wife wishes to discuss the matter. It was most distressing.' Matt glanced at Kitty.

She guessed his thoughts reflected her own.

'Monsieur Fetherington, you have been warned many times about disturbing our guests.' The maître d' placed a firm hand on the journalist's arm. 'My apologies, madame, monsieur.' He bowed his head in apology to Kitty and Matt.

'Here, take my card.' Mr Fetherington dropped a slightly grubby looking card onto the pristine white tablecloth as the maître d', assisted by the wine waiter, began to bundle the reporter out of the dining room. 'I'll only take a few minutes of your time,' he called over his shoulder as he was removed.

'Goodness me.' Kitty glanced at the card quickly before collecting it up and slipping it into her bag. She couldn't be certain, but she thought Mr Fetherington had been the man with the camera following the doctor at the scene of the murder. That had to be why he had seemed familiar.

'That was most peculiar.' Matt frowned as he watched the unlucky journalist being escorted from the hotel.

'Very,' Kitty agreed, her attention once again caught by the group on the next table.

The younger woman looked distressed and the older one angry, or annoyed. Kitty got the impression that they had been watching the interaction with Mr Fetherington. Indeed, it would have been hard for them to miss it. Perhaps they considered such a disturbance unseemly in such a high-class hotel. She knew her grandmother would not have been amused if something like that had occurred at the Dolphin.

'Shall we go through to the ballroom before anything else happens?' Matt asked.

Kitty smiled her agreement and took her husband's arm to walk out of the dining room. She wasn't sure that she still felt like a dance, but the thought of a cocktail was suddenly most appealing.

The dance floor was busy with couples moving to the music from the small band. The female singer sparkled and shimmered in a gold-lamé dress. There were several small tables and chairs set out in front of the dance floor. White-jacketed waiters bustled about delivering glasses of champagne and cocktails to the elegantly dressed occupants of the seats.

Matt spied an empty table and steered Kitty in that direction before it could be taken. Within moments of being seated a waiter had appeared to take their order. After a restorative sip of an expertly made negroni Kitty started to feel much more herself again.

She decided that they may as well make the most of their stay at the Le Negresco. After all, once they managed to alert the brigadier to the death of the agent they had come to meet, they were likely to be recalled straight back to England.

The thought of having failed their mission before it had even properly begun was quite depressing, but they did still have the key and that book of matches. Perhaps all was not yet lost.

CHAPTER FOUR

Matt swallowed a sip of his cocktail and looked around the busy room at their fellow guests. He didn't like the attention the hotel manager had brought upon them by presenting him and Kitty with champagne. For that matter, he hadn't enjoyed that journalist tracking them down to pester them with questions either.

Finding the man they had been supposed to meet dead in the alley had been distressing. The only clues to possibly obtaining the documents were the objects they had found in his pockets. He had studied Kitty's guidebook on their return to their room but couldn't see Vue Bleu marked anywhere on the map. He had guessed it to be a road but thinking about it now, he supposed that it could be the name of a house. The Casino Plessy, however, was noted, standing on what seemed to be a small promontory overlooking the sea on the edge of town.

Whoever had murdered Federico had obviously seen through the agent's disguise. Had they been following him? Did they know where Vue Bleu might be? By the time he and Kitty worked out where it was, if the papers Federico had been carrying had been stowed there, they might be too late.

He knew that Kitty was worried too about Federico's death.

He had seen her tense when the reporter had come towards them wanting to ask questions about the murder. He glanced at his wife, relieved to see that she seemed to have started to relax again, the toe of her patent black evening shoe tapping on the floor in time to the music.

'Fancy a spin around the floor, old thing?' he asked, setting down his glass. Perhaps dancing to the band might help both of them to relax.

'I thought you'd never ask.' Kitty smiled as she stood, and they joined the other couples moving about the dance floor.

One dance turned into three or four and they were both flushed with their exertions when they returned to their table.

'That was lovely.' Kitty picked up her drink as she retook her seat.

'It was rather.' Matt smiled back at her. He always enjoyed dancing with Kitty.

He noticed the group who had been seated near them in the dining room had also moved into the ballroom. They were being seated with the same amount of fuss that they had attracted earlier. The waiters scurrying to arrange chairs with a good view of the singer, drinks being brought immediately and much bowing and scraping.

He could only assume that they were either very important, or very rich, or both. The brigadier had mentioned a suspicious party of influential people staying at the hotel. Kitty noticed the direction of his gaze.

'Do you know them at all? The staff seem to be making a lot of fuss over them. I wondered if they were famous. If Alice were here, she would know,' Kitty said.

Matt shook his head. 'No, I can't say that I do. The hotel clearly values their custom though, whoever they are.' He was certain that Kitty and her grandmother didn't fuss over their important guests in such a way. He was also certain that Alice, with her love of films, would have recognised anyone remotely well known.

'Why are you smiling?' Kitty asked.

'I was just thinking that the woman, whoever she is, would give your grandmother's friend Mrs Craven a run for her money.' Matt's smile widened. Mrs Craven and Kitty did not see eye to eye, despite her long-standing friendship with Kitty's grandmother. The older woman being fond of giving her opinion on anything and everything, even when her opinion had not been asked for.

Kitty gave him a baleful look. 'Mrs C would enjoy the attention,' she agreed.

Matt finished his drink and signalled to a passing waiter.

'Kitty, darling, another negroni?' he asked as the man paused to take their order.

'Oh yes, please.' Kitty finished the last drop of her current drink so the man could clear their glasses.

'By the by, my wife and I are supposed to meet some friends tomorrow near the Vue Bleu, do you know where it is?' Matt asked.

'*Mais oui*, monsieur, but it is not so good there. Perhaps monsieur's friends have mistaken the place? It is, um, in a not nice area.' The man gave directions, his expression clearly doubting that they had the correct address.

'*Merci*, my dear fellow. Perhaps you are right, and they are confused. We shall have to check the instructions they gave us.' Matt dropped some notes onto the waiter's tray.

The waiter's expression brightened when he saw the money, and he hurried off to the bar to refresh their drinks.

'Nicely done, Matt. At least we know where to go now,' Kitty murmured, her voice barely audible above the music.

'I think our best bet is to go early tomorrow morning before anyone is around,' Matt suggested.

'Before breakfast you mean?' Kitty raised her neatly arched eyebrows.

'I'm afraid so. We can go out and be back in time for a croissant and tea without arousing suspicion.'

Kitty seemed to be considering the plan. 'We can always say we went for an early morning walk if anyone notices,' she agreed. 'But I'll hold you to that croissant.'

* * *

After the helpful waiter had delivered a fresh round of cocktails, Kitty happily agreed to take to the floor once more. She was much happier now that they had a plan. At least once they had followed up the clue of the mysterious key, they would have done their utmost to fulfil the task set by the brigadier.

She presumed that they would also have to pay a visit to the casino. There had to be a reason why Federico had been carrying a matchbook from there in his pocket. There had been no evidence that he smoked, no pipe or cigarettes, so why matches?

The music finished and they started back to their seats.

'Oh, my apologies, madame.'

Kitty was brought up short by the dark-haired, good-looking man from the table that had been near them in the dining room bumping into her.

'That's quite all right,' Kitty assured him. He had managed to avoid standing on her toes or spilling anything on her frock, so no damage had been done.

The man bowed his head towards her and Matt. 'Forgive me, I am always told I am very clumsy. Permit me to introduce myself, I am Comte Malfiore, Luciano to my friends.'

'Captain Matthew Bryant and my wife, Kitty,' Matt acknowledged the introduction.

'I am seated with some friends: Mrs Eunice Delaware and

her daughter, Candace, and Miss Delaware's friend, Sir Montague Savernake. Forgive my curiosity but did we hear Monsieur Corot say earlier that you had been caught up in a murder today here in Nice?' the comte asked.

'Oh, it was all quite, quite dreadful. We only arrived this afternoon, so we went for a walk in the town to get our bearings. Well, of course we got lost and found ourselves in this alleyway. There was the body of a tramp, murdered, stabbed to death.' Kitty widened her eyes and did her best to sound shocked and distressed.

'My dear lady, of course. I am so sorry it must have been terribly shocking. Is this your first time here in Nice?' the comte asked with an expression of concern on his handsome face.

'Yes, it was quite awful. Kitty's uncle arranged the trip for us as a belated Christmas present and we have been looking forward to the holiday,' Matt explained, giving the story that they had decided upon before leaving England.

'A most happy thought from your uncle, madame. Please, why do you not join us? Mrs Delaware is American and longs to converse more with English speakers. We can all reassure you that such things are very rare in this lovely town.'

Before they could protest Kitty discovered they had been incorporated into Mrs Delaware's entourage and were swiftly being introduced to the other members of the party. Mrs Delaware, her daughter Candace, and Sir Montague Savernake.

The comte lost no time in telling Mrs Delaware of Kitty and Matt's afternoon adventures.

'Oh my.' Mrs Delaware pressed a heavily bejewelled hand to her bosom. 'One would think Nice was a civilised place. How ghastly, a tramp, you say?' Her kohl-lined eyes gleamed with interest.

'Yes, we can only assume it must have been a falling out amongst thieves or something. Why else would a man such as that be murdered? He couldn't have had anything worth taking,' Kitty said.

'No, I suppose not. Not a very nice start to your holiday if you have only just arrived,' Mrs Delaware agreed.

She had a distinct American accent and close up, despite her clever use of cosmetics, Kitty could see that she was older than Kitty had first assumed.

'I suppose that was why that dreadful reporter chappie was bothering you? Blooming nuisance. I've told Corot before they should ban him.' The man who had been introduced as Sir Montague Savernake huffed.

He was older than Candace, probably closer to Matt and the comte's age. Well dressed in clothes Kitty guessed were from Savile Row and with expensive shoes and gold monogrammed cufflinks.

'Mr Fetherington is merely doing his job, Monty, as you would know if you had one,' Candace muttered.

Sir Montague didn't appear to hear her, but Kitty noticed Mrs Delaware glaring at her daughter.

'Luciano tells me this holiday is a gift from your uncle? How very thoughtful,' Mrs Delaware probed.

'Yes, my uncle is very generous and has always been very kind to me and Matt,' Kitty agreed.

'That's so sweet.' Mrs Delaware smiled at her. 'You will enjoy it here, I'm sure, despite the bad start. Just mention my name in any of the good restaurants and shops and I'm sure you will get the best attention.'

'There are many lovely sights to see here too. You must, of course, go to see the old fort. The view from the top is well worth the climb,' the comte assured them.

'Thank you, we do intend to go there. Kitty has a guidebook and we have marked off a few things we would like to see during our stay,' Matt replied, before taking another sip of his cocktail.

'We have been told that the Casino Plessy is fun for a night out,' Kitty said.

'Of course! It's delightful, my dear, you must go. We were planning to go tomorrow night. Say, why don't you join us? A party is always more fun, we shall introduce you to Monsieur and Madame Dupont. They own the casino and are old friends of Luciano's.' Mrs Delaware beamed at the comte.

'Thank you, that's most kind of you.' Matt exchanged a quick glance with Kitty.

'Jerard and Helene will be delighted to make your acquaintance I am certain,' Luciano said.

The evening continued with more chatter and dancing, until Matt and Kitty were able to make their excuses and slip away upstairs to their room.

'Well, I feel quite exhausted after all of that,' Kitty declared as she closed the door and slipped off her evening shoes. She wriggled her stocking-clad toes with relief.

Matt chuckled. 'Our new friends are certainly very talkative.'

'And inquisitive.' Kitty sat down in front of the dressing table and unclipped her ruby earrings.

'You noticed?' Matt chuckled as he undid his bow tie and his collar studs.

'It's so hard to know if it's just the usual kind of getting to know new people in a strange place kind of conversation, or if there is more to it. I rather think they may be the people the brigadier told us about.' Kitty swivelled around on the dressing stool to look at Matt.

'I think you're right. Still, that was a good bit of work about the casino. Interesting that the comte appears to have connections there.' Matt dropped his cufflinks back in their box.

Kitty stood and stepped out of her evening gown. 'Do you think they may be connected to Federico's murder?'

Matt sighed. 'The comte is Italian so I suppose he may have

connections with the Italian government. As for Mrs Delaware, it's too early to say.'

Kitty laughed. 'She is very keen on ordering her daughter around. I think she intends Candace to make a match with Sir Montague.'

'Hmm, I had noticed that,' Matt agreed.

'Candace seemed quick off the mark to defend that reporter, Mr Fetherington.' Kitty had been pondering the girl's muttered remark. It crossed her mind that perhaps Candace might prefer the young reporter to her older, wealthier suitor. Now that would not amuse Mrs Delaware very much at all.

'Oh?'

Kitty told Matt what she had heard Candace say.

'You could be right. He seemed a bit of a dry stick, Sir Montague.' Matt finished hanging up his evening attire and prepared his clothes ready for the morning.

Kitty yawned and followed suit. She set her travel alarm clock before tumbling into the large comfortable bed. It seemed that tomorrow would be another busy day.

The sun was already up when Kitty's alarm clock sounded. They dressed quickly and slipped out of the hotel. Kitty felt somewhat self-conscious as they set off through the virtually empty streets.

Lucy had persuaded her to borrow a pair of beach pyjamas from her to take on the trip. Kitty thought that perhaps wearing trousers rather than a skirt might make it easier should they have to get away from somewhere in a hurry. Therefore, she thought this early morning excursion might be a good time to try them out.

It felt strange though after always wearing skirts. She knew her friend Alice would have laughed at her and told her all the Hollywood film stars wore them. It still didn't help to quiet the disapproving voice in her head, that sounded suspiciously like Mrs Craven, saying it was unladylike. Matt, however, had told her she looked very chic when she had put them on.

Matt had the key they had taken from Federico in his jacket pocket, and they followed the directions the waiter had provided the previous evening. The route took them away from the still shuttered and closed high-class shops and bars through to the seedier side of the town.

'According to the waiter it must be around here.' Matt halted at the end of a street where the cobbles petered out onto a dirt track. The buildings around them appeared more residential and run down.

'There's a small building down there.' Kitty indicated a shabby building further along the dirt track. The lime-washed walls were dirty and the blue painted shutters faded from the sun. Like the rest of the street, it appeared deserted.

'Let's go and take a closer look.' Matt started towards the villa with Kitty at his side.

They paused once more at the front of the house. It looked derelict and locked up with no signs of life. Vines covered the far side of the house and a small green lizard skittered over the cracked stone doorstep.

'Is this it, do you think?' Kitty asked. 'There is what seems to be a number two scrawled in chalk on the door.' She peered more closely at the almost vanished mark.

The door had a small brass padlock securing it shut. Kitty thought the metal appeared quite new and shiny compared with the rest of the building. Matt leaned forward to examine it.

'This seems recent, and there is a trace of oil. Someone has been this way.' Matt took the key they had found on Federico's body from his pocket. 'It looks as if this may be a match.'

Checking there was no one around, he slid the key into the lock. Kitty watched as the padlock sprang open.

'I doubt anyone is inside. My only hope is that there

was only one key, and no one has beaten us to it.' Matt twisted the door handle and prised open the warped wooden door.

Kitty peered inside the gloomy interior. 'It doesn't look very safe. There are holes in the floorboards.'

'I think you should stay here, Kitty. Keep a look out in case anyone else comes this way.' Matt didn't wait for her to agree, slipping inside the dark hallway to carefully commence his search of the house.

Kitty's protest died on her lips, and she folded her arms as she waited for him to return. She could hear the ancient floorboards creaking and the opening and closing of various doors as Matt searched the house.

Outside the villa, everything was still. She peered back towards the run-down shacks at the end of the paved road. There was still no one in sight, just a thin and scruffy stray cat licking its paws in a patch of sunlight. But the fine hairs at the nape of her neck prickled and Kitty couldn't shake off the feeling she was being watched.

She retreated back towards the side of the villa into the sparse shade offered by a scrubby oleander bush and looked around. She tried to identify what was making her feel as if she was being observed. The windows of the other houses further along the road were shuttered and blank, the front doors firmly closed.

The uncomfortable feeling persisted, however, so she turned her attention to the surrounding hillside above the villa. Small groups of shrubs and trees were sited on the various rocky outcrops. Still nothing, she looked carefully, at first not spotting anything untoward.

Then a gleam of sunlight flashed and blinked at her from a group of boulders beneath an olive tree. Kitty adjusted the wide brim of her straw hat to shade her face and looked to see if it happened again. There, another glint of sunlight on glass.

Someone was up there watching them through binoculars, she was sure of it.

Kitty heard more creaks and bangs within the house before Matt emerged from the front door into the sunshine brushing dust from his hands.

'Anything?' she asked.

'Nothing. Someone has been staying there, sleeping rough in the back room but it looks as if a shutter had been forced at the rear of the house. Someone has searched the place from top to bottom before we got here. If those papers were here, they've gone now,' Matt said.

He turned to re-secure the door and padlock.

'Don't look now but up on the hillside to your left is a rocky outcrop under a tree. Someone up there has binoculars and is watching us,' Kitty said.

Matt completed his task and casually glanced around before turning back to Kitty.

'Yes, you're right. Interesting, perhaps that means they don't have the documents yet and hope that we might lead them to them. I can't think of any other reason why they would be watching an empty house.' Matt fell into step beside her as she took his arm to walk back to the hotel.

'So good news if the papers are still out there, but bad news for us if they now know we are looking for them.' Kitty didn't like that idea at all.

CHAPTER FIVE

The town was livelier on their walk back to the hotel. Some of the cafés and bakeries were open and the shops were preparing to welcome visitors. Steps were being swept and mopped and there was a bustle on the streets. They made it to the dining room just in time for a late breakfast.

Kitty was quite hungry now after their morning walk and happily filled up her plate with delicious-smelling freshly baked croissants and pastries. They had secured a table near a window where they had a good view of people walking past. Sunlight streamed in across the white-linen tablecloth making the glassware on the table sparkle.

'Isn't that Candace Delaware over there?' Kitty asked as she poured some freshly squeezed orange juice from the jug into her glass.

The girl was dressed smartly in the latest fashion but appeared to want to avoid attracting attention.

'She seems to be in quite a hurry,' Matt remarked.

Kitty had a slightly better view of the girl as she moved quickly along the path.

Matt leaned forward to peer through the window to see where the girl might be going in such haste.

'Hmm, well that looks very much like Mr Fetherington,' he said, relaxing back in his seat as he presumably lost sight of his quarry.

Kitty's brows raised. 'A clandestine meeting, do you think?' It wouldn't surprise her if that were the case. She had suspected there was something between Roland and Candace last night.

Matt gave a slight shrug. 'It would certainly appear that way.'

She spread butter and jam onto her pastry before glancing out of the window once more. 'Now here comes the comte. Candace was in luck. He must have just missed seeing her. I have a feeling her mother would not be happy to discover she is keeping company with Mr Fetherington.'

The comte spotted them in the window and gallantly raised his smart white panama hat in acknowledgement.

Kitty and Matt smiled back politely.

'It seems that everyone is out and about this morning,' Matt observed as Mrs Delaware, dressed in a pink-print dress and white hat stepped out to greet the comte. She was followed a second or two later by Sir Montague.

Kitty watched as the group huddled together for a minute. They appeared to be having some sort of discussion. She wondered if they were looking for Candace since Mrs Delaware kept looking around her as if expecting her daughter to appear. Eventually they moved off together in the direction of the town. Mrs Delaware holding the comte's arm and Sir Montague trailing along behind them with his walking stick in hand.

'What are our plans for the day?' Kitty asked after she had swallowed the last delicious bite of her breakfast. She felt nicely full, but her feet ached from the walking they had done the day before and on their earlier adventure.

The dining room was quiet for now with only another

couple of tables still occupied. The waiters were busy clearing away and preparing for the lunchtime service.

'I wish we could let the brigadier know about Federico,' Matt murmured as he held a linen napkin to his lips.

'I could telephone Enderley, speak to my uncle. He would pass on a message, I'm sure,' Kitty suggested.

'I suspect there are ears at the switchboards and any attempt via telegram or post could be intercepted. We do need to let him know but we shall have to be careful how it's done.' Matt frowned as he considered her suggestion.

'Hmm, I see what you mean. Perhaps we should wait until after we have been to the casino? You didn't find anything at the villa so perhaps we may find something when we go out tonight. Then at least we can hint if we still have a chance to recover the parcel,' Kitty said.

'That's a good point. Perhaps we should have a lazy day today then? Yesterday was rather strenuous and we were up early this morning.' Matt dropped his napkin back onto his empty plate as the waiters started to clear the table next to them.

'An excellent suggestion, and we are out again this evening. I have a book to read, and I could write those postcards to Grams and Alice.' Kitty knew they would both be very surprised to discover she and Matt were in France instead of Devon. Unless, of course, Lucy had already spoken to Alice.

Half an hour later they were duly installed on comfortable rattan steamer chairs in the shade of a jaunty striped parasol with a view of everyone entering and exiting that part of the hotel. Matt had acquired an English newspaper from reception and Kitty applied herself to her postcards.

They had not been there for long before Kitty spied a familiar figure entering the hotel.

'I think Inspector Villier has just arrived.' She looked at Matt.

'I wonder if he is calling with an update about Federico? You did ask him to keep us informed on his progress.' Matt's brow creased in perplexity.

Kitty couldn't help feeling slightly anxious about the possible purpose of the policeman's visit. Had the police discovered the man's identity? If they had, then could they link him to them in any way?

'It appears he has come to see us,' Kitty said when the inspector re-emerged accompanied by Monsieur Corot, who then pointed him in their direction. The inspector nodded to the hotel manager and Monsieur Corot returned to his duties inside the hotel. The policeman made his way along the terrace towards their table.

'Inspector Villier, this is an unexpected pleasure.' Kitty indicated a vacant seat at their table.

The inspector shook their hands before taking a seat and removing his hat. 'My apologies for interrupting your holiday once more, Madame Bryant, Captain Bryant. I trust you are both recovered from yesterday?'

'Everyone has been most kind to us, and I am feeling much better this morning,' Kitty said.

'*Bien sur*, I am delighted to hear it.' The inspector leaned forward in his chair slightly, his grey eyes suddenly sharp. 'I thought you might wish to know there are some complications regarding the poor fellow you found yesterday.'

'Oh, how so?' Matt asked in a politely enquiring tone.

Kitty was aware of a subtle change in her husband's posture. His shoulders had stiffened and his gaze had sharpened and she knew he was on his guard.

'The tramp had no papers, no money, wallet, watch, nothing that could identify him. I think I may have mentioned this to you yesterday. Do you not think this is a little strange?' Inspector Villier asked.

'I suppose so, but if he had been robbed by whoever killed

him, they may have taken anything he had,' Kitty said.

'It is possible, madame, any valuables maybe, but why take his papers? No, I think perhaps it was so he could not be identified easily.' The inspector rested his gaze thoughtfully on her for a moment.

Kitty resisted the urge to nervously lick her lips which had dried under his perusal. Her palms had grown clammy, and she shifted uncomfortably in her chair.

'That seems something of a stretch, Inspector. He could have left them in his lodgings, unless perhaps you think he may have been a fugitive?' Matt suggested.

The inspector nodded his silver head thoughtfully. 'A possibility, Captain Bryant. You may not have noticed but there were aspects of this so-called tramp's appearance which gave me pause.'

Kitty swallowed and pinned a smile to her lips. 'Oh, what was that?'

'His shoes, madame, were those of a gentleman and his hands were very well kept beneath the grime.' Inspector Villier fixed his attention back on her once more.

'Then surely that lends credence to the fellow being a fugitive of some kind. No doubt whoever he was hiding from must have caught up with him and exacted their revenge,' Matt said.

There was a moment of silence before the inspector spoke again. 'There is a story going around Nice that this man was perhaps English.'

'I suppose he could be any nationality since he was without any papers.' Matt gave a small shrug.

'You and Madame Bryant are both very certain this man was not known to either of you?' Inspector Villier asked.

'We had never met him before until we discovered him in that alley, and I must admit I did not care to look too closely. The sight of all that blood made me feel quite ill.' Kitty closed her eyes momentarily and shuddered.

When she opened her eyes again, she discovered the inspector was still studying her face as if trying to determine if she was telling the truth.

'Of course, madame, forgive me, I did not mean to distress you,' the inspector apologised. 'Monsieur Corot tells me that you plan to remain at the hotel for a few more days?'

'That was our intention, yes. Our plans are fairly fluid. We have never visited this area before so there is a lot for us to see,' Matt said.

'Of course, and we are not so far from the Italian border here also. Many people take the opportunity to pass backwards and forwards,' the inspector said. 'Very well, I must return to my duties. I wish you a peaceful remainder of your holiday.'

He rose and shook hands with them once more, before collecting his hat from the table and making his way out of the hotel gardens.

'He knows, doesn't he? That we know who his murder victim is?' Kitty murmured as they watched the inspector depart.

'Inspector Villier is clearly no fool,' Matt agreed.

'Ugh, I hated not being able to tell him what we know. Do you think they will be able to identify Federico?' Kitty asked. Deceiving a police officer did not come easily to her. She was sure the inspector had known that she was keeping something from him. It made her feel quite uncomfortable.

'I'm sure they will work it out. It sounded as if the inspector had already been doing a lot of digging. Federico had dual nationality remember, hence the two names.'

Kitty wasn't comforted by Matt's words. Before they had left for France the brigadier had been very clear that they would be on their own during this mission. The government could not afford to be seen to be meddling in the affairs of another country. They had been instructed to collect the papers and get back.

Now the man due to deliver those papers was dead, the

documents were missing, and the police seemed, to her, to be eyeing them up as suspects.

She picked up her fountain pen once more. 'I have one post-card left to write. I think I ought to send it to my uncle. I know we said we would wait until after we had been to the casino, but the inspector's visit has made me uneasy.' Kitty looked at Matt.

'Very well, but remember that it may be seen by anyone so choose your words carefully,' he cautioned her.

Kitty nodded.

Dear Uncle,

Arrived safely and weather splendid. However, you'll never guess! We have become embroiled in a most ghastly murder investigation! The local police seem to be very on the ball so I'm sure they will apprehend the chap responsible quite quickly. We haven't found a suitable gift yet for Mother so will keep looking. Have met some interesting people.

Much love, Kitty x

She read out what she had written to Matt, and he nodded approvingly.

'Perfect, I'm sure your uncle will interpret that and relay it to the brigadier.'

Kitty applied the stamp to the corner of the card and added the address for Enderley Hall.

As Kitty set down her fountain pen, she saw Roland Fether-ington entering the hotel grounds. He spotted them and came along the terrace towards their table. 'Oh dear.'

Matt, who had just folded his newspaper ready to commence the crossword, followed her gaze. Mr Fetherington pulled up the vacant chair and sat himself down uninvited at their table.

'Good morning, Captain Bryant, Mrs Bryant. I just spotted Inspector Villier leaving the hotel. What news on the murder?' Mr Fetherington whipped out a battered, brown leather-covered notebook and licked the end of his pencil in anticipation.

'Mr Fetherington, we are on holiday.' Matt glared at the unrepentant-looking reporter.

'Please, Captain Bryant, just a quote from you or Mrs Bryant. This could be a big break for me with my editor. It's my first opportunity to get a real scoop and a front-page byline.' The man looked pleadingly at them.

'There is really nothing we can add to what you probably know already.' Kitty glanced at Matt.

'Yes, but you found this mystery man. First on the scene and all that. The police are printing posters to try and identify him. Please, Mrs Bryant, give a bloke a break,' the reporter begged.

'Very well, you may say we were both very shocked and distressed. The townspeople have been most kind to us and we have every confidence in the efficiency of the police in apprehending the murderer,' Kitty said. 'There, will that do?'

Mr Fetherington scribbled furiously in his book. 'Ta ever so, Mrs Bryant.'

'By the by, did you have a pleasant walk this morning with Miss Delaware?' Kitty asked casually as the reporter started to tuck his book back inside his jacket pocket.

'Miss Delaware?' Mr Fetherington paused in his actions.

'Miss Candace Delaware.' Kitty fixed the man with a firm gaze.

A hint of dark red tinged Mr Fetherington's cheeks and some of his usual slightly cocksure manner appeared to desert him momentarily.

'Ah, yes, that Miss Delaware. Yes, very pleasant, thank you.' He shifted uncomfortably as Kitty continued to look at him.

CHAPTER SIX

Kitty bit back a smile and waited. It had occurred to her that Mr Fetherington could be quite a useful person to get to know. He appeared to be acquainted with everyone who was anyone and he was clearly on top of the inspector's investigation into Federico's death.

'I rather got the impression last night that Miss Delaware was intended for Sir Montague,' Matt remarked mildly.

The red colouration in Mr Fetherington's face deepened as he shifted uncomfortably at the table. 'That is what Mrs Delaware intends for Candace.'

'And Candace herself?' Kitty asked.

'Candace and I have an understanding. She can marry whoever she wishes when she turns twenty-five. If she marries before then without her mother's blessing, then she loses her inheritance.' The reporter sighed heavily as he finished speaking.

'I take it that Mrs Delaware does not approve of you as a match for her daughter.' Kitty nodded understandingly.

'I've no money or title. I'm a journalist. Mrs Delaware intends Candace to marry that boring old stick, Savernake. He has a country estate and a title. Mrs Delaware would like Candace to become Lady Savernake. Candace has the loot to reel him in, her late father was big in ball bearings apparently. Candace was their only child,' Mr Fetherington explained.

'I presume then that until her birthday her mother holds the purse strings,' Matt mused.

'I've known Candace for ages. She's a really tip-top girl. I'd marry her tomorrow and hang the money, but it wouldn't be fair to Candace.' The reporter gave them a worried look. 'Please don't say anything to Mrs Delaware or she'll have Candace locked up in a nunnery or marched down the aisle to Savernake.'

Kitty exchanged a meaningful glance with Matt. 'It's really none of our business. We were merely curious since Mrs Delaware seems to be quite a force to be reckoned with, judging from our brief acquaintance.'

Roland Fetherington gave a bitter laugh. 'Candace's mother is quite a piece of work. If I were you, I'd be very careful around her. Definitely, if you go to the casino with her don't play poker against her. She's a card fiend.'

'We are going with them to the casino tonight. The comte has offered to introduce us to the owners, Monsieur and Madame Dupont,' Kitty said.

Roland's brows raised. 'An interesting pair, the Duponts. They have fingers in every pie in Nice. They are at the top of the society heap, friends of the mayor and all that jazz.'

'It promises to be an interesting evening then,' Matt said.

'I may well see you there. I regularly camp out front with Marc Lapin, a photographer friend of mine. The great and good like to see themselves in print looking glamorous. He takes the pictures, I do the write-ups.' Roland collected his hat and rose from his seat. 'Please do let me know if you hear any more on the murder from the inspector. It's the biggest story I've had in ages.'

Kitty sighed as she watched the reporter make his way out of the grounds, carefully avoiding the waiting staff.

'That was interesting information about the Duponts, don't you think?' Matt looked at Kitty.

'Yes. That matchbook Federico was carrying had to mean something. He'd obviously been to the casino, and I don't think from everything we've heard about it that it's the kind of place that would have admitted a tramp,' Kitty said.

'I think your new chum, Mr Fetherington, might prove useful to us,' Matt said as he raised his hand to signal to one of the waiters.

'Those were my thoughts exactly,' Kitty agreed.

Once their order had been placed for a jug of iced lemonade, Kitty sat back and popped on her round metal-framed sunglasses. The air was much warmer now and a faint heat haze shimmered over the marble slabs of the terrace. A cicada chirped noisily from somewhere in the tree above her head and there was a subdued hum of chatter as the tables nearby filled with people lunching.

'I suggest we wait until later this afternoon to go and post your cards, unless there is a box in the lobby,' Matt suggested as the waiter placed their order down on the table in front of them.

'Yes, it feels much warmer than when we arrived yesterday. I really don't fancy walking out in this heat.' Kitty smiled her thanks at the waiter as he poured their drinks before leaving. 'I do feel a tad guilty though, sitting here doing nothing,' she said after taking a sip of her drink.

'There is nothing much we can do for now. We shall have to wait and see what we can discover tonight at the casino.' Matt adjusted his hat, so that the brim shaded his eyes.

Kitty wondered what they would find out. Certainly, Monsieur and Madame Dupont sounded interesting, but would they lead them to the missing papers?

They were debating ordering lunch when there was a

kerfuffle on the terrace and Mrs Delaware, accompanied by the comte, approached them.

'Oh, my dears, such a trying morning.' Mrs Delaware waited for the comte to pull out the vacant chair so she could be seated. A waiter scuttled forwards with an extra seat so that the comte too could join them.

Kitty moved her postcards and her book to make room for Mrs Delaware to deposit her floral silk scarf, sunglasses and silver monogrammed cigarette case onto the tabletop. 'It's certainly very warm out there today,' Kitty remarked politely.

'Too warm for me.' Mrs Delaware settled into her chair while the comte ordered dry white wine, iced water and the luncheon menu from the waiter.

Kitty could see they were about to have company for lunch whether they wanted it or not. Mrs Delaware took out a small enamelled compact and checked her flushed complexion, patting her blonded curls in place under her wide-brimmed, white straw hat.

'Have you been out in the town?' Matt asked. He had risen from his seat to greet the newcomers but was now settled back down.

'I had so many errands that I simply had to run. I had hoped that Candace would assist me, but she apparently had made her own arrangements this morning.' Mrs Delaware was obviously annoyed by her daughter's defection. 'The difficulties of travelling when one doesn't have reliable help. Has your maid accompanied you, Mrs Bryant?'

Kitty couldn't meet Matt's gaze at this question. She knew he would find it a humorous enquiry given that Kitty's usual maid was in fact her best friend.

'Not on this holiday, Mrs Delaware. It's just the two of us,' Kitty responded politely.

The waiter returned with refreshments and menus while the American woman took out her small folding fan to waft air onto her face. She directed the waiter to return in five minutes to take their lunch order while the comte poured her some iced water to accompany her glass of wine.

'That is so much better,' Mrs Delaware declared after taking a sip alternately from each glass.

'Have you spent your morning here?' the comte asked.

'Yes, we went for a walk early this morning, before breakfast whilst it was cool. It was very pleasant, although we got hopelessly lost again,' Kitty said. She thought it best to say that since someone had been observing the villa and had seen them there. Not that her story would hold water, but it might muddy any suspicions a little.

'I hope this time at least you did not stumble upon any more bodies.' The comte smiled at her.

'No, thank heavens. We decided we should have a lazy day since we have the casino to look forward to tonight,' Matt agreed.

'I've been writing my postcards and reading my book.' Kitty indicated the neat pile of her possessions that she had moved to make room for Mrs Delaware's things.

The older woman glanced at the cards. Kitty realised too late that the upper one showed the address for Enderley Hall.

'Oh but, my dear, do forgive me, but is your uncle Lord Medford? I do believe I met him and your aunt at a reception at the American Embassy in London a few months ago. What a delightful coincidence.' Mrs Delaware patted Kitty's hand.

Kitty noticed, however, that her gaze had suddenly sharpened, and she was certain she was attempting to read the message on the card. Kitty collected up her things and placed them out of view inside her large straw bag.

'Yes, that's my uncle. I was just writing to tell him what happened yesterday. Poor darling, he will be so upset. It was very kind of him to send us on this holiday, he really wanted us to relax for a few days. I was concerned that if he saw a report in the newspaper and our names were mentioned he might worry. You know how the press can be.' Kitty was quite pleased with herself that she had flipped the situation around to probe a little into Mrs Delaware's views on Mr Fetherington.

'Snakes, the lot of them. I saw you were accosted yesterday evening at dinner by that ghastly boy, Roland Fetherington. He hops around one like a flea. Poor Candace has been the subject of his unwanted attentions.' Mrs Delaware shook her head in despair.

'Oh dear. Yes, Mr Fetherington wanted to talk to us about the murder. That was why I was worried in case my uncle might read something in the press. I think Mr Fetherington said he worked for an English newspaper.' Kitty looked at Mrs Delaware and the comte for confirmation.

'I believe that is where he sells most of his news stories. He travels around a lot it would seem. We have encountered him in Venice and in Rome before we came here.' The comte frowned.

'You travel extensively I take it, Mrs Delaware?' Matt asked.

'Yes, I feel it my duty to ensure that Candace has experience of the world. My dear late husband was a wealthy man and Candace will be a rich young woman in her own right very soon. I'd be failing in my duty as a mother if I didn't make certain that she was exposed to the cream of society and, of course, if she should meet someone suitable well, that would be most delightful, don't you think?' Mrs Delaware turned wide, blue but icy eyes on Kitty.

'She seems friendly with Sir Montague Savernake,' Kitty responded.

Personally, she felt it was up to Candace who she wished to befriend or court. On the one hand she could see Mrs Delaware's reasoning that she didn't wish her daughter to fall prey to a man only interested in Candace's fortune. However, she suspected that Sir Montague's title was what was most appealing to Mrs Delaware. Sir Montague didn't seem, on their brief acquaintance, to be the most intelligent of men.

'Monty is a doll, isn't he? And he adores Candace. He has a very fine estate you know in Wiltshire. Yes, it would be nice to see Candace settled as Lady Savernake.' Mrs Delaware beamed at Kitty and Matt.

'Eunice, my dear, we should make our selection for lunch, the waiter is returning.' The comte passed the menu across.

Their orders chosen and given, they returned to their conversation once the waiter had departed.

'Monty accompanied us this morning for a short time. I think he too hoped that Candace would join us. I rather think we lost him somewhere near the cathedral.' A frown puckered Mrs Delaware's brow.

'I believe he had some business at the bank, my dear,' the comte said.

'Oh yes, of course.' Mrs Delaware appeared relieved by her companion's reminder.

They were just finishing their main course of a light green salad, baby potatoes and veal cutlets when Candace arrived to join them.

A waiter produced another chair and more glasses, and the girl took her place at the table.

'Candace, darling, wherever have you been? We waited for you this morning. Have you eaten lunch?' her mother asked as Candace poured herself a glass of wine.

'I'm really not hungry, Mother. I had a good breakfast, and I did tell you I wouldn't be going out with you this morning,' Candace replied, before taking a large sip of wine.

Kitty noticed the girl didn't answer the first part of her mother's question. The girl was dressed like Kitty in beach pyjamas. Candace's were primrose yellow and covered with a jolly print of cacti and donkeys. Her face was carefully made up and

Kitty suspected the girl had made an effort for her earlier meeting with Roland Fetherington.

It was plain from their earlier conversation that Mrs Delaware would definitely not be amused if she learned of her daughter and Roland Fetherington's 'understanding'.

Candace did, however, consent to ordering a dish of lemon sorbet when the waiter came to clear the plates from the main course.

'You'll never guess, darling, but Mrs Bryant is related to Lord and Lady Medford. You remember, we met them in London at the embassy reception,' Mrs Delaware informed her daughter. 'I was saying it's a small world.'

'I suppose it is,' Candace agreed politely.

'Where did you meet Sir Montague?' Kitty asked the girl.

Her mother answered for her. 'That was London too, wasn't it, darling? At that jazz club in Mayfair?'

'Yes. I think so.' Candace's answer wasn't brimming with enthusiasm.

'And you, my dear comte, where did you make the acquaintance of our delightful new friends?' Matt asked.

Kitty too was interested in this answer. From what Mrs Delaware had said earlier it had sounded as if the party had been travelling together for a while.

'Rome, my dear?' the comte suggested to Mrs Delaware as if slightly uncertain of his answer.

'I think it was in Berlin.' Candace took out a silver monogramed cigarette case and inserted a cigarette into a small ebony holder.

The comte immediately furnished her with a light. 'Oh yes, perhaps it was. You may be right.'

Kitty wondered if it was just her imagination or if the usually suave and debonair comte seemed a little annoyed at Candace's correction.

'A fascinating city, Berlin,' Matt remarked.

'Oh, have you visited there?' Mrs Delaware asked.

'It's been some years ago now.' Matt kept his answer light.

Kitty assumed it must have been after the end of the war when Matt had first begun working for the brigadier. She knew he had travelled extensively on various diplomatic and other missions.

Their desserts arrived and conversation ceased momentarily while they gave their ice creams and sorbets their full attention.

'I take it that you also travel a lot?' Kitty asked the comte as she set her spoon back down in her now empty delicate glass boat-shaped dish.

'Indeed. I am a buyer for an auction house in Rome. My work takes me to many different places appraising works of art.' The comte bowed his head towards Kitty.

'He has given me such good investment advice regarding paintings and sculptures. I have acquired some lovely things and had them shipped home. I've heard that your uncle has an exceptionally fine old mural at his house.' Mrs Delaware looked at Kitty.

'He has indeed.' Kitty suppressed a small shiver at the memory of the fate of the Jewish woman who had restored the mural during her first ever visit to Enderley.

'I should love to see it in person. I do so adore antiques and you have so much history in England,' Mrs Delaware hinted.

Kitty smiled back politely. She had no intention of prompting her uncle and aunt to invite Eunice and Candace to Enderley. Something about them and their recent travel itinerary suggested to her that they were not the kind of guests her family would welcome.

CHAPTER SEVEN

Matt and Kitty excused themselves from their companions once lunch was completed and headed back to their room. They had agreed to meet the Delawares before dinner at the bar downstairs for drinks. After dining, the comte had said that he would secure cars to transport the group to and from the casino.

'Mrs Delaware dropped some substantial hints about visiting Enderley, didn't she?' Matt slipped off his shoes and reclined himself on the large bed.

'Yes, she did seem very interested.' Kitty frowned as she turned to face him. 'There is something odd isn't there about the whole set up? You know, Mrs Delaware's friendship with the comte, and then her pushing Candace at Sir Montague.'

'They certainly aren't the kind of people we would usually choose to socialise with,' Matt agreed.

He knew what Kitty meant. It was as if their acquaintance had been forced upon them ever since they had discovered Federico's body in the alleyway.

'I can understand their curiosity when they heard about the murder, but there is something else that I can't quite put my finger on.' She paused in her pacing up and down the sumptuously appointed room. 'Do you think I'm overthinking things, Matt? I fear the brigadier's warnings about not trusting anyone might be playing on my mind,' she confessed.

Matt sat up and pulled an extra pillow behind his head. 'No, you're wise to be cautious. We were warned too, remember, that there was a group within the hotel that we needed to be wary of. These are strange times at the moment politically, and we are not on English soil. That business this morning at the villa where someone was watching us through binoculars means we do need to be very careful.'

Kitty perched herself on the edge of the bed next to him. He scooted over to give her a little more room and took hold of her hand.

'Darling, we can go home if you're frightened. The brigadier would understand. We have no guarantee now of finding those papers. They may be long gone and this poking about is for nothing.' He could see that Kitty was troubled by the events of the previous day and the morning's escapade.

'No, Matt, that wouldn't be right. We agreed to take this job on, and we need to see it through to the best of our ability. If there is no new information to be found tonight, then we may have to give up and go home anyway but we owe it to the brigadier to try.'

Matt patted her hand reassuringly. 'Very well. We'll see what we can discover tonight. There seems little we can do at present though to find out who may have killed Federico. That will have to be a job for the inspector. He knows Nice far better than we do.'

'Do you think he may ask us again about the murder?' Kitty asked. Her gaze was troubled.

'Because we think he knows that we know the victim's identity?' Matt frowned. 'No, I think he suspects that there is espionage afoot. He made the point about not being too far from the border. I don't think, however, that he will wish to rock the diplomatic boat.'

* * *

Kitty felt suitably well rested and refreshed after her afternoon nap and dressed with care for the evening ahead. Luckily, she had packed a few of her nicest evening gowns for her visit to Enderley and Lucy had loaned her a couple more for the unexpected trip to France.

She decided on one that Lucy had persuaded her to borrow, an expensive gunmetal-grey satin sheath with diamanté straps. Matt let out a low whistle of approval, bringing a blush to her cheeks when she showed it to him for his approval.

'*Très chic*, darling.'

Kitty grinned at him and collected her silver-metallic evening bag and Lucy's white fur stole ready to go downstairs.

'All set for tonight?' she asked, thinking her husband looked equally dashing in his evening attire.

'I think so,' Matt responded, locking the room door behind them as they ventured out onto the landing.

When they arrived downstairs the Delaware party was already assembled in the bar. Mrs Delaware and the comte were seated at one of the tables. Eunice was dressed in a dark-blue satin gown and a profusion of diamonds. The comte looked very debonair in an exquisitely cut evening suit as he smoked his cigarette.

Candace was standing nearby, dressed in a gold-lamé gown, holding an almost empty cocktail glass. She was accompanied by Sir Montague who appeared to be holding forth on something. Not that Candace seemed to be paying any attention to him. She was twirling the cocktail stick in her drink and gazing rather absently at the contents at the bottom of the glass.

'Captain Bryant, Mrs Bryant, do come and join us.' Mrs Delaware patted the seat of the empty chair next to her in invitation.

'Please call us Matt and Kitty,' Kitty said, taking the chair, while Matt offered to order more drinks.

'Then you must call us Eunice and Luciano,' Mrs Delaware insisted.

'I have arranged the cars to collect us at nine o'clock. My friends, the Duponts, are holding a drinks reception at the casino tonight and are delighted that we are to join them,' the comte said.

'I must confess I have never been in a casino before,' Kitty remarked as Matt returned with a glass of champagne for her.

'Oh, my dear, you'll love it, I'm sure. It's such fun. Do you play any card games?' Mrs Delaware asked.

Kitty shook her head. 'I'm afraid not. Not really. I think I'll probably just watch everyone else tonight to learn what to do.'

'I shall take you under my wing. *Vingt et un* is very straightforward and a spin at roulette would start you off nicely,' Mrs Delaware declared. 'How about you, Matt? Do you play cards at all?'

'I have some experience of casinos, but I must confess I am not really a gambler,' Matt said.

'Well don't play cards with Mother.' Candace joined the group, seating herself near the table. 'She is quite a shark.'

'Candace, really!' Eunice admonished her daughter. Her tone was playful, but Kitty saw there was a flintiness in her gaze when she looked at Candace.

Once they had gone through to the dining room, Kitty found herself seated next to Sir Montague at the dinner table.

'Sir Montague, are you enjoying Nice?' she asked him as the first course of consommé was delivered. She was curious to find out more about him and his rather lacklustre pursuit of Candace.

'Yes, it's quite a lark here. The nightlife is rather fun and, of course, the weather is nice. I was saying to Candace I was thinking of buying a yacht. There are some rather fine ones in the harbour.' He picked up his linen napkin and shook it out onto his lap.

'How fun, do you sail?' Living in Dartmouth Kitty was well versed in boats and knew it to be quite an expensive hobby. Perhaps Sir Montague thought it might be something Candace would pay for if they were to marry.

'Not really. I was thinking I might take it up. Bit of a hobby, you know.' He gave a slight shrug and delved into his soup.

Kitty abandoned any hope of furthering her acquaintance with Sir Montague until the first course was finished. Mrs Delaware was deep in conversation with the comte, and Matt, seated on her other side, was talking to Candace who was opposite him.

She took a sip of her wine as the soup bowls were cleared and the fish course was served. She noticed Sir Montague's gaze resting on Candace as the girl laughed at something Matt had said.

'Miss Delaware is very pretty, don't you think?' Kitty remarked, determined to discover if the man did admire Miss Delaware or if he was purely interested in the girl's trust fund.

'What? Oh yes, she is rather.' Sir Montague flushed slightly.

'Where did you meet? I thought Mrs Delaware said something about a club in London?' Kitty asked.

'Um, yes, I think it was. I was on a night out in Mayfair with some chums and was at a bit of a loose end. Ran into Candace at a club. You know, friend of a friend kind of thing.' Sir Montague gave a small smile.

'And here you are together in Nice.' Kitty leaned back slightly to allow the waiter to place her plate in front of her.

'Yes, indeed. I called on her a few times in London and Mrs Delaware suggested I join her party on their travels in France. I know Cannes and Nice quite well, so I was happy to offer my services as a guide.' Sir Montague picked up his cutlery.

'Did you know the comte too?' Kitty asked as she started on her fish.

'No, ran across him quite quickly though. He's very thick with Candace's mother. I think they had been to several places in Europe together. He's been advising her on some artistic purchases. I know they have been to several auctions. I had thought I might get him to look at a couple of pictures knocking around at home, see what he thought.' Sir Montague turned his attention to his food.

Kitty waited until the course was finished before picking up the thread of the conversation once more.

'You must have been to the casino before, Sir Montague, do you know Monsieur and Madame Dupont?' Kitty asked as the plates were cleared.

'Yes, indeed, although Luciano is rather better acquainted with them than I. Very pleasant people,' he confirmed.

'I must confess, I'm rather afraid of making something of a fool of myself tonight. I've never visited a casino before,' Kitty said.

'Oh, there's no need to worry about it. Just have a look around the place if you are uncertain about trying any of the games. It has the most marvellous view and since the town has gained more electric lights, it's quite a sight from the terrace.'

'That reporter, Mr Fetherington, said that there was a photographer that snapped pictures outside the entrance on certain evenings.' Kitty picked up her wine glass and waited for Sir Montague to respond.

'Oh Fetherington. Don't believe a word he tells you, my dear. He's a regular nuisance about the place.' Sir Montague's tone was sharp, and Kitty saw she had struck a nerve. 'What did he want anyway?'

'He was asking about that poor chap who was killed. You

know, if the inspector had told us anything.' Kitty waved her free hand in a dismissive gesture.

'Oh yes, of course, a terrible business. There's a rumour going around the town that he was a spy. The police have put up posters trying to identify him. I saw one outside the town hall this afternoon.'

Kitty almost choked on her wine. 'Goodness, how peculiar. He was just a tramp as far as we could see. I wonder if they will find out who he is.'

Sir Montague shrugged. 'It seems he had no papers on him. A fellow at the café said he'd heard he had crossed the border from Italy. I suppose that's where the spy story has come from.'

'How extraordinary. Gosh, I would never have guessed.' Kitty was aware from the sudden stillness of Matt's body next to her that he had been listening in to the conversation.

'What was that, Monty?' It appeared that Candace too had caught what he had said.

'I was saying to Mrs Bryant, Kitty here, that fella they found in the alley, rumour has it in town that he was a spy of some sort,' Sir Montague said.

'A spy?' Mrs Delaware repeated.

'Ah rumours, the life blood of towns and villages. I'm sure he was probably just some unfortunate down and out.' The comte seemed disinclined to take Sir Montague's remark seriously. 'What say you, Captain Bryant?'

'I'm sure you're right. I suppose with the way the world is at the moment there are bound to be these kinds of stories whenever something unpleasant occurs. I expect someone will identify the poor fellow and it will turn out to be no great mystery at all,' Matt replied.

'I suppose so,' the comte agreed.

The conversation turned back to the evening ahead and by the time dessert had been consumed and coffee taken the cars had arrived to transport them to the casino. Kitty and Matt found themselves sharing their car with Candace and Sir Montague, while Mrs Delaware and the comte took the other large black Rolls Royce.

Kitty gazed out of the car window as the car swept them through the streets of the town, past the brightly lit bars and cafés and along the seafront. They continued on towards a glittering white building, styled like the Acropolis in Athens, floodlit on top of a small promontory at the far edge of the town.

Butterflies fluttered in her stomach and her grip tightened on the silver chain handle of her evening bag. Would they learn anything new at the casino? The cars turned off from the main road and up the steep drive to the front of the building where they halted. A uniformed doorman, smart in burgundy livery and grey top hat, rushed forward to open the car doors for them.

A red carpet was in place down the short flight of marble steps and a gleaming brass handrail was there to assist less able guests. The faint strains of classical music reached her as she took Matt's arm ready to enter the building.

The comte and Mrs Delaware were already out of their car and waiting for them. Candace and Sir Montague followed them in under the stone canopy supported by substantial Doric-style marble pillars. Large green-fronded palms in gold-coloured pots filled the entrance way and Kitty spied a discreet mahogany and glass cashier's booth in the corner.

There was a sudden flash from a camera and Kitty glimpsed what appeared to be Roland Fetherington and his photographer friend lurking in the background near the marble columns.

'*Mon cher ami.*' A middle-aged man in immaculate evening wear and oiled hair came forward to greet the comte in the continental style. He was accompanied by a woman of a similar age, rail thin and elegant in a draped-style eau de Nil silk gown.

'My dear Jerard, Helene, may I present Captain Matthew Bryant and his wife Kitty.'

Introductions were made and Kitty found herself being

somewhat sweatily embraced by Monsieur Dupont and air kissed by his wife, before being led inside the casino.

CHAPTER EIGHT

Kitty wasn't sure what she had expected the interior of the casino to look like. Her only impressions had been from a film she had seen at the picture house with Alice ages ago. She vaguely remembered it had been a film about gangsters and there had been a gunfight at one point. Hopefully this evening's outing would be less dramatic.

The Duponts led their group through what seemed to be the main hall. There were various green baize-topped tables surrounded by glamorously dressed men and women, smoking and drinking cocktails. Music was provided by a small three-piece group playing away on a stage in the corner.

Each table was lit from above with a separate light producing small islands of activity in the room. Some appeared to be playing a card game. Others were throwing dice or placing red, blue and white counters at the roulette table. There appeared to be as many people watching the games as there were taking part. That at least was reassuring.

There was a hum of chatter and laughter mixed in with the faint strains of the classical music she had heard on the way inside. A faint bluish haze of smoke mingled with the perfume worn by the women and the scent from the large vases of lilies and roses dotted around the room.

A polished mahogany well-stocked bar was at the far end of the room with the two white-jacketed bar stewards busy shaking cocktails and pouring champagne for the guests. Everything spoke of glamour and comfort.

'Come, *mes amis*, come.' Monsieur Dupont ushered them through the room to another space accessed by a marble archway. This area was cordoned off by thick red cord suspended between brass stanchions with a card saying *privé*.

A large man in evening dress moved the barrier as the Duponts approached and allowed them all to enter. The new room was furnished with black leather and chrome chairs and sofas in the latest style. Large Grecian-style marble statues framed a huge plate-glass window and a door overlooking the terrace, which ran around the outside of the building.

It also afforded a view of the bay. Although dark outside now, the stars were bright, and the full moon was creating a pathway over the sea. In the distance a couple of ships were showing as dots of yellow light on the water.

Several people were already in the room nibbling on the canapés being circulated by the smartly dressed waiters, who also bore trays of champagne. Kitty soon found a glass being pressed into her hand by Monsieur Dupont.

'*Mon cher madame*, welcome to Casino Plessy, any friend of Luciano is, of course, a friend of ours. He tells me this is your first time in Nice and your first visit to a casino? I trust you like this?' He waved a slightly pudgy hand expansively at their surroundings, clearly expecting her to admire it all.

'It all seems most delightful and well appointed. It's extremely kind of you to invite us,' Kitty said.

Monsieur Dupont beamed with satisfaction at her reply. 'It is our pleasure, madame, besides *mon ami* Luciano tells me that you and your husband had a very unfortunate introduction to our beautiful town. The death of that poor vagrant, I hear.'

'Yes, sadly, it was all rather ghastly, poor fellow.' Kitty wondered what else the comte had been telling his dear friend Monsieur Dupont.

'A tramp, I believe, and no one seems to know who he was or where he came from.' Monsieur Dupont shook his head in a sorrowful fashion.

'Yes, although I have now heard a rumour that people are saying he was a spy and had come from Italy.' Kitty waited to see how Monsieur Dupont might react to this suggestion.

'Ha, I detect the voice of Inspector Villier. The poor fellow is obsessed with the idea of espionage.' Monsieur Dupont chuckled but Kitty thought she noticed a sudden sharpening in the casino owner's gaze.

It was apparent to Kitty that if Federico had come to Casino Plessy he would not have been disguised as a vagrant. Everything about the casino and its guests spoke of money and the higher echelons of society. No, if the dead man had visited here, he would have been dressed as the other guests.

'I confess that I am relieved to hear that. The whole thing has been very distressing and this rumour about spies, well...' Kitty gave a delicate shudder as she sipped her champagne.

'I understand completely. It is not an experience a lovely young lady like yourself should have encountered. But come, my dear madame, and I will introduce you to some people. You will enjoy yourself and forget such horrid things.' Monsieur Dupont guided her towards a group of elegantly dressed men and women.

The party it seemed consisted of guests of various nationalities: American, French, Italian and German. All of whom appeared to know the Duponts, and in varying degrees it seemed, each other. Some were regular guests in the town and several appeared to have yachts moored in the harbour.

'Are you having fun?' Matt murmured in her ear having finally extricated himself from an elderly Frenchman who appeared to have been enjoying the opportunity to practise his English.

'It's all terribly glamorous, isn't it?' Kitty replied, looking around at their fellow guests.

'I've found the matchbooks.' Matt had his head close to hers so that it would appear to the casual observer that he was whispering sweet nothings in her ear.

'Where?' Kitty breathed back.

'On the bar over there. We need to check to see if they are available in the main room as well or just in here,' Matt said.

Kitty glanced towards the small bar in the corner where the waiters were collecting and depositing their silver trays. She could see a small artistic arrangement of blue matchbooks identical to the one they had found on Federico's body.

'Madame Dupont has kindly offered to show us around the main part of the casino so that we may try our luck on the tables, should we so wish.' Matt spoke a little more loudly and Kitty realised that the lady in question had moved nearer to them.

'How very kind of her.' Kitty picked up on his cue and raised her voice slightly.

Madame Dupont came to join them. 'What a lovely fur.' She touched Kitty's borrowed stole with the tip of her fingers.

'Thank you, my cousin, Lady Thurscomb, has loaned it to me for this holiday. She thought white more of a spring colour,' Kitty replied.

'It is very lovely. Do you just have the one cousin?' Madame Dupont asked.

'Yes, Lucy, she and her husband are at Enderley now visiting my aunt and uncle.' Kitty set her half-drunk glass of champagne down on the empty tray of a passing waiter.

'A country estate is always charming,' Madame Dupont replied.

Kitty had started to feel a little light-headed and decided it might be wise to avoid having anything else to drink.

'Enderley is rather lovely,' Kitty agreed.

Matt followed suit and deposited his glass on a tray too. He took Kitty's arm as they prepared to accompany Madame Dupont into the main hall of the casino.

Candace seemed to have disappeared and Kitty wondered if the girl might have risked slipping away to meet up with Roland Fetherington. The comte was standing with Monsieur Dupont by the window, ostensibly looking at the view across the bay as they smoked their cigarettes. Kitty noticed, however, that the two men were conversing heatedly but discreetly about something.

As the casino employee unclipped the thick, red rope to allow them into the hall Kitty noticed Sir Montague was already at the roulette wheel. His usually rather sheep-like face flushed with excitement as he placed various coloured chips on the numbered squares on the green baize cloth.

Madame Dupont took them around the room, graciously explaining the various entertainments which were on offer.

'Well, my dear Kitty, Matt, which game do you think you would like to try first?' Madame Dupont asked.

'It all looks so interesting. I think I'd like to just continue watching for a while before I decide. If that's all right, of course?' Kitty asked.

'*Absolument*, you will find the booth is in the foyer should you require any markers.' Madame Dupont smiled graciously at them and excused herself to return to her other guests.

Mrs Delaware had already slipped away from the side room to take her seat at one of the card tables. Her attention now seemed to be solely on the cards she had in her well-manicured hand.

'Let's circulate around the room and try to get nearer to the bar.' Kitty pressed Matt's arm gently to indicate a gap in the crowd and they started to make their way past the roulette table towards the bar at the far end.

They paused to watch the action at the wheel so as not to draw any attention to themselves. Kitty suspected that the Duponts probably had eyes everywhere within the casino. Both to watch those gambling and also to watch the croupiers on the tables. She recalled from the film she had seen with Alice that one of the croupiers in the movie had been stealing from the house.

Sir Montague appeared to be having a run of good luck at the wheel. He now had a sizeable stack of coloured counters in front of him. Two attractive young women in revealing silk dresses had also appeared by his side, cheering him on.

After watching for a few minutes, they walked away towards the bar where Kitty requested a fruit juice. One of the bar stewards swiftly obliged, pouring her an orange juice and adding several cubes of ice to her glass.

'No matchbooks here,' Kitty murmured to Matt as they wandered back out into the room.

That meant the matches could only have come from the private area of the lounge which was guarded by a casino employee. A shiver ran down Kitty's spine. The Duponts had to have known Federico or he would not have been able to gain entrance to that area of the room. What had he been doing there? Had he arranged to meet someone, and if so why?

Mrs Delaware was still engrossed in her card game and the comte had joined her, standing behind to watch her play. Kitty sipped her juice, the cold drink refreshing her.

'We should get some chips and at least try one or two of the tables,' Matt said.

Kitty nodded in agreement. It would look very odd if they didn't and she didn't wish to cause any offence to their hosts. They wandered back out into the foyer to the glass-fronted cashier's booth in the corner where Matt exchanged some francs for gaming chips.

'I fear we are rather low stakes compared to the amounts many of the others here are risking,' he said with a wry smile.

Kitty was unsurprised. Judging from the clothes and the jewels sported by the other guests she had suspected as much.

'The air is cooler at least out here,' Kitty said.

Another large limousine pulled up at the foot of the steps and the doorman sprang into action to open the door ready to escort the occupants inside. Kitty noticed the flash from the photographer snapping the new arrivals. She didn't see Roland Fetherington though or any sign of Candace.

'We can take the air for a moment before returning to the tables if you like.' Matt offered her his arm to stroll around the terrace.

Several other couples seemed to have had the same idea and Kitty discovered that there were a couple of glass panelled doors which opened from the main room. The cooler air did much to clear the muzzy feeling from her head.

Matt paused in front of a shallow flight of lit stone steps leading down to a path into the gardens between the palms and oleander bushes.

'I expect it is just as delightful a spot in daylight as it is at night,' Kitty agreed.

Did Federico come up this path and enter the casino via one of the doors on the terrace or had he too arrived by car, perhaps as part of a party? she mused.

'I wonder where this path leads?' Matt asked, glancing at Kitty.

'We could walk down a little way. It seems to be lit on this top part,' she suggested.

They set off down the steps and along the stone pathway, passing a shadowy recess housing a marble bench. The scent of roses and the sound of the cicadas both seemed magnified on the night air. The garden went down towards the sea with the path curving back around towards the front of the casino on the road side.

'It seems to lead back around to the front of the casino near where the cars park. I can see some kind of wrought-iron gate. That's probably where it meets the road. Wait here a minute.' Matt extracted his arm from her grasp and hurried off towards the gate.

He returned a few minutes later. 'It's securely locked, with a padlock. I was right though, it does lead onto the main road.'

'Interesting. We should go back inside and take a turn on the tables,' Kitty suggested, resting her hand back on her husband's arm.

They turned and had scarcely gone more than a few steps when a piercing scream sounded on the path just ahead of them.

CHAPTER NINE

Kitty clutched at Matt's arm. 'What was that?'

They hurried back up the stone path until they reached the area containing the marble bench. A man's body lay sprawled face down on the ground in front of the seat, blood oozing stickily from a large wound on the back of his head.

Candace stood to one side, her hands pressed to her lips, her body trembling.

'I just found him here.' Her words were barely audible.

Matt dropped to his knee to check the man's vital signs. Feeling for a pulse in his neck. 'He's alive.'

Kitty placed her arm around Candace's shoulders as people started to appear, alerted by Candace's scream. One of the first amongst them was Roland Fetherington.

'Candace?' Roland looked first at the girl as if to ensure she was safe before fully taking in the man on the ground. 'That's Marc Lapin, the photographer. What's happened?'

'He's been badly hurt. We need an ambulance and the police. It looks as if he has been attacked.' As Matt spoke two large men in evening attire pushed their way through the small chattering knot of guests who had gathered on the path.

Kitty guessed from their demeanour they must be part of the security team for the casino. They took one look at the man on the ground and began to take charge. Roland addressed them in fluent French. One of the men nodded and rapidly departed back towards the casino. The other man began to clear the crowd, ushering them away back inside the building.

'They are calling for assistance. The police and an ambulance will be here soon,' Roland said. He went to Candace and placed his arm tenderly around her waist, guiding her to sit beside him on the bench. The girl sobbed and buried her face in his shoulder.

Freed from her immediate responsibilities, Kitty went to join Matt beside the wounded man. She looked around the site for any clue as to what might have happened to him.

It didn't take long for her to spot something. 'There is a large piece of stone with blood and hair on it over there.' She bent down to where Matt was still attending to the injured photographer.

'Hit from behind, I'd say,' Matt agreed.

'Where is his camera?' Kitty asked.

She could see no sign of it anywhere. She thought it unlikely that he would have set it down somewhere. Had he been robbed for it? Or had he not had it with him?

In the distance she heard the wail of sirens drawing closer.

'That must be the police or the ambulance or both,' she said to Matt.

'Why would anyone wish to hurt Marc? He's worked this patch for years. Two nights a week, taking pictures. He sends them to the local newspaper and sells copies to anyone who wants to purchase their own photograph as a souvenir.' Roland appeared almost as shaken as Candace.

Monsieur Dupont appeared on the scene flanked by the man who had apparently summoned the police and ambulance.

His plump face creased in distress when he saw the man on the ground.

'*Zut alors! Mon cher* Mademoiselle Candace, Captain Bryant, Madame Bryant, what has happened? Come, come inside. The police and ambulance are here, with the *docteur*.' He appeared to ignore Roland Fetherington.

There was a stir above them, and Inspector Villier arrived, accompanied by a uniformed gendarme and the man in the checked suit who Kitty had seen attending Federico's murder scene.

'Captain Bryant, Madame Bryant.' Inspector Villier appeared surprised to see them.

Matt straightened up and stepped away from the injured man so that the doctor could attend to him.

'The injured man is the casino photographer. Mr Fetherington there identified him.' Matt nodded towards Roland. 'He seems to have been hit on the back of the head with a large stone.' Again Matt indicated with his head the rock Kitty had located earlier. 'We were strolling on the path lower down when we heard Candace scream. We arrived to find the poor fellow like this.'

Inspector Villier nodded his head slowly at Matt's concise description of events. Monsieur Dupont stood to one side wringing his pudgy hands in despair. Yet Kitty thought she saw a sharp gleam in the man's eyes, which was at odds with the image he was presenting to the inspector.

'You found this man, mademoiselle?' Inspector Villier turned to Candace.

The girl nodded miserably. 'I was hot inside the casino and had a bit of a headache. I came out here to smoke a cigarette and get some air. When I turned the corner, there he was.' She broke off into a sob and immediately opened her evening purse to retrieve a lace-edged handkerchief.

'A tragic accident, no doubt. The man must have slipped,

fallen and banged his head on one of the edge stones,' Monsieur Dupont suggested.

The inspector gave him a scathing glance at this suggestion and turned to the doctor, asking a flurry of questions. The doctor replied and two men bearing a stretcher came down the path. They lifted the wounded man under the doctor's instruction and departed with the victim. The doctor said a few more words to the inspector and hurried after them.

Inspector Villier's expression was grave. 'The doctor is not hopeful about the man's prognosis. He fears there is bleeding in the brain from the blow he sustained.'

Candace winced and turned her head into Roland's shoulder with a small cry of despair. Matt placed his arm around Kitty's waist offering her his silent support. A uniformed gendarme came down the path and greeted the inspector.

Inspector Villier issued a stream of instructions to the policeman before turning to Monsieur Dupont who stood fidgeting at the side of the path.

'Perhaps, Monsieur Dupont, there is a quiet, private space where we may all go so that I can take some more details of what has happened here this evening?' The policeman's request sounded more like an order and Monsieur Dupont sprang into action.

'But, of course, my dear inspector. Come, come. No doubt Mademoiselle Candace's *maman* will be most concerned for her daughter.' The casino owner started to lead them back towards the building.

'I think it best for a moment if the *maman* of Mademoiselle Delaware could perhaps wait outside until I have ascertained an account of this evening,' Inspector Villier replied firmly.

Candace and Roland followed behind Matt and Kitty as they re-entered the casino through the small crowd that had formed in the foyer. Monsieur Dupont led them to a well-concealed door in the marble-tiled wall beside the cashier's booth. He produced a key from the pocket of his waistcoat and unlocked it.

'Please, Inspector, use my private office, come inside.' Monsieur Dupont stood aside and allowed them all to enter.

The room was a large square space. A magnificently carved and gilded desk with a marble top was at the one end with several gilt chairs, ornately carved around the edges. A woven tapestry depicting a hunting scene hung on the wooden panelled wall behind the desk.

Monsieur Dupont waved the inspector to the larger, throne-like seat behind the desk. The rest all took their place on the gilt chairs, bringing them closer to the desk. They had scarcely sat down when there was a hammering on the door of the office and Mrs Delaware's voice could be heard stridently demanding to be allowed in.

The inspector placed his hands on the desktop to lever himself up and went to open the door, using his body to bar entrance.

'Mademoiselle Candace will be out shortly, madame. I must insist that you return to the lounge.' He closed the door in Mrs Delaware's face and turned the lock.

'Now, if I may proceed. I shall endeavour to be as quick as possible since I know that this is most distressing.' He retook his seat behind the desk.

'Monsieur Fetherington, you know the details of the injured man?' Inspector Villier took out his notebook while Roland gave the photographer's name and address to the policeman.

'Marc Lapin, Eight Rue De Poire.'

Monsieur Dupont busied himself at a small gilt and marble trolley, pouring shots of brandy into crystal tumblers and handing them out to everyone in the office. The inspector frowned when one was placed before him.

'I have asked my gendarme to search for Monsieur Lapin's

camera, which appears to be missing, along with the rolls of film he was no doubt carrying with him.' The inspector looked at Roland for confirmation.

'Marc always carried his film in his pockets. New film in his right pocket, spent film in his left,' Roland said.

Kitty thought the journalist seemed dazed by the events of the evening and his hand trembled as he raised the tumbler of brandy to his lips. Candace appeared to have recovered some of her colour and her composure since they had come into the office, placing her hand reassuringly on Roland's leg.

'*Eh bien*, and you and Monsieur Lapin were on good terms? No arguments between you?' the inspector asked.

'I say, are you implying it was me that bashed poor old Marc over the head? That's utter tosh! We have been working together for a few weeks and are on perfectly good terms. He's a decent fellow, a widower. He lost his wife in the influenza epidemic a few years ago.' Roland glared at the inspector.

The inspector merely made notes in his book. 'Do you know anyone who had quarrelled with Monsieur Lapin? Did he owe money to anyone, or did someone owe him money?'

'No, Marc was on good terms with everyone as far as I know. He kept himself pretty much to himself. Like I said, he was a decent fellow.' Roland paused.

The inspector looked up from his note-taking. 'You have thought of something, Monsieur Fetherington?'

Roland's brow furrowed. 'It was just something Marc said when I arrived this evening. We were talking about the man Captain and Mrs Bryant found in the alley. You have started to circulate posters around the town to try and identify him?' He looked at the inspector.

'*Oui*, what of it?' Inspector Villier asked.

'Marc said he had seen him before, here at the casino. He had taken his picture the day before he was killed,' Roland said.

'*C'est impossible!*' Monsieur Dupont erupted. 'A hobo in

my casino. No, my clientele is most select. A tramp would not be allowed anywhere near these premises.'

'Silence!' Inspector Villier smacked the top of the desk with the palm of his hand. 'Monsieur Fetherington, explain your statement, please.'

The creases on Roland's brow deepened. 'Marc said the man was well dressed in evening wear. He arrived alone, late on and went inside. He said he planned to call in at the police station in the morning to take in the photographs.'

'What does Monsieur Lapin do with his photographs? The ones he does not sell?' the inspector asked.

Kitty tightened her grip on Matt's hand. This sounded as if it could be a possible clue. If the photographs showed Federico meeting someone, well, it might lead to the missing papers or to his murderer.

Roland shrugged. 'He keeps all of them in a file with the date for about three months. He has a darkroom at his house as he uses the front room as a studio for passport pictures and things.'

The inspector picked up the receiver of the ivory Bakelite candlestick phone on the desk and dialled. He barked out orders into the receiver and hung it back up.

'I have asked my gendarmes to go to Monsieur Lapin's home to look for this photograph. It may give us a clue to who the man in the alley was. It is plain he was no ordinary hobo.' The inspector looked at Monsieur Dupont. 'It is possible that he did in fact visit here.'

'It is ridiculous,' Monsieur Dupont huffed, but in a quieter tone. He clearly resented the policeman's unspoken reprimand.

'Mademoiselle Candace, your details please,' the inspector continued.

Candace provided her information.

'I see that you are acquainted with Monsieur Fetherington?' Inspector Villier asked.

Candace removed her hand from Roland's leg as if she had been burnt. 'Yes, we have met before, several times,' she said.

Kitty raised her brows at this fudging of the truth. Candace clearly knew that Monsieur Dupont was likely to inform her mother of anything that was said inside the room.

'You said you went outside to take the air and smoke a cigarette in the garden?' Inspector Villier focused his gaze on the girl.

'Yes, that's right, I had a slight headache.' Candace fidgeted slightly in her seat.

'You also intended to meet with Monsieur Fetherington? An assignation *d'amour*?' the inspector asked.

Candace's cheeks pinked and she licked her lips nervously.

'Come, Mademoiselle Candace, a warm starlit night, a pretty girl, a young man?' The inspector looked at her.

'Roland and I have been seeing one another but Mother doesn't approve of our friendship,' Candace said. 'Roland had said he would get away to meet me, so I went to the bench to wait for him, only as I turned the corner that poor man was lying on the ground bleeding.' The girl's voice wobbled into a sob.

'There, there, it's all right, darling,' Roland soothed her, offering her his own handkerchief when the girl was unable to find where she had placed hers.

The inspector looked at Candace. 'Did you see anyone else there, mademoiselle? Did anyone pass you on the path?'

Candace shook her head and sniffed. 'No. There were people on the terrace but no one on the path.'

'Monsieur Fetherington when did you last see your colleague this evening? Did he say he was going into the garden also? To meet anyone, perhaps?' the inspector asked.

'He said he was taking his break. The arrivals had pretty well slowed down and he often went for a wander and a smoke around that time. It would be about ten minutes I suppose before I heard Candace scream,' Roland said.

'And where were you in those ten minutes?' The inspector's steely gaze rested on the journalist.

'I was hanging around near the foyer. I saw Candace go out and I was waiting a minute or two before I followed her. We didn't want her mother to see us together, so I waited until I thought the coast was clear. I was about to go and find her when I heard her scream.'

The inspector added to his notes. '*Eh bien*, and did anyone see you when you were hanging around in the foyer?'

Roland shifted on his chair. 'I don't know. The girl in the booth maybe.'

'We shall speak to her,' the inspector said. '*Vraiment*, Mademoiselle Candace, you may go to your *maman*. Monsieur Fetherington, please stay within Nice as I may wish to speak to you again. *Et* Monsieur Dupont, no doubt you are anxious to return to your guests.' He dismissed them and they filed out, Roland looking back curiously at Matt and Kitty.

'Now, if I may, a few moments of your time, Captain Bryant, Madame Bryant,' the inspector said as the office door closed.

CHAPTER TEN

The inspector leaned back in his chair making the gilded wood creak as he shifted his weight. He surveyed them with a level stare.

'I will be frank with you both. I have on my hands at *ce moment* two problems. A man who definitely was not a vagrant, stabbed to death in an alley. Now a photographer who claims he may have witnessed our not-really-a-hobo attending this very casino. This same photographer is now seriously injured and may not survive. The only common link between these two events at present appears to be you.'

Kitty's pulse speeded at the icy tone of the policeman's voice. How she longed for the familiar friendliness of Chief Inspector Greville back in Devon. Matt, however, seemed to be perfectly composed.

'I agree, that is quite a dilemma, Inspector.'

'These are unsettled times, Captain Bryant, both here in France and indeed further afield. I have remarked before on our proximity to Italy. There has been an increase of late in visitors travelling both ways, so my colleagues at the borders tell me.' The inspector's words seemed to hang in the air. He paused and continued. 'I think you know very well who our murdered man might be and possibly the reason he was killed.'

The butterflies inside Kitty's stomach felt the size of elephants. She was sure her face had paled under the inspector's stern gaze.

'A most interesting theory, Inspector, but alas you are mistaken,' Matt replied calmly. Kitty wondered how her husband could be so collected.

'Now there is this assault on Monsieur Lapin. Did someone not wish him to link our deceased friend to the casino, perhaps?' the inspector asked.

'It would be a possibility, I suppose, hypothetically speaking. Or maybe to someone else here tonight, perhaps,' Matt responded.

The inspector nodded and his gaze locked with Matt's. Kitty felt as if she could scarcely breathe.

'You and Madame Bryant saw nothing this evening? No one approached Monsieur Lapin? No one else on the path?'

'No, Inspector, no one passed us going up or down,' Kitty said.

'And you did not speak to Monsieur Lapin at all this evening? Or arrange to meet him?' Inspector Villier asked.

'No.' Kitty now rather wished that they had thought of talking to the photographer. He might have given them some important information about Federico.

The inspector closed his notebook and returned it to his jacket pocket. He looked at Matt. 'I am a simple man, Captain Bryant. I have little interest in politics. However, I have a duty to my fellow citizens to keep the peace and to ensure justice is served. I suggest that your stay from here on in is uneventful and preferably short. I would ask, however, that you inform me should you intend to leave Nice. You understand my concerns for your safety and welfare?'

'Of course, Inspector Villier.' Matt rose from his chair and

Kitty followed suit. It was clear the inspector had his suspicions about why she and Matt were in Nice. Matt shook hands with the policeman, and they exited the office to re-enter the now quiet foyer. After the drama of earlier, everything appeared to have gone back to normal.

Matt placed his arm around Kitty's waist and hugged her. 'Are you all right, darling? That was a bit intense in there.'

Kitty took a shaky breath. 'It was just a touch. I suppose we should go and find the others. We should see if Candace is all right, she was very upset.'

Before they had taken many steps Madame Dupont was advancing towards them. '*Mon cher amis*. Come with me to the lounge. Such dreadful things tonight. My dear Jerard has told us what has happened. *Pauvre* Candace.'

The main hall was as busy as before as they followed the woman back into the private area, which was now empty of all other guests except the party they had come with. There was no sign of Roland Fetherington and Kitty wondered where he had gone. Candace was being roundly scolded in hissed whispers by her mother in a corner of the room.

The comte was deep in conversation with Monsieur Dupont and Sir Montague had rejoined the party. He was at the bar ordering a large brandy from the staff.

'My dear Matthew, Kitty, are you both all right? Jerard has explained what happened in the gardens and poor Candace is most upset.' The comte advanced towards them, his brow furrowed with concern.

'It was very distressing. It seems that Nice is a hotbed of crime.' Matt attempted to lighten the situation.

'Oh no, my dear Captain Bryant. You have indeed been most unfortunate. That such a thing could happen here on our premises is most terrible. We have such good security. Our clientele is of the best social standing.' Madame Dupont seemed most distressed.

'Is there usually security in the garden, madame?' Kitty asked.

'We have persons employed to patrol the casino and the grounds. Many of our guests have valuable jewellery and money with them, so we are most careful of their safety. I cannot imagine how this assailant got past them.' Madame Dupont frowned. 'Jerard will speak with them no doubt.'

Her husband had disappeared from the room. Kitty wondered if he had gone in search of his employees or to lock his office, if the inspector had finished with it.

'This was not the pleasurable evening out we had intended.' The comte glanced towards Mrs Delaware and her daughter.

'No, it's such a shame. Perhaps we can visit again on another occasion?' Matt suggested.

'But, of course, you and Madame Bryant would be most welcome,' Madame Dupont said.

'Luciano, darling, do you think we might call the cars? Candace and I would like to return to the hotel.' Mrs Delaware joined them. Candace remained seated in the corner.

'But, of course. I expect you also would like to return, Kitty?' the comte asked.

'I would rather if that's all right. I do feel rather shaken up,' Kitty agreed.

'I shall make arrangements for you; you shall use our private cars. It is the least Jerard and I can do.' Madame Dupont pressed her bony bejewelled fingers on Luciano's arm and went over to speak to one of her staff.

The cars were brought around to the front of the casino before Sir Montague had time to finish his drink. He had concurred with the rest of the party's decision to return to the Negresco. He seemed somewhat belatedly to remember that he was supposed to be courting Candace and fussed about placing her mink stole around her slender shoulders.

This time on the drive back to the hotel Luciano accompanied Matt and Kitty, while Candace, her mother and Sir Montague travelled in the other car. Matt, as usual, had cracked the rear window open to allow a flow of cooler night air into the car. His time during the war had left him with a strong dislike of enclosed spaces, amongst other things.

Kitty leaned her head on her husband's shoulder. She would be glad to get back to their room so that she could ask Matt what he thought of the evening's events.

'You have been most, what is the English expression? Stoic, Kitty. This cannot be your usual life?' the comte said.

'One encounters many situations as a hotelier, but I must admit I had expected our little holiday to be relaxing. One doesn't expect so much violence in such a lovely place,' Kitty responded.

'Quite so, darling. This was supposed to be a chance to compare the French Riviera to the English one,' Matt added.

'The inspector, he has found the camera of the poor Monsieur Lapin. Jerard informed me that the gendarme's discovered it broken on the rocks lower down the hillside,' Luciano said.

'Oh dear, the poor man. If he recovers how will he make his living?' Kitty asked. 'I'm sure his equipment must be expensive.'

'Perhaps he has a spare one,' the comte suggested. 'Jerard also said the inspector seemed to think this attack was linked to the murder of this alleged spy that you discovered.'

'He said something about that to us. I don't know though. It all seems very far-fetched to me,' Matt said. 'Was Monsieur Lapin employed by the casino, or was he someone your friend allowed on the premises to take pictures?'

Luciano gave a small shrug. 'I believe Jerard merely permitted him to be there. He was not an employee. I believe he had worked there for some years taking photographs. You know, for souvenirs and for the society column of the local paper. Mr Fetherington joined him recently.'

'Did he work alone before then?' Kitty asked.

'I think from time to time a journalist would come if there were very wealthy or well-known people attending the casino. When the yachts are in the harbour over the summer, we see many film stars here. Actors and actresses, some from America,' Luciano explained.

The car pulled to a stop behind the first car at the front of the hotel. The burgundy-liveried chauffeur nipped out smartly to open the door for them. Kitty accepted Matt's hand to help her out of the car. Mrs Delaware and Candace were already standing with Sir Montague by the entrance.

Kitty glanced at her dainty gold evening wristwatch, surprised to discover the time was only a little after midnight. She had expected it to be much later, as so much had happened.

'We are retiring for the night. I hope we shall see you in the morning, Matthew, Kitty?' Mrs Delaware asked.

'I expect so,' Kitty answered.

'Come, Candace.' Mrs Delaware escorted her daughter away.

'I rather expect I should turn in myself,' Sir Montague said.

'Yes, us too,' Matt agreed and followed the comte and Sir Montague into the lobby of the hotel. 'It's been quite an evening. That poor man. Were you still at the tables when it happened?'

Sir Montague frowned. 'I think so. I seem to recall hearing a dreadful kerfuffle and people saying there had been an accident in the garden. Of course, if I had realised Candace was involved, I would have gone right there.'

'Of course,' Matt agreed.

'Were you at the tables too, Luciano? Eunice was at the card table, I believe, when we stepped outside?' Kitty asked.

'Oh, when Eunice gets into her card game she plays like a demon. I think I had gone to get more chips from the booth when I heard the commotion.' Luciano smiled genially at her. 'I intended to join Monty at the roulette wheel since he seemed to be having quite a run of luck.'

'Yes, indeed. Not often one leaves better off at these places.' Sir Montague patted his pocket.

'I expect Monsieur and Madame Dupont will be most distressed by all of this. I hope it won't affect their business. Were they nearby when it happened? Monsieur Dupont came quite quickly,' Kitty asked.

She was as interested as Matt in trying to subtly discover where everyone was when the unfortunate Monsieur Lapin was assaulted. She was aware that anyone could have attacked the photographer, but she couldn't shake her suspicions that it was all connected somehow to the group they were with.

'I saw Jerard attending to some of his staff near the bar just before everyone rushed out. I think Helene Dupont was still in the private lounge with some guests from Germany. I'm sure there will be no repercussions on the casino, Madame Bryant, have no fears on that score. It really is a most unusual event,' Luciano assured her.

'I do hope so,' Kitty said and placed a satin-gloved hand in front of her mouth as she yawned. 'Do please forgive me, I really think I should retire to bed. I feel quite exhausted.'

'Of course, madame.' The comte gave a courteous little bow and clicked his heels together.

Kitty and Matt said good evening to Sir Montague and the comte and walked slowly up the magnificent staircase, leaving the two men to follow behind at their leisure.

Kitty had barely entered their suite before she slipped off her evening shoes with a sigh of relief. 'Goodness me, what a night. What on earth do we do now?'

* * *

Matt seated himself on one of the armchairs, his long legs spread out in front of him. He considered Kitty's question. It had been the same one that had been at the front of his mind ever since they had discovered Monsieur Lapin.

'I think we need to review everything and make a plan.' He rubbed his eyes wearily. As he looked at Kitty something behind her caught his attention.

'What is it?' Kitty turned her head to see what he was looking at.

'I'm not sure.' Matt stood and went over to the large rosewood chest of drawers.

One of the drawers had not been closed properly. The line of the drawer running slightly out of kilter with the rest. He frowned as he pulled open the offending one. It contained his underwear, and handkerchiefs, nothing of any value.

'Have you been in this drawer for anything, darling?' He knew that Kitty wouldn't have been. Her things were in the one next to his.

'No, why?' She came over to join him.

'Check your things,' he said.

She opened her drawers and looked carefully at the contents. 'Someone has searched our room, haven't they?' she asked as she pushed it closed again.

Matt nodded. 'Everything has been put back neatly but not quite as we left it.'

Kitty shivered. 'What a horrid thought, having someone pawing through our things.'

She crossed over to the dressing table and unlocked her shagreen vanity box where she kept her cosmetics and the small amount of jewellery she brought with her when she travelled.

'Everything is here so nothing has been stolen.' She examined the lock of the box. 'I rather think someone has picked this, however. There are some scratches that I am certain weren't there before.'

'I suspect they were hoping that either we had recovered the documents, or were looking to see if they could find out who had sent us.' Matt undid his bow tie and dropped it down on the top of the dresser.

Kitty paused as she unclipped her earrings. 'This is so horribly complicated. Are they Italian agents trying to get their papers back, or agents from another country who would also like to get their hands on them?'

Matt continued preparing for bed. 'It could be either, but if I had to guess I would think it is most likely to be the Italians.'

'Yes, that would make sense, I suppose. Even if another country knew of their existence, they probably wouldn't know that Federico had taken them.' Kitty removed her jewellery and placed it safely back in her vanity box.

'Someone worked it out though and has been watching us once they thought Whitehall had not sent one of their regular agents to make the pickup.' Matt climbed into bed.

Like her husband, Kitty too continued to prepare for bed. Once she was tucked up beneath the sheets and the light had been extinguished, she turned to him.

'Do you think that was why we were invited to the casino tonight? To get us out of the way while someone searched our room?'

'It's very possible. Or again, if we are being watched then someone took the opportunity to make a search.' Matt had been thinking the same thing.

'Hmm,' Kitty murmured sleepily. She hoped a fresh day would help them figure it out.

CHAPTER ELEVEN

Kitty woke the next morning to bright sunlight filtering around the edges of the lined silk-damask curtains into their room. Despite the events of the previous evening, she had slept surprisingly well.

Matt was still asleep when she slipped out of bed and padded over the tiled floor to the large panoramic window to peep outside at blue skies and shimmering sea. The promenade was already busy with people up and about in the early morning sunshine. Well-dressed ladies walking small dogs passed by, which made her homesick for Bertie. She hoped he was behaving himself for Lucy.

Kitty stepped back from the window and turned to her wardrobe. It looked as if it was going to be a lovely day. The only cloud currently on her horizon was that they had said they would see Mrs Delaware and her party at breakfast. She selected a pretty cotton frock in a cheerful primrose-yellow sprigged with tiny white flowers and dressed quickly.

Matt was just stirring as she combed her short blonde curls and applied her lipstick. What she really wanted to do was to have time alone with Matt to go over everything they had learned so far. Hopefully they could then try and work out who might be behind both Federico's murder and the attack on Monsieur Lapin.

It would be even better still if they could work out where the documents that they and everyone else was searching for might have been hidden. She was quite certain that Federico had hidden them, and they had not yet been discovered. Or why else would Monsieur Lapin have been assaulted and their suite searched?

Federico must have only been in Nice for a couple of days before they had arrived. The brigadier had come to Enderley as soon as he had received the telegram and they had flown to France the day after that. He had to have visited the casino on that first evening and presumably realised he was in danger and assumed his tramp disguise afterwards. Had he felt safe until then? Had he sent the telegram before or after his visit to the casino? She wished they knew the answers.

Matt got up and came over to where she was still sitting deep in thought in front of her dressing table mirror.

'Morning, darling, you look very pensive.' He kissed the top of her head.

'Just mulling things over.' Kitty smiled up at him as she spoke.

Matt smiled back and headed off to the bathroom to prepare for the day ahead.

Kitty picked up the small silver evening purse she had taken to the casino. She had placed the blue matchbook they had discovered on Federico's body inside it, along with the key to the derelict villa. It seemed this had been a good decision since their room had since been searched.

She took the matchbook out to examine it more closely. The only place they had seen them had been on the bar in the private lounge area of the casino. Federico could only have obtained it from there, unless someone else had given it to him, but she thought that seemed unlikely. Especially since Monsieur Lapin had told Roland Fetherington that he believed he had taken his photograph. That surely proved Federico must have been personally to the casino.

There was nothing unusual on the front or back of the flimsy cardboard matchbook. It looked to her like the others they had seen last night. She opened it up. Three matches were missing, torn out. The striking strip at the bottom, however, showed no sign of being used. Federico had no cigarettes on his body when they had found him so why were the matches missing?

Matt came out of the bathroom and opened the curtains covering the large window of the suite. A shaft of sunlight flooded into the room and Kitty realised that in the blank space where the missing matches had been there were some indentations. Her pulse speeded as she realised the marks were deliberate.

'Matt, come and look at this.'

Her husband came to join her, alerted by the urgency in her voice. She showed him the marks in the cardboard turning the matchbook around so they could see them more clearly.

'It looks like twenty-eight.' Matt frowned as he squinted at the small matchbook.

'Twenty-eight what though? A room number, a house number?' Kitty was sure it must have some significance. Why else would Federico have gone to so much trouble to jot the number in a secret place? He had to have done so anticipating he might be killed before he could deliver the papers.

'Keep those matches safe and we'll go down for breakfast. Let's see what everyone is up to this morning. Well done, Kitty. At least that might give us something to go on.' Matt grinned at her.

Eunice and Candace Delaware were already at breakfast with Sir Montague. There was no sign of Luciano. Mrs

Delaware, as always, was immaculately made up, while Candace looked pale and heavy eyed, picking at a plate of cold ham and cheese. Sir Montague was tucking into a cheese omelette, appearing none the worse for wear after the previous night.

'Good morning.' Kitty took her seat on a chair pulled out for her by one of the ever-attentive waiters, while Matt took his place beside her.

The others greeted them, and Matt placed an order for coffee and croissants for himself and Kitty.

'No Luciano this morning?' Kitty asked brightly as the waiter immediately reappeared bearing a tall chrome coffee pot and a matching jug of steamed milk.

'No, not as yet. I thought I saw him talking to some fellow in the lobby when I came downstairs but he hasn't been in here for breakfast, I don't believe.' Sir Montague finished his food and set his knife and fork down neatly on his empty plate.

'What are your plans for today? It looks delightful outside this morning,' Mrs Delaware asked, looking at Kitty.

'We aren't quite certain what to do just yet. To be honest, we had thought of cutting our stay short after everything that's happened,' Matt replied, glancing at Kitty.

She guessed he was trying to see how they would receive the idea that they might return to England earlier than planned.

'Oh, my dears, but you haven't seen anything of the area really. At least stay and see a couple of the sights. It would be such a shame to go home early with a bad impression of the place,' Mrs Delaware said.

'That's very true. You must at least visit the old fort and go to the Russian orthodox cathedral. It's very picturesque, no one leaves Nice without having been to either of those.' Sir Montague dabbed at the corners of his mouth with his napkin.

The waiter returned and deposited a basket of freshly

baked croissants and two crystal dishes, one of jam and one of butter, in front of them. Kitty sniffed the aroma appreciatively.

'I don't know. Darling, what do you think?' Matt asked her.

'We can take you both out, show you the sights. We can make an outing of it. We know the most wonderful place for lunch. They have the most marvellous seafood,' Mrs Delaware declared before Kitty could respond. The American woman spotted the comte approaching their table. 'Ah, Luciano, we were just saying we should take Matthew and Kitty out today, show them the sights, the old fort and the cathedral. It would be too bad if they were to cut their holiday short and leave without seeing everything.'

Luciano took his place on the vacant seat. 'That sounds very agreeable. It would be a terrible pity not to see the beauty of Nice before leaving.' He requested a dish of fruit from the waiter and more coffee.

Kitty could see that their plans for the day were now settled. 'Well, perhaps another day or so would be nice,' she agreed.

She was not averse to seeing either of the sights the group had mentioned. Perhaps more time spent in the company of the others might help them to work out if any of them had been involved in Federico's murder or the assault on the photographer.

'I saw a man I know in the lobby earlier. He told me he had heard that Monsieur Lapin died in the early hours of this morning.' Luciano shook his head sorrowfully and poured himself a coffee.

'How awful,' Kitty said. The doctor had warned that Monsieur Lapin's injuries might prove fatal, but it was still distressing news. The other's murmured agreement with her statement.

'There is also a rumour that Inspector Villier has taken that journalist, Roland Fetherington, to the police station for questioning,' the comte continued.

Candace gave up all pretence of eating any breakfast and dropped her cutlery down on her plate with a clatter. 'Poor Roland, of course he didn't hurt Monsieur Lapin. He is just being victimised,' she said forcefully.

'Really, Candace, that's quite enough. I warned you not to befriend that young man.' Her mother's tone was sharp. 'A most unsuitable person for you to become acquainted with.'

Candace's cheeks flushed pink and Kitty could see the girl's eyes had filled with tears.

'I dare say asking him to the station is just a precaution. After all, it did sound as if he may have been the last person to see the chap alive. The inspector probably just wants to go over his statement and check he hasn't missed anything,' Matt said as he spread more strawberry jam on his croissant.

Candace looked grateful for the reassurance while her mother glared at Matt.

'I wonder if the police found the photographs that they were looking for at Monsieur Lapin's house?' Kitty asked.

'Photographs?' Sir Montague looked up from where he was adding sugar to his cup of tea.

'Yes, apparently Mr Fetherington told the inspector that Monsieur Lapin thought he had taken a picture of the man we found in the alley. He thought he had visited the casino.' Kitty waited to see how this information would be received by the others. She also had the uncomfortable feeling that she had mentioned the photographer to Sir Montague before their visit to the casino.

Candace had known about the picture, but the others hadn't been present in Monsieur Dupont's office when Roland had told the inspector he thought Federico had been at the casino. Although she strongly suspected that Monsieur Dupont may have told the comte afterwards since he had been present at the time.

'A vagrant at the casino?' Mrs Delaware looked as if this

news was a personal affront. 'Nonsense, Jerard and Helene would never countenance such a thing. The security men would have not permitted such a person anywhere near the premises.'

'I did tell you, Eunice, my dear, there was a rumour that the man found in the alley was a spy,' Luciano remarked, before taking a sip of his coffee.

Mrs Delaware continued to look discomfited. 'Well, I know these things do go on. I mean when we were in Berlin we heard from some of the highest officials in the German government that there were countries who still had a grudge against their nation.'

Kitty thought it wise to keep a diplomatic silence on the subject, although she noticed a pulse beating in the side of Matt's temple.

'You will forgive me from speaking on that matter, Mrs Delaware. My own experiences of the conflict are still very fresh in my memory,' Matt said.

The older woman's mouth dropped open and snapped shut again as she realised what she had just said.

Sir Montague coughed. 'Well then, back to our plans for today. I suggest we visit the cathedral first, since the restaurant for lunch is not too far away, and then we can go on to the old fort later.'

'I think I would rather stay here. I have a bit of a headache,' Candace said.

'Then some fresh air will be good for you,' her mother responded firmly. 'I have no desire to sit and play nursemaid to you for the sake of a mild headache.'

'I should be perfectly all right by myself, Mother,' Candace objected, glaring at her parent.

Eunice snorted. 'And have you running off to the police station after that worthless young man as soon as my back is turned. I think not, darling.'

Candace folded her arms, her lower lip set in a mutinous pout.

'That seems to be settled then. Shall we all meet back in the lobby in say thirty minutes?' Sir Montague remarked in a mild tone.

'I wonder what we will discover on this outing today,' Kitty murmured to Matt as they returned to their room to collect the things they needed for a day sightseeing. 'Do you think Roland Fetherington could be the man behind Federico's death and the murder of Monsieur Lapin?'

'I suppose it is possible. He seems to have travelled around a fair amount and he said he has been in Italy. He could have encountered Federico there, I suppose,' Matt said as they entered their room.

'Mrs Delaware seems to have connections with Germany, and strong feelings on the matter.' Kitty glanced at Matt as she picked up her straw sun hat. She admired her husband's restraint with the woman, given what he had suffered during the war.

'I noticed.' Matt placed his white panama hat on his head. 'I also saw that Madame Dupont spent a lot of time last night with her German guests.'

'Would the Germans be the other party interested in these Italian documents, do you think?' Kitty looked around for her sunglasses. 'The Duponts could be the go-betweens?'

'I think it very likely. They may be hoping for allies or simply to discover the Italian government's plans after this business in Ethiopia.' Matt found her glasses and handed them to her.

'Then Mrs Delaware and the Duponts may both have a vested interest in the papers Federico was carrying.' Kitty frowned.

'And, of course, there is the oh-so charming and obliging comte. Luciano has also been accompanying the Delawares and as an Italian he would no doubt want to get the documents back before any other nation could see them.' Matt added their sun cream to the contents of Kitty's bag.

'He does seem to have a finger in every pie. Mind you, Sir Montague also appears to know a lot of people locally. He must know that Candace prefers another man, so why is he still accompanying them? Does he need the money she is due to inherit, I wonder?' Kitty asked.

'If he were to convince Candace to marry him? I expect if she is as wealthy as they say then it would no doubt be very useful. Or he could have other motives for staying close to them.' Matt patted his pocket to check he had his wallet safely stowed away.

'The papers you mean? He could sell them for money, couldn't he? He did seem very at home at the gaming tables.' Kitty was thoughtful as she prepared to leave the room.

'Well, let's enjoy the day and see if we can spot anything that might link to the number twenty-eight while we are out and about,' Matt suggested.

It might also be the case that none of the people they had met were involved in either the murders or the missing documents. Although Kitty couldn't see that being likely. There were too many coincidences for her taste, and they would need to stay alert.

CHAPTER TWELVE

Mrs Delaware strolled along the promenade at the head of the party. A jaunty jade-green Chinese style parasol shading her head as she leaned on the arm of the comte. Luciano was sporting white linen trousers and a striped red and white blazer with a straw boater.

'He looks like he's lost his gondola,' Matt murmured in Kitty's ear, and she was forced to stifle her giggles.

Sir Montague was attired in the English style, like Matt, with a white panama hat, cream trousers and a light jacket. He carried a silver-handled walking cane and was accompanied by a reluctant-looking Candace who was dressed in a pretty, pale-blue frock with white polka dots. She appeared to have declined to take Sir Montague's arm preferring to walk alongside him.

Their walk took them along the Promenade des Anglais and through the town in the vague direction of the station. They paused a couple of times on the way for Mrs Delaware to examine various trinkets in the shop windows and for Sir Montague to acquire more cigarettes at the tobacconists. Presently they arrived in a small treelined square.

'Here we are, the Cathedral of St Nicholas.' Mrs

Delaware halted at the front of the cathedral so the party could admire the red and cream structure, topped by its green onion-shaped domes. Kitty and Matt dutifully admired the church.

Sir Montague produced a guidebook from his jacket pocket. He cleared his throat and read aloud from the book. 'There was a miracle here only last year, on the feast of Saint Nicholas. An icon that is said to relieve suffering in children.' He squinted at the guidebook as if to make sure he had read the correct paragraph.

'I think you'll find it is just as magnificent on the inside as it is on the outside. Let us go in and we can look for the icon,' the comte agreed. He and Mrs Delaware led the way inside the church. Kitty could immediately see why so many people came to visit the cathedral. The icons and intricate gold work was fascinating to see and there were already several visitors looking at the various features. She couldn't help thinking about St Saviour's Church in Dartmouth where she and Matt had married.

St Saviour's was much smaller and centuries older but with the same air and feel as this marvellous modern church. She and Matt broke away from the others to wander around quietly on their own. Candace placed herself on the end of a pew and sat cooling her face with a small folding fan which she had produced from her handbag.

Sir Montague had pulled his guidebook out once again and appeared to be trying to interest her in the history of the building and the various important icons. Candace's mother and Luciano were looking for the icon of St Nicholas the wonderworker who was said to perform miracles for children.

'I think we could use a miracle,' Kitty whispered to Matt once they were out of earshot of the others.

He smiled at her and squeezed her hand sympathetically. They continued to look around for a while longer, before Mrs

Delaware started to hint that she was bored, meaning that it was time for them all to leave.

Kitty had enjoyed her visit but had seen nothing that might have any bearing on where the missing documents may have been placed or anything to link to the number twenty-eight. She had thought that if Federico had left the matchbook as some kind of clue, then the number had to be somewhere obvious or be something that would leap out at them as a possibility. Hence her idea that there might be something at the church which might spark an idea.

She had discreetly counted various things inside the cathedral and looked at all the shops, cafés and bars on their way towards the older part of the town, but nothing had struck her as a possibility. Whatever Federico had meant by those numbers hidden in the matchbook remained elusively out of her reach.

While they had been inside the cathedral the streets had grown busier and the sun had climbed higher in the clear blue sky. The trees in the small park, although providing a little shade, were not fully up to the job. When Mrs Delaware proposed that they go to the restaurant she liked for a drink before lunch, Kitty and Matt were both happy to agree.

It was not far to walk, and the interior of the restaurant was cool and shady. It was also clear that Mrs Delaware and the comte were valued customers. The white-jacketed waiters showed them to a table laid with pastel-pink linen and sparkling silver cutlery. Jugs of iced lemonade garnished with sprigs of mint were procured and Kitty discreetly slipped off her sandals under the table.

Her feet ached from all the walking they had done recently, and she was glad of the opportunity to sit and rest before they were to tackle the steps to the old fort. She relaxed as the cold tiled floor under her bare feet eased the discomfort.

'It is so warm today. I do think, Luciano, darling, it will be too far to walk in this heat to the old fort.' Mrs Delaware took a long drink from her glass.

'It is quite hot,' the comte agreed as he removed his hat.

'I must admit, my feet are aching rather,' Kitty said.

Sir Montague produced his guidebook once again. Kitty saw it was the same one she had procured on her first day in Nice, which she had left on her nightstand back at the hotel.

'Let's have a look at the map.' Sir Montague unfolded the larger map from inside the book and spread it out on the tablecloth for Kitty and Matt to see. 'Now, we are here.' He dabbed at a point not far from the cathedral.

'And that is the old fort over there?' Matt leaned in to take a closer look. He pointed to a spot that was some distance from the restaurant.

'That looks much further than I thought,' Kitty said.

'We could always just go to the Colline du Château. It's got a marvellous view from there and it's much more accessible. You can see right over the harbour,' Sir Montague suggested, pointing to another spot closer to the sea.

'There might even be a breeze.' Mrs Delaware perked up at the suggestion. 'There is much more shade there with the trees, despite the steps, and the waterfall is most attractive. I'm sure you'll enjoy it.'

The suggestion seemed to meet with approval, and everyone assented to the change to the plan. With the matter decided, they settled down to enjoy a leisurely lunch. Even Candace appeared more cheerful by the time she spooned up the last of her trio of sorbets.

The heat of the day had started to diminish a little by the time they left the restaurant to begin the stroll towards the château. Sir Montague's guidebook had said it was a picturesque ruin sited in a leafy park. Once more Luciano and Mrs Delaware led the way, with Candace and Sir Montague following and Kitty and Matt bringing up the rear.

Their route took them back towards the Promenade des Anglais and closer to the sea again. Kitty clutched Matt's arm as she spotted something interesting. 'Look, over there,' she said quietly, not wishing to attract the attention of the others.

Matt followed her direction with his gaze. 'Bar Twenty-Eight,' he muttered.

The bar had a few rattan tables outside on the cobbled streets and a board implied there would be live music each evening.

'It could be the place,' Kitty said. Although what they were expected to find there, she had no idea. Perhaps Federico had left the papers there, or maybe there was someone there who he had entrusted to look after them. It might not have anything to do with Federico at all, but they would need to investigate.

'We need to return this evening, after supper,' Matt agreed quietly.

'It has to be worth checking out.' Kitty's spirits lifted now she felt there was at least a possibility of a clue. After all, those numbers in the matchbook had to mean something.

Soon they were walking slowly up the winding steps between lush, green trees dotted with palms. Sir Montague's book was proved right about the vista overlooking the bay, with the red tiled roofs of the buildings spreading out below them. The blue sea was sparkling in the afternoon sun.

Candace found herself a bench overlooking the water with the harbour below. Sir Montague lit a cigarette and contented himself with pottering about the ruins. Kitty walked off to take in the distant views beyond Nice itself that lay shimmering in the heat. Matt indicated that he wished to explore more of what was left of the château and left her to her own devices.

Kitty wandered along the path taking her a little away from some other visitors who had also made the climb to the château. The shade from the trees was a welcome relief after the hot walk through the streets to get to the hill.

Eventually she reached a nice, peaceful spot with a view of the sea and sat down on a large flat-topped grey rock in the shelter of some bushes. The sound of the cicadas was loud all around her and she breathed in the faint scent of mimosa and sea air. It was nice to escape from the rest of the party for a few minutes to drink in the beauty of the place in solitude.

After a moment or two she realised she could hear two people talking. Two male voices that were both quite familiar. She moved very quietly from where she was sitting to ensure she could not be seen as she shamelessly eavesdropped on the conversation.

'Dupont says the deal will be off if we do not have the goods for him soon.' Kitty recognised Luciano's voice.

'I'm not sure what more we can do, old boy. I'm keeping my eyes and ears open.' Sir Montague's lazy drawl sounded unconcerned.

'We need to stay with these two. The girl's uncle is well connected with your government, and I don't think they are here for a holiday, First, they found Benedetto in the alley and then there was the debacle at the casino,' Luciano responded.

Kitty heard the sound of gravel crunching underfoot as the two men moved closer along the path. Luciano and Sir Montague had both known Federico's identity. Her pulse speeded up and she hoped they wouldn't decide to leave the path to come closer to her hiding place.

'I agree, although there was nothing in their room I hear. Then Jerard will have to be patient for a little while longer and so will his clients,' Sir Montague said.

'I don't think they will be patient for long,' Luciano warned.

Something flew through the air and landed near her foot. It took all of Kitty's self-control not to squeak aloud in fright. The discarded cigarette butt glowed briefly and extinguished itself and she breathed a long slow sigh of relief.

The footsteps moved on and Kitty waited for a few minutes

to make sure the men had gone before emerging from her spot. She brushed the stray blades of grass and dried leaves from the skirt of her dress. At least she knew now who had arranged for the search of their room while they had been at the casino.

From what she had heard it sounded as if Luciano and Sir Montague were working together and that Jerard Dupont was acting as some kind of middleman. Did that mean that they had killed Federico and Monsieur Lapin? But why, when they didn't have the documents?

She felt quite shaken by her discovery as she took a different route back to where she had left the others. Candace was still sitting on the bench, but her mother had now joined her.

'This is a fascinating place and the views are quite something,' Matt said as he approached them.

'Yes, I'm so glad we decided to come here this afternoon,' Kitty agreed. Her gaze met Matt's and he walked closer to her slipping his arm around her waist.

'Come and see this view from over here,' he suggested, leading her to a private point on the path where no one else was around.

'What's wrong?' he asked in a low voice once they were sure they couldn't be overheard.

Kitty quickly recounted the conversation she had listened to a few minutes earlier.

'Interesting.' Matt rubbed his chin.

'It answers a few of our questions,' Kitty said.

'And raises a few more. Well done, old thing.'

They sauntered back to the bench together in time for the comte and Sir Montague to rejoin the group.

'We had better start back.' Luciano offered his arm once more to Mrs Delaware and they set off back down the hillside towards the Promenade des Anglais.

They paused for tea at a café en route to the hotel, in need of refreshment after the climb up and down the hill. Mrs

Delaware sank down on a chair declaring she was all in after so much activity in one day. Candace who had been quiet and uncommunicative for much of the expedition suddenly sprang to life. She leapt to her feet and hurried off from the table before her mother could say or do anything to stop her.

'Candace!' Mrs Delaware frowned and folded up her fan. 'That girl! Running off like that! Where has she gone?'

Kitty suspected that Candace had spied Roland Fetherington, and had gone to find him. If that were the case, then it would seem that the inspector had released him.

'Don't fret, Eunice, darling, she'll be back soon enough,' Luciano reassured her.

Kitty and Matt continued to drink their tea and nibbled on the delicate almond biscuits that had accompanied their drinks. Kitty's thoughts had already turned to the evening ahead. She knew there was only a very slim chance that the number scribbled so faintly in the matchbook referred to the bar. Still, it had to be worth investigating. But how to shake off the comte and Sir Montague though in order to do it?

* * *

Matt's thoughts were also on the comte and Sir Montague. It sounded from what Kitty had heard that Monsieur Dupont was acting as a broker for some unnamed client who had a vested interest in obtaining the documents Federico had been transporting. He had thought that Luciano might have wished to obtain them so they could be returned to Italy.

Now though it seemed that the comte's interest in them was purely financial. It certainly explained why Sir Montague was travelling with the group and didn't seem affronted by Candace's preference for the company of Roland Fetherington. Candace was merely providing cover for him to move around while he too searched for the missing documents.

In Matt's mind he could only see that the murder of Federico must have been in error, unless it was a gamble that hadn't paid off. It had been madness to kill the man before knowing where the documents were. Whoever killed him must have believed they were secreted about his person or had been stashed at the semi-derelict villa he and Kitty had found and searched. That provided a small amount of good news, as it meant he and Kitty still stood a chance of recovering them.

Then there was the deadly assault on Monsieur Lapin. Had that been the work of Monsieur Dupont? Perhaps he hadn't wanted the inspector to make the connection between Federico and the casino. Or was it that perhaps he or someone else may have realised that perhaps Monsieur Lapin may have not only captured a picture of Federico, but maybe someone else who was there too.

Matt drained his cup and rested it back on the saucer. This job was becoming very dangerous, and he didn't like it. Their new friends appeared to know much more than they'd hoped. Even if he and Kitty got lucky and managed to get hold of the papers, they then had to get them out of France. They also had to make sure they weren't killed in the process.

What did that twenty-eight mean that had been written inside the matchbook? Was there a connection with the name of the bar they had seen earlier? Or was it a house number or room number somewhere?

He glanced across the table to where Kitty was sitting calmly finishing her tea and listening to Mrs Delaware's complaints about her daughter. One thing he was sure about was that he was not going to allow Kitty to be put at risk during this operation. He would never forgive himself if she was hurt in any way.

CHAPTER THIRTEEN

Kitty was not at all sorry to see the back of the Delaware group when they finally arrived at the hotel. It had been a struggle to continue to make polite social chit-chat with Sir Montague and Luciano, knowing how treacherous they both were.

'Ugh, I am utterly exhausted.' Kitty dropped down on the bed with a huge sigh when they reached their room.

She had also developed another small blister on her heel, and she suspected she might have sunburnt the tip of her nose. Matt dropped down onto the bed beside her and tugged the pillows more comfortably under his head.

'I was thinking on the way back, about tonight.' He paused and looked at her.

Kitty had a feeling from his expression that she was not going to like what he was about to say.

'Yes, what about tonight? We need to get out of here and over to that bar without the comte or Sir Montague noticing,' Kitty said. It had been on her mind too.

'That may not be very easy. We know that they are both watching us, and they also have connections all over Nice,' Matt said.

'As does Monsieur Dupont it seems.' Kitty's stomach flipped over. Getting to the bar to snoop around was going to be much harder than she had anticipated. Every time they ventured out of their room it seemed a member of the Delaware group was waiting for them.

'Two people have died already. This is going to be very dangerous. Even if the documents are at the bar, or with someone there, then we have still to smuggle them safely out of France.' Matt's eyes seemed a brighter blue than ever as he looked at her.

'We have to get ourselves out safely too,' Kitty agreed.

'I suggest that we go to dinner as normal and go to dance afterwards. I'll spy my chance and slip away to go out to the bar. With any luck since you are still there, I can be back before they realise there is anything amiss,' Matt suggested.

'I am to be the decoy?' Kitty couldn't help feeling disappointed. Despite her sore feet she had quite fancied stepping out into Nice at night to do some sleuthing.

'My French is much better than yours.' The dimple flashed in Matt's cheek.

'And I'm prettier than you,' Kitty countered with a smile.

'So you will make a much better decoy,' Matt chuckled as he replied. 'Seriously though, Kitty. It'll be less noticeable if I go. A pretty girl in an evening gown at a seedy bar with a band is likely to attract a lot of attention. And not the sort of attention we want.'

'You'll be gone for at least an hour by the time you've walked there and back. Do you think I can divert them for that long?' Kitty asked.

'You won't have to. By the time they have realised I've stepped out the chances are I'll be on my way back.' Matt gazed up at the ceiling.

'Supposing you get attacked on your way back here if they think you've managed to retrieve the documents?' Kitty didn't like the sound of his proposal at all. It was very risky. He could be followed and attacked before reaching the safety of the hotel.

'I don't think they would risk it. They already messed this up when they killed Federico by not making sure he had the documents before he was killed. They won't know where I've gone so they won't know if I have the papers, or have merely gone to look for them,' Matt reasoned.

'Possibly.' Kitty was doubtful about this line of thought. Whoever had killed the photographer and Federico had seemed to her to be exactly the kind of people who acted first and thought about it later.

'There is also an increase in the number of gendarmes about the town. Did you notice we passed three on our way back here? I think the inspector is trying to reassure everyone that Nice is a safe place. Two murders in two days is not going to go down well with either the tourists or local citizens,' Matt said.

'I don't like it,' Kitty said. She wasn't certain how she was going to pull off keeping Luciano or Sir Montague from noticing that Matt was missing.

'We can't both go. The comte and Sir Montague are determined to stick to us like glue and we wouldn't manage to find anything out. No, separating is our only hope to see if this bar is linked to Federico in some way.'

Kitty sighed. 'Very well, but promise me you won't take any stupid risks and will get back here as quickly as possible.' Her eyes filled with tears and she was forced to blink in an effort to dispel them before Matt noticed.

'I promise.' He turned his head and kissed her cheek.

Kitty dressed with care for dinner, choosing an older midnight-blue crushed velvet gown that allowed her to wear a pair of slightly lower, more comfortable silver shoes. They made their way downstairs and, even though they had not agreed to meet the Delawares, Eunice was waiting for them. The comte was with her, although there was no sign of Candace.

'Darlings, you both look divine. What are your plans for the evening?' Mrs Delaware asked.

'Dinner and a few twirls around the dance floor. The walking today has left us feeling quite fagged out.' Matt smiled politely at the American woman. 'No Candace tonight?'

'Oh, she'll be along in a minute. I left her styling her hair,' Mrs Delaware said. 'Such a nuisance when one doesn't have a maid to assist.'

Sir Montague strolled up to join them, dapper in his evening attire. 'Drinks?' he asked, looking at Eunice and Kitty.

'That would be lovely.' Kitty smiled brightly at him. 'A negroni cocktail would be rather nice.'

'I'll come with you,' Matt offered and went with the other man to the bar.

'I think we shall have a quiet night too. After the dreadful events yesterday, I must admit it's left me feeling rather unsettled.' Mrs Delaware adjusted the diamond clasp on the pearl collar around her neck. 'I mean, if something so awful can happen at a place as well managed as the casino, it makes one wonder where is safe.'

'I do agree,' Kitty said.

Candace joined the group as Matt and Sir Montague returned with the drinks. She had clearly taken care over her appearance and was wearing a very lovely dark-grey taffeta silk dress with diamond-studded combs in her hair. Sir Montague immediately returned to the bar to collect another drink for her. Candace seemed to be in a much more cheerful mood and her eyes were sparkling as she accepted a glass of champagne from Sir Montague.

'Chin, chin.' She clinked her glass against those of the others.

'We were discussing our plans for the evening.' Mrs

Delaware glared at her daughter. 'I was saying how I felt it was terribly unsafe to be out at night in Nice with these dreadful murders.'

'Matt and I are going dancing after dinner in the ballroom,' Kitty said.

'A splendid idea,' Eunice agreed. 'Don't you think so, Luciano? I am very fond of dancing.'

'I should be delighted to escort you, as always, my dear,' the comte agreed with a smile.

'Topping idea,' Sir Montague said. 'Candace, darling?'

'It sounds as if you'll all have a wonderful time, but I have other plans for tonight,' Candace announced in a cheerful tone.

Colour climbed in Mrs Delaware's cheeks at her daughter's rebellion. 'You are not to set foot outside of this hotel. It's far too dangerous. I forbid it.'

Candace downed the rest of her drink. 'Sorry, Mother, enjoy your evening. I'll probably be back after midnight so don't wait up for me.' She placed her empty glass down on the table, collected her fox fur stole from the back of the chair, gathered her evening purse and left.

'She's going out with that journalist, isn't she?' Mrs Delaware looked as if she was about to cry.

'Shall I go after her?' the comte offered.

Sir Montague said nothing.

'Yes, no, oh she's making her bed she will have to lie in it.' Mrs Delaware appeared to pull herself together. 'I'm so sorry, Sir Montague, you know how girls of today are. I'm sure she'll come to her senses soon enough.'

'Think nothing of it, Eunice, my dear. I may go out myself this evening after all, perhaps to the casino for a spell. My luck was running hot yesterday, despite what happened to that photographer chappie.' Sir Montague excused himself after finishing his drink.

'Kitty, my dear, you and Matthew are not going to run away

too, are you?' Mrs Delaware placed a satin-gloved hand on Kitty's arm.

'We shall be delighted to dine with you both,' Kitty assured her with a smile.

Privately she wondered how she could divert the comte's attention after dinner so that Matt could get out of the hotel. At least it seemed as if they wouldn't have Sir Montague to worry about. That is if he was telling the truth about going to the casino.

They finished their drinks and entered the dining room, where they were immediately shown to one of the best tables.

'Now then, Kitty, my dear, you must tell me more about yourself. Do you stay often with your uncle or your cousin?' Mrs Delaware asked as she patted her linen napkin in place on her lap.

Kitty exchanged a fleeting glance with Matt. 'We visit them regularly. Enderley Hall is just the other side of Exeter so just a couple of hours away really. Lucy and Rupert, of course, live in Yorkshire so sadly we don't see as much of them these days unless they are at Enderley,' Kitty said.

'Or we are visiting my parents or my aunt. They all live in Yorkshire,' Matt added.

'Your uncle does a great deal of work for your government, I believe? I have seen his name in the newspapers and, of course, Eunice has told me much about him,' the comte said.

'He has done in the past but, of course, he is really pretty much retired now. He just does a little tinkering in his workshop. My aunt is very passionate about her garden. She grows roses and is quite an expert.' Kitty crossed her fingers under the table hoping it would offset the whopping great fib she had just told about her beloved uncle.

'You must know a great many interesting people with all of your travelling?' Matt turned the tables back on Mrs Delaware.

'Oh yes, of course. Travel really does broaden the mind you

know. I met Luciano here for one thing.' Mrs Delaware patted Luciano's hand. 'And Sir Montague too, of course. Both such charming men.' She smiled archly at the comte.

The waiters set down bowls of consommé forcing a temporary break in the conversation.

'You also seem to know a great many interesting people.' Kitty turned her gaze on the comte.

'It's the nature of my work, my dear. I am fortunate that my circumstances are such that I can enjoy myself travelling and, of course, one visits many lovely places.' Luciano smiled at her.

'You work for an auction house, you said?' Matt asked.

'Yes, I'm based in Rome, I appraise paintings mainly. You know to establish provenance and to assist with valuations. Since the war and the events on the stock markets, many families have sadly been compelled to dispose of some of their artworks.' Luciano gave a small shrug as he spooned up the last of his soup from the delicate white china bowl.

'Do you encounter many forgeries in your line of work?' Kitty asked. She had read something recently which had said that there had been a spate of works with forged signatures entering the market.

'If one has the eye for such things, forgeries are easy to detect. The temptation is strong I am certain for people to claim any old picture as one completed by a master, but I have not found many. It is a buyer's market at the moment, so I suppose people wish to get the most they can,' Luciano said.

It crossed Kitty's mind that if Luciano were willing to possibly betray his country for money, he would probably be open to other means of increasing his income. His position in the art world might provide just such an opportunity.

'I have acquired several pieces myself under Luciano's guidance. Investments for the future, and, of course, a talking point back home.' Mrs Delaware smiled smugly as the soup dishes were collected and the second course served.

'A fortunate meeting for both of you, then,' Matt replied mildly.

Kitty suspected her husband was probably thinking along the same lines regarding the comte.

The rest of the meal was mainly spent discussing Nice and whether or not Kitty and Matt should hire a car with a driver to explore further afield before returning home. Kitty took a surreptitious glance at her dainty gold evening watch as they sipped their after-dinner coffees.

Time was moving along, and Matt had to escape from the hotel and get across the town to the bar. He would need to be there for when the place was busy but not overcrowded, so he could look around and investigate properly.

If Federico had left the documents with someone, that person would surely have learned by now that he was dead. Had he been told to hold on to them until someone else arrived to claim them if that happened?

The films she watched at the picture house with Alice always suggested that, in the movies at least, a code word was required. She wondered if Matt had thought about this, or perhaps it was just something that happened in the film studios and not in real life.

They finished their coffee and went through to the area set aside for dancing. As usual Mrs Delaware was shown to a table at the front and to the side of the stage. More drinks were ordered, and Kitty took to the dance floor in Matt's arms.

'When are you going to try and leave?' Kitty asked quietly as he expertly guided her around the small space.

'After a few more dances. We need to lull them into thinking we are remaining here all night. I want you to ask me to get something from our room. Then when I'm gone for a while say you are going up to look for me. Take your time once you are up there, then return and make an excuse for my delay,' Matt murmured in her ear as they danced past the band.

'Very well, I'll do my best,' Kitty promised as the song ended and they returned to their seats to catch their breath.

The nervous tension in her abdomen grew tighter as the time ticked by. She danced twice more with Matt and then with the comte, before returning to the table.

Presently she opened her silver evening purse and started to hunt inside as if missing something. 'Oh no, Matt, darling, I've left my tablets in our room.' She looked at her husband.

'Don't worry, I'll go and fetch them for you. Where are they?' Matt rose from his seat.

'They might be on the nightstand or possibly in the bathroom. I'm not certain.'

'That means they could be anywhere,' Matt replied with a mock groan. 'All right, I'll go and have a hunt.'

'Thank you, darling.' Kitty tried to sound grateful as he departed from the ballroom. She hoped she had sounded convincing and not anxious.

Now all she had to do was keep her companions distracted while Matt went to Bar Twenty-Eight to see if that might be where Federico had left the documents. She crossed her fingers discreetly and hoped for an uneventful evening.

CHAPTER FOURTEEN

Matt hurried away from the hotel keeping a sharp look out for anyone who might be interested in his whereabouts. He took care to look around for any sign of Sir Montague. The man might have said he intended visiting the casino but that didn't mean he was telling the truth. Hopefully Kitty would be able to keep Eunice and Luciano occupied.

He had studied the street map in Kitty's guidebook before dinner, so he had worked out the quickest route to the bar they had seen earlier that afternoon. The Promenade des Anglais was busy still with couples taking an evening walk after dinner in the warm evening air.

Matt turned into the side roads as soon as he could, checking to make sure no one appeared to be following him. It was quite likely that the comte or Sir Montague may have employed people to keep tabs on both himself and Kitty. He passed two of the uniformed French gendarmes patrolling the streets as he hurried to the bar.

The sound of jazz music met him before he rounded the corner to his destination. A saxophone was playing, and a female singer was crooning along, while another man played the piano. Light spilled from the large, engraved plate-glass windows onto the tables outside on the cobbled street. The scene inside was clearly illuminated and Matt could see there were several men perched on stools at the bar, while couples held hands across the tables inside.

It was clearly a busy and popular spot. Matt slowed his pace to appear more casual in his approach as he went inside. He walked into the bar and made his way to the long wooden counter. There was a vacant stool next to an older man in a beret who, from his appearance, looked as if he might be a regular there.

Matt ordered a cognac from the bartender, and drew out his cigarette case, offering a cigarette to the man next to him.

'*Merci*, monsieur.' The man accepted.

'The music is good in here tonight.' Matt thought Kitty would have enjoyed it. He lit his own cigarette and provided his new companion with a light as the bartender placed his cognac before him.

'*Oui*, the band are regulars here. The people like them and they draw a good crowd,' the man answered in French.

'You too come here regularly?' Matt asked, before taking a sip of his drink.

'Every night. My wife passed a couple of years ago. It gets lonely in the house on your own, you know,' the man replied with a sigh.

'I understand. My first wife died some years ago. It took me a long time to get over it,' Matt replied.

The man nodded. 'You are English?'

'Is my French so bad?' Matt smiled. 'Yes, I am just a visitor here.'

'We have many visitors from many countries.' The man blew out a thin stream of smoke, clearly relishing his cigarette.

'I was recommended to come here by a friend, Federico.'

Matt's tone was casual, although he watched to see if there was any recognition of the name.

'Your friend lives in Nice?' the man asked. His face betrayed no recognition of the name.

Matt shook his head. 'No, he is only a visitor like me. I had hoped he might have left a parcel for me here.'

This was something of a gamble and Matt could only hope it wouldn't place him at any risk.

The man chuckled. 'I think you are mistaken, my friend. No one has left anything here. I am here all the time, more than Alain there.' He inclined his head in the direction of the young bartender who was busy pouring beers for a small group that had just come in.

'*Eh bien*, perhaps I misunderstood him,' Matt replied with a smile.

'Alain, no one has left a parcel with you to be collected from here?' the man asked the bartender when he came near to where they were sitting.

'*Non*, monsieur.' The bartender shook his head and continued wiping down the bar, before returning to the other end to serve more customers.

'*Merci*,' Matt thanked his new companion and finished his drink. It seemed the trip to the bar had been a red herring after all. Kitty would be disappointed; she had been convinced that they had solved the clue. Now he needed to get back to the hotel before he was missed.

He said goodnight to his companion and set off once more through the darkened streets. He had not gone far before he realised someone was behind him. Someone who seemingly didn't wish to be noticed. Matt tested his supposition by speeding up a little. Sure enough, the soft footsteps behind him also increased in pace.

Matt halted near a shop window on the pretext of looking inside. In the distorted reflection of the glass under the streetlight he made out the figure of a man ducking into the entrance of an alleyway. His heart thudded in his chest, and he wished he had brought his gun with him.

The man appeared to be dressed in dark clothes, evening wear like himself, and Matt wondered if it might be Sir Montague. He continued on his way, this time heading for the more brightly lit busier areas. He had no wish to risk his safety by taking one of the shortcuts he had used on his way to the bar, even if it did mean it took longer for him to get back.

The man continued behind him but fell further back as they encountered more people and entered the Promenade des Anglais once more. He passed one of the gendarmes and whoever was tailing him seemed to disappear. Matt quickened his pace again until he was outside the hotel. Once at the entrance he nodded a good evening to the doorman and ducked into the lobby to wait and see who came through the front doors.

If Sir Montague appeared it would confirm that he was the person who had been following him. If no one entered, then it would indicate that someone else had been on his trail. He positioned himself discreetly behind one of the large potted palms where he could have sight of the door and the area outside.

He waited for a few minutes, but no one entered the hotel. He was about to leave to return to Kitty when someone he did recognise walked past his hiding place. Roland Fetherington in evening attire and without Candace at his side.

* * *

Kitty engaged in light conversation with Mrs Delaware and Luciano after Matt had gone.

'I do hope he'll be able to find where I put my tablets. I'm so dreadfully disorganised with them and it makes Matt so cross.' Kitty smiled brightly at her companions.

'This is the problem when one doesn't have a maid,' Mrs Delaware sympathised. Kitty had learned that Eunice's maid had left her employment in Paris, and she had been unable to recruit someone else that met her standards. It explained much of her grumbling.

The comte asked Mrs Delaware to dance, and they stepped out onto the dance floor, leaving Kitty alone at the table. She took a sneaky peek at her watch. It was going to be difficult to keep them from noticing Matt's absence for a whole hour or so. She would have to get her thinking cap on.

'Has Matthew not yet returned?' Eunice asked a few minutes later when the comte delivered her, looking slightly flushed and breathless, back into her seat at the end of the dance.

'No, I think he must be unable to find them. It's such a nuisance, please excuse me for a moment and I'll go and see where he is.' Kitty slipped out of her seat quickly before either of them could object and headed for her room. She deemed it best to do as she had said, in case one of them watched to see where she went.

She let herself in to the room and turned on the lamps. Another look at her watch told her that Matt had been gone almost fifteen minutes. She hoped that meant he would have reached the bar safely by now. It was very worrying and she wished she could have gone with him.

She waited for five minutes before heading back downstairs where she encountered the comte in the lobby.

'My dear Kitty, Eunice and I were becoming concerned. Is everything all right?' Luciano greeted her.

'Perfectly, thank you. Matt couldn't find my tablets. I'd left them in the stupidest of places.' Kitty affected a slightly distressed smile and gave a pathetic little sniff as if about to cry. 'I'm afraid we've had a bit of a tiff about it. I'm sure he'll be down shortly when he's cooled off.' Kitty placed her hand on the comte's sleeve. 'I'm sure you'll think me quite foolish, but I hate it when we argue. It's horribly upsetting.'

'I'm sure your husband will always be quick to forgive a wife so charming,' Luciano assured her.

While his words were soothing Kitty noticed his gaze had sharpened as if suspecting her of hiding something.

'I hope so. His time in the war affected him and sometimes he does get awfully upset. I find the best thing to do is to leave him to himself for a while.' Kitty gave the comte another disarming smile. 'We should rejoin Eunice. I would hate to alarm her with our silly little squabble.'

'Of course, my dear lady.'

Luciano was left with no choice but to do the gentlemanly thing of escorting Kitty back to their table.

More drinks were ordered, and Kitty gave Mrs Delaware the same story she had given the comte. As she dabbed her eyes with her handkerchief Kitty hoped her acting was convincing.

'You poor thing. I do sympathise. My late husband, Hiram, could be just the same. His temper would blow up out of nowhere, but he always came to when I gave him some space.' Mrs Delaware patted her hand sympathetically.

The drinks had just been delivered when Candace entered the room and came over to their table.

'I thought that you had other plans this evening,' her mother remarked somewhat sniffily as the comte stood to pull out a chair for the girl.

'I've had a very pleasant evening, but Roland does have to make a living and something urgent came up.' Candace took a seat and Luciano signalled to the waiter to order an extra drink.

Her mother snorted. 'A man who abandons you at the dinner table. I hope he paid the bill before he left.'

'I'm sure it must have been something terribly important to interrupt your evening,' Kitty soothed, seeing that the girl looked as if she were about to snap at Eunice.

'Oh, it was. He's very involved you know in investigating what happened to his photographer friend the other evening. He was dreadfully upset by Monsieur Lapin's murder. Then he got taken to the police station earlier today and was questioned for ages. So, when this man appeared while we were having dinner who had information for him, well...' Candace looked distressed.

'Oh dear. I think the police thought that Monsieur Lapin's death may have been connected to that poor soul Matt and I found.' Kitty sensed the comte and Mrs Delaware were now paying close attention to the conversation.

'Yes, Roland said the police had been to Monsieur Lapin's house to look in his files for a picture on the night he was attacked. They thought he may have taken one of the man that you found, Kitty,' Candace said.

'Did they find such a picture?' Luciano asked in a casual tone.

'No, the house had been ransacked, the files were in disarray even though they got there quickly. Roland said the inspector had told him he thought the gendarmes had just missed whoever had been there. The front door had been forced and as the police entered, they thought they heard the back door slam.' Candace's eyes were wide as she told her story.

'Good heavens, what on earth is going on in this town?' Mrs Delaware frowned in disapproval.

'It is quite extraordinary,' Kitty said. 'What with talk of spies and things it's all very queer.'

'And you say Mr Fetherington abandoned you to pursue some information regarding this investigation?' the comte asked.

Candace shrugged her slender shoulders. 'We had just finished dinner when a man knocked on the windowpane. We were seated by the window, you see. Roland excused himself and went out to speak to him. He looked quite a disreputable sort of fellow, so I was a little concerned. When

Roland came back in, he said he had to go, the man was one of his informants. He saw me into a taxi and hurried off into the town.'

'Really, the man has no manners at all.' The creases on Mrs Delaware's brow deepened.

'I wonder where he went?' Kitty mused. She hoped it had nothing to do with Matt's errand.

'I don't know,' Candace said. 'This story could be his big break though. To get his name on the bylines of some major newspapers. An exclusive.' She looked quite proud.

'I suppose so. It would also mean that he could clear his name completely with the inspector. I presume he must have been a suspect for the police to question him for so long?' Kitty said.

'Really, it gets worse. Candace, I think you have taken leave of your senses.' Mrs Delaware glared at her unrepentant-looking daughter.

Candace took a sip from her cocktail. 'I do wish you would face facts, Mother. I love Roland and we intend to be married. There I've said it.' She leaned back in her chair and glared defiantly at Mrs Delaware.

The colour drained from Eunice's cheeks leaving only unbecoming patches of rouge. 'I was right. You have taken leave of your sense. I forbid it, Candace. If you go ahead with this wild scheme to marry that man, you'll never see a dime from your father's trust fund.'

Candace swallowed the rest of her drink and banged the empty glass down on the table. 'Fine. I don't care what you say. I only have to wait a few more months until my birthday and the money is mine anyway and there is nothing you can do about it. Roland and I will get married, with or without your blessing.' She jumped up from her chair and swept out of the room.

Mrs Delaware appeared to be frozen in her seat. She clutched at her heart and gasped for breath. 'That wicked, ungrateful child, after all I've done for her.' Her words came out between pants.

Kitty summoned a waiter and requested water and brandy urgently since she was sure Eunice was about to faint. The waiter took one look at the stricken woman and was back in seconds.

'Here, take a sip of this.' Kitty pressed a glass of cognac to the woman's lips.

Mrs Delaware's hands shook as she held the glass with Kitty's assistance. 'Hiram will be turning in his grave,' she wailed.

'Eunice, my dear, do not fret. There is plenty of time for Candace to change her mind,' the comte assured her. 'Perhaps it is only because you disapprove that she feels the need to defy you.'

'What are you suggesting, Luciano? That I give them my blessing?' Colour started to return to the older woman's cheeks.

'Just the appearance of it, at least for a while. You know what they say, dearest, forbidden fruit is the most attractive. Perhaps if he is around more often then he will not be so appealing. What do you think, Kitty?' The comte looked at her.

'I suppose it could do no harm,' Kitty agreed.

She wondered if the comte's sudden desire to welcome Roland Fetherington into the fold was prompted by the idea that he might discover a lead for the whereabouts of the documents.

Mrs Delaware appeared to be recovering from her shock. 'I don't know. I had such plans for her. She is so like Hiram though sometimes.' She sniffed.

Kitty consoled her as best she could, while the comte continued to press brandy as a remedy for the upset she had just sustained.

'Whatever will Sir Montague think?' Mrs Delaware produced a tiny, dainty handkerchief from her evening bag and dabbed at her nose. 'He was so suitable, a title and a large estate. She could have been Lady Savernake and been presented at court.'

Kitty was saved from having to answer this by Matt's reappearance in the ballroom.

'Oh, darling, you're back. I'm so sorry, I hope you've forgiven me.' Kitty stood up and flung herself on her unsuspecting husband.

CHAPTER FIFTEEN

Matt just about caught his wife's murmured instruction to play along as she hugged him. She buried her face in his shoulder, and he just caught the muffled word, 'Argument.'

'Steady on, old thing, of course I forgive you.' He wasn't quite sure what he was to forgive Kitty for but guessed it must have something to do with whatever tale she had told the other two people at the table. Presumably she had made up a row to explain his absence.

'It really was so silly of me to leave my medication in the pocket of my coat. I should have thought.' Kitty sniffed as she looked up at him with limpid blue-grey eyes.

'No harm done, darling. Least said, soonest mended.' He kissed the top of her blonde head.

Clearly something had happened whilst he had been chasing his tail all over Nice trying to work out the meaning behind the figures in the matchbook.

'I think, if you will all excuse me, I need to retire to my room to lie down. This business with Candace and Mr Fetherington has been horribly distressing.' Mrs Delaware rose from her seat and, refusing Luciano's offer to accompany her, departed from the ballroom.

'I think I too shall turn in, as you English say.' The comte bade them goodnight and followed Mrs Delaware.

Matt took one of the vacant seats as Kitty sat down again.

'Phew, I think I need another drink, that was terribly dramatic,' Kitty said. 'I have been quite the actress this evening.'

Matt flagged down a waiter and ordered them each a nightcap of a small cognac. 'I gather things kicked off while I was gone?' Matt asked, keeping his voice low just in case anyone might be trying to eavesdrop on their conversation.

'I'll say. I've lots to tell you. How about you? Any luck at the bar?' Kitty asked in the same low tone.

Matt shook his head. 'No joy. Whatever those numbers in the matchbook mean, that wasn't it.'

Kitty looked disappointed as she sipped her drink. 'I know it was a long shot, but I had rather hoped we might have cracked it. It just seemed like a sign when we walked past there today.'

'Me too. I have got lots to tell you though,' Matt said, before taking a good sip of his cognac.

'Then shall we finish these and get out of here?' Kitty suggested. She finished her drink and collected her bag and her stole.

Once safely back in their room, Matt told her what had happened at the bar and about Roland Fetherington following him back to the hotel.

Kitty's expression was grave as he finished his story. 'Goodness, that makes sense now of what Candace told us just before you returned.'

She explained what Candace had said about Roland cutting short their date. She also told him what she had learned about the police visit to find Monsieur Lapin's photographs of Federico at the casino.

'And you say that Luciano suggested Eunice make nice with

Roland, to try and dissuade Candace from marrying him?' Matt paused from where he was taking off his cufflinks.

'Yes. But I think he wants to keep an eye on Roland in case he discovers something which could lead to the papers,' Kitty's voice came from the bathroom where she was washing her face.

'Or was he the one who killed Monsieur Lapin and possibly Federico?' Matt suggested.

'He could have, but so could Sir Montague, if they were in it together. Do you think the comte will try and cut Sir Montague out of whatever deal he might have going on with the Duponts, now that he really has been cast aside by Candace? I mean, Sir Montague can hardly keep hanging about with Mrs Delaware now surely?' Kitty wandered back into the bedroom and slipped under the covers.

Matt considered Kitty's questions. 'In ordinary circumstances I would say no, but he's on the brink of losing potentially two paydays. Marriage to Candace and all her lovely money and being levered out of the money from Dupont for the documents.'

He finished preparing for bed and joined Kitty under the covers.

'He could become desperate you mean?' Kitty asked.

'It depends how parlous his finances are. We know he has a large estate and he seemed very fond of the gaming table. I wonder if he has debts at the casino?' Matt switched off the bedside lamp.

'I suppose we might find out tomorrow what's going to happen. Either way, I am so very glad you came back safely tonight. I was so worried all the time you were gone.' Kitty snuggled closer to him.

'You did really well, keeping everyone distracted.' Matt just wished the mission had been more successful.

* * *

Kitty had no clear idea now what their plan of action was to be when they went down for breakfast the following morning. There was no sign of Mrs Delaware and Candace or of the comte.

Only Sir Montague was there, dining alone at a small table. Kitty raised her hand in greeting and called good morning as the waiter led them to a table for two.

'What shall we do today?' Kitty asked, after shaking her linen napkin out onto her lap.

'We really need to try and crack that twenty-eight business. It's the only thing we have left to go on,' Matt said.

Kitty agreed, but she had been thinking about it ever since they had discovered it and she had drawn a complete blank.

'The only thing I can think of is the casino. Is it to do with the gaming table? The roulette wheel?' she suggested. 'Is that why it's a matchbook from there?'

Matt cracked the top of his hard-boiled egg with a spoon. 'Shall we go again tonight? I still have the gaming chips we didn't use.'

'I think we should, just to see if there is anything. The Duponts are definitely involved in this somehow, aren't they? So, we may discover something of use.' Kitty poured them both a cup of coffee.

'I agree. We'll give it a shot.' Matt picked up a slice of toast and started spreading it with butter.

'It may be dangerous though.' Kitty could already feel a prickle of unease running through her at the thought of returning to the scene of Monsieur Lapin's murder.

'Yes, we'll have to be very careful,' Matt agreed.

After finishing breakfast, they ventured back outside onto the terrace. Kitty took her book to read, and Matt acquired an English language newspaper from the reception desk. The air was warm, and the sea twinkled in the distance. Kitty thought perhaps a paddle might be in order later on. They had just comfortably installed themselves in a shady spot with a good view of all the comings and goings when the shadow of a now familiar figure loomed over the table.

'*Bonjour,* Madame Bryant, Captain Bryant, may I join you for a moment?' Inspector Villier asked politely, before seating himself after a nod of assent and a greeting from Kitty and Matt.

'Can we get you a drink, Inspector?' Kitty asked as she placed her bookmark inside her novel and closed it.

'Thank you, Madame Bryant, a cup of tea would be most welcome.' The inspector removed his hat and mopped his brow with a clean white-cotton handkerchief.

Matt summoned a nearby waiter and placed their order. Kitty could see the policeman appeared unusually hot and bothered, considering the early hour of the day.

'Forgive me, Inspector, but are you all right?' Kitty asked, concerned the man looked so flustered.

'These murders, Madame Bryant, are causing quite a stir in the town, and the mayor is not happy. I have been out and about already for several hours this morning with various tasks.' The inspector tucked his handkerchief back into his pocket and took out his notebook and pen.

'I take it we can assume this is not a mere social call then, Inspector?' Matt said as the waiter placed a tray containing tea things in front of them.

'Unfortunately not, Captain Bryant, although the main purpose of my visit is to see Mademoiselle Candace Delaware.' The inspector settled himself in the rattan chair as Kitty set out the cups and saucers to pour the tea.

'Candace? I presume this call then is to do with the murder of Monsieur Lapin?' Kitty placed the tea strainer over the top of one of the delicate modern geometric-shaped cups.

'A mere formality, Madame Bryant. I wish to revisit her statement. Indeed, that is also why I wish to speak to you both too. You have had the misfortune to be present at the discovery of both of the victims.' Inspector Villier looked first at Kitty and then at Matt.

Kitty poured the inspector's tea before pouring a cup first for Matt and then for herself. 'Yes, as you have pointed out before we have been particularly unlucky in that regard,' she agreed calmly.

'I think you should know, Madame Bryant, that we have now finally managed to identify the man you discovered masquerading as a vagrant in the alleyway.' Inspector Villier carefully added milk to his cup.

'Gosh, so he wasn't a tramp then after all? You were right, Inspector. Who was he?' Kitty added milk to her own cup once the inspector had set down the jug.

'It seems he was a businessman who possessed dual nationality. In Italy he was known as Federico Benedetto. In England we believe he used an anglicised version of his name, Frederick Bennet.' The inspector's gaze sharpened.

'How interesting.' Kitty stirred her tea with a steady hand.

'I have already had discussions with the British Embassy and the Italian Embassy about this man.' The inspector paused and took a careful sip of his tea. 'Both establishments had little to say on the matter.'

Matt picked up his own cup and saucer. 'Do you know what he was doing here in Nice? Why he was, as you say, masquerading as a tramp?'

Kitty admired Matt's nonchalant tone. As she endeavoured to keep her voice light, her heart hammered against her ribcage, and she was surprised her hand had not been shaking as she'd stirred her tea. The inspector had already heavily hinted that he knew of Federico's business in Nice and that Kitty and Matt were somehow connected to it.

'I believe we all here at this table know why this man may have been here and why he had adopted this disguise.' The policeman's tone hardened. 'I cannot therefore exclude you from involvement in his death. Nor, for that matter, the death of Monsieur Lapin.'

'But we had only been in Nice for a few hours when we discovered this Mr Benedetto, and surely the doctor who examined him would have known he had been dead for some time before we stumbled across him?' Kitty protested. 'We had no motive to wish either him or Monsieur Lapin any harm. We didn't even speak to Monsieur Lapin.' She thought it best not to address his other suspicions about their knowledge of Federico's identity.

The inspector took another sip of his tea before replacing his cup back on the saucer with a very deliberate air. 'In my experience, Madame Bryant, it is very unusual for the same persons to stumble across two murders in two days. For that reason alone, it makes you persons of interest. I therefore would formally request that you remain in Nice now until I have concluded my investigations into these deaths.'

'Obviously, we are happy to try and assist you as much as possible, but we have told you all we can about both incidents.' Matt met the inspector's gaze and held it.

'This Benedetto man must have been photographed by Monsieur Lapin before he changed his guise to that of a vagrant. Those pictures were stolen from the photographer's home before my gendarmes could retrieve them. I think the purpose of this theft was twofold. One, to try and delay identification of Mr Benedetto, and second, I think he was pictured with someone who knew very well why he was in Nice and who was either his murderer or is somehow linked to his death,' Inspector Villier said.

Matt nodded. 'That seems to be a reasonable supposition based on what you have told us. Do you have any idea who that person may have been?'

The corners of the inspector's mouth lifted in a small half-smile. 'When we reorganised Monsieur Lapin's photographs, we found several other pictures taken on the same evening that Mr Benedetto visited the casino.'

'I expect that would be very helpful,' Kitty said. Her interest was suddenly piqued. It was clear the inspector was an intelligent and thorough man and she hated deceiving him.

'There were several people who were present both on the evening Mr Benedetto visited and who were also present the night Monsieur Lapin was attacked. I have already interviewed some of those people this morning and excluded them from the inquiry,' Inspector Villier said.

Kitty assumed that was why the inspector had looked so hot and bothered when he had arrived at the hotel.

'I presume that the Delaware party, Comte Malfiore, and Sir Montague Savernake were present both nights?' Matt suggested.

'You would be correct in that assumption, Captain Bryant,' Inspector Villier confirmed.

'And I assume Monsieur and Madame Dupont are also likely to have been present since they own the casino,' Kitty added.

'*Naturellement*, madame,' the inspector agreed.

'So all of these people are persons of interest, along with Roland Fetherington,' Matt said. 'I take it he too was present that evening, although I seem to recall he said he arrived late.'

'I am very anxious to resolve this case quickly. I have a certain amount of pressure, as I told you, the mayor is most concerned. I also wish that there are no more deaths.' The inspector looked at them once more.

'We sincerely also hope that will be the case, Inspector,' Kitty said.

As she spoke Candace Delaware emerged from the hotel dressed in a smart navy and white dress. She glanced over to where Kitty and Matt were sitting on the terrace and went to hurry away.

'Mademoiselle Delaware, *un moment*!' The inspector spotted her and leapt to his feet. He grabbed his hat from the table and waved it in the air as he called to the girl.

Candace was forced to acknowledge him and reluctantly changed her course to come and join them at their table.

'I am so pleased I caught you, Mademoiselle Delaware.' The inspector courteously pulled out a chair so Candace could sit down. 'I was on my way to see you.'

'Good morning, Inspector Villier. I hope this won't take long, I have an appointment in town.' Candace accepted the seat with a show of impatience, clearly annoyed that she had been unable to avoid the policeman's summons.

'Of course, mademoiselle, I shall do my best not to impede your day.' The inspector dropped his hat back down on the table and took up his notebook and pen again. 'Perhaps, you would be so kind as to go through once more for me the events at the casino leading up to the discovery of poor Monsieur Lapin?'

Candace repeated her previous story of having agreed to meet Roland and having slipped away from her mother to go outside and into the gardens.

'May I ask, mademoiselle, when you were leaving the casino to meet Monsieur Fetherington, where were the rest of your party?' Inspector Villier asked.

'Mother was at the card table as usual. Luciano had been with her watching the game.' Candace screwed up her face as she tried to remember. 'He had moved away though then. I presume he was bored as Mother ignores everyone and everything when she is engrossed in a game. Monty had been at the roulette table, but he wasn't there when I came out. I remember because I was worried in case one of them saw me and reported back to Mother later on.'

'Thank you, Mademoiselle Candace. You know Monsieur and Madame Dupont, I believe?' the inspector asked.

Candace looked puzzled. 'Yes, I've met them several times at the casino. They are friends of Luciano's, although Monty seems to know them very well too.'

There was something in the girl's tone when she mentioned Sir Montague's friendship with the Duponts that caught Kitty's attention.

It clearly caught Inspector Villier's notice too.

'Sir Montague Savernake is also a friend of theirs?' he asked mildly.

Candace smiled and rummaged in her bag for her cigarettes. 'I'm not sure that friend is exactly the term I'd use.' She took out her ebony cigarette holder and inserted a cigarette.

Inspector Villier felt in his jacket pocket for his lighter and lit her cigarette for her. 'And why do you say that, Mademoiselle Delaware?'

Candace pulled on her cigarette and blew out a thin ribbon of smoke. 'Because I overheard Jerard Dupont threatening Monty, the night that poor man was attacked.'

CHAPTER SIXTEEN

Kitty looked at Matt. *This was interesting information.* Inspector Villier made a note in his book.

'Can you tell me what happened, mademoiselle?' the policeman asked.

'It was just before Monty went to the tables. He was at the bar in the private room getting a drink. He always made the most of the free drinks in there.' Candace paused to flick the ash from the end of her cigarette into a large white ceramic ashtray in the centre of the table. 'I was standing nearby but I think they thought I couldn't hear them over the music that was playing in the other room and everyone talking.'

'You say Monsieur Dupont threatened Sir Montague?' Inspector Villier prompted.

'Yes. He came up to Monty and said something like, "I hope Lady Luck will be on your side tonight. The debt you have is growing very large and I believe that the means you have to repay it are out of reach at present. We are unable to further extend your credit without a payment to reduce the capital." Monty said that he would be able to deliver the goods soon and Jerard was not to worry. He said he was good for the money.

Monsieur Dupont said he hoped that would be the case since the consequences of a bad debt could carry a severe penalty.' Candace broke off and gave the inspector a worried look. 'It wasn't what he said but how he said it.'

'I see.' Inspector Villier finished scribbling the information in his book.

'I felt as if it had a double meaning, and I could see Monty was uncomfortable all the while they were talking. Those security guards were standing close to them too and kept looking at Jerard, almost as if waiting for some kind of instruction. Monty kept looking at them and fidgeting with his collar, and he looked all pale and sweaty.' Candace extinguished her cigarette.

'I take it that you believe Sir Montague owes a great deal of money to the casino?' Inspector Villier asked.

Candace laughed. 'I know that he owes a lot of money and not just here in France. Mother was so keen to foist me off on Monty; she wants to boast about her titled daughter and her English estate to her friends back home. But Monty is flat broke, he barely has a cent to his name, and I would be expected to pay all of his debts if we married. I'm not as naïve as Mother thinks where money is concerned. I guess I'm my father's daughter after all. I made some enquiries back in England when we were in London. Monty's family money was eaten up in death duties. He was the youngest son, and his older brothers were in line to get the estate. One was killed in the Great War and his other brother died in a motoring accident in Switzerland.'

'And Sir Montague, you think he has a gambling problem?' Inspector Villier asked.

'He'd bet on two flies crawling up a windowpane, so I guess he would owe the Duponts money. His luck hadn't been that good at the tables, everyone knows the house always wins. No, Monsieur Dupont had this sort of, well, sinister tone when he was talking to Monty that night,' Candace said. 'It made me feel uncomfortable and I wasn't even involved.'

'You left the private area and went from the casino foyer out onto the terrace. Then you immediately walked straight along the path through the gardens? You did not pause for any reason or notice anyone while you were doing this?' Inspector Villier asked.

'I saw Madame Dupont near the cashier's booth, she was assisting some of her guests. There were people out on the terrace, you know walking and smoking, that kind of thing but no one else that I knew personally,' Candace said. 'It was quiet when I set off along the path, I didn't see anyone else there until, well, until I found that poor man lying on the ground.' Her voice wavered and she came to a halt.

'Captain Bryant, Madame Bryant, please can you confirm for me your account of the evening?' the inspector asked.

'We had walked down to the bottom gate which was locked. We were on our way back up to the terrace and came as soon as we heard Candace call for help. No one passed us on the path, and we didn't see or hear anyone until we found Monsieur Lapin with Candace standing next to him,' Kitty confirmed.

'And Monsieur Fetherington was the first person to appear after you and Captain Bryant had come to Mademoiselle Delaware's aid?' Inspector Villier lifted his gaze from his notes as if to confirm this statement.

'Yes, Rolly came straight away. I think he had seen me go out onto the terrace and had been on his way to meet me when he heard me shout for help,' Candace agreed.

'*Eh bien, merci*, mademoiselle, you have been most agreeable.' The inspector closed his notebook.

Candace collected her things from the table. 'Then I'm free to go now?'

'Of course, mademoiselle.' The inspector watched as the girl bade them a hasty farewell and hurried from the terrace and out onto the Promenade des Anglais.

'I take it that Candace's statement supports the information that Roland Fetherington gave you when you interviewed him yesterday?' Matt asked as the inspector replaced his notebook in his jacket pocket.

The corners of the inspector's mouth twitched upwards in a brief smile. 'Monsieur Fetherington has said he had just left the foyer and had gone out to the terrace and was at the entrance of the garden path when he heard Mademoiselle Delaware call out.'

'Had he seen any of the others outside at all or in the foyer?' Kitty asked.

'You are very interested in the statement of Monsieur Fetherington, Madame Bryant?' Inspector Villier looked at Kitty.

Her cheeks warmed under his gaze. 'Human curiosity, Inspector, especially as we seem to have become entangled with all of this.'

'I see. Well as you heard from Mademoiselle Delaware, Helene Dupont was in the foyer and Monsieur Fetherington also believes she may have been outside the casino. He also said he thought he saw Sir Montague emerge from one of the other openings onto the terrace.' The inspector sighed. 'It all is very complicated.'

'There is Sir Montague now.' Kitty noticed the Englishman leaving the hotel, a newspaper tucked under his arm and his silver-topped walking cane in his hand.

'Sir Montague!' The inspector leapt into action once more. His bellow causing the other occupants on the now busy terrace tables to look up from their various occupations.

Sir Montague appeared unperturbed by the inspector's summons and made his way along the terrace to their table in a leisurely fashion.

'My dear Inspector Villier, good morning. Kitty, Matthew. This is quite the surprise.' He doffed his hat to Kitty and accepted the chair recently vacated by Candace.

'If I may take a moment of your time, Sir Montague, I should greatly appreciate it.' The inspector's notebook made a reappearance once more.

'Of course, my dear fellow!' Sir Montague placed his newspaper down on the table and rested his cane across his knees. 'How can I assist you?'

'I have just concluded my interview with Mademoiselle Delaware regarding the events of the night of Monsieur Lapin's death,' the inspector said.

'Ah yes, the photographer chap at the casino. Dashed bad show that business.' Sir Montague adjusted the cuffs on his smart navy-blue blazer.

'As you say, Sir Montague, it is indeed very bad. I am just checking the statements you were all so good as to give me around the time of the incident. I wonder if you can confirm to me where you said you were during that evening up until Mademoiselle Delaware discovered Monsieur Lapin in the gardens.' The inspector had his pen poised over the open page of his notebook. His expression was suitably bland, and Kitty wondered what he was thinking.

'Well so far as I can recall, we all travelled to the casino together. Luciano had arranged the cars. We had drinks in the private area that Jerard and Helene use to entertain special guests. After a while I went onto the old roulette table. I had a bally good evening. Lady Luck was with me that evening.' Sir Montague paused and frowned as if trying to recall the next part of the night.

'Ah yes, that was it. My luck was holding, but I didn't want to push it. It's been a while since I'd finished on the plus side. I came away from the table and got another drink from the bar. It was getting quite warm, so I stepped outside for a time, have a smoke you know and cool off. There were some very pretty fillies there that night and they had been jolly attentive, if you catch my drift.' He winked at the inspector.

Kitty's brows rose at this, and she wondered if Sir Montague had forgotten she was present.

'Any hoo, I couldn't see them out on the terrace, so I was about to go back inside. I thought I might just chance another couple of spins when I heard a bit of a commotion. Nobody seemed to know what was happening and several people went to take a look. Two of Jerard's men went dashing past me into the garden. I found out the rest later.' Sir Montague looked at the inspector.

Inspector Villier had been writing rapidly while Sir Montague had been speaking. So far as Kitty could tell his tale supported what Candace had said. Although she could see that it could have given him time to follow Monsieur Lapin, attack him and return before the alarm was raised.

'*Merci*, Sir Montague. While you were on the terrace, taking the air and having a cigarette, did you see anyone out there that you knew at all?' the inspector asked.

Sir Montague's brow creased in concentration. 'Luciano was out there, I think. I saw him talking to Jerard, but I could have been mistaken.'

'You were familiar with Monsieur Lapin, the photographer? You had met him before?' Inspector Villier looked at Sir Montague.

'Well, I wouldn't say familiar. I mean I've been photographed a few times by him, of course, got his card somewhere probably.' He patted his jacket pockets as if half expecting to discover that item somewhere about his person.

'Did Monsieur Lapin give his card out to people that he photographed?' Kitty asked. It should have occurred to her that if people wanted their picture they could then call on him. Roland had said he sold them as souvenirs.

Sir Montague blinked as if suddenly remembering that Kitty and Matt were present. 'Yes, that's how he got more sales. I believe he displayed them in his studio window usually.'

Kitty realised it would also be how the burglars who broke into his home would have known where he lived if they had not been familiar with his studio. It also meant that Sir Montague and the comte would have known his address. No doubt the Duponts would have known it already.

'May I ask if you are on good terms with Monsieur and Madame Dupont?' Inspector Villier returned to questioning the peer.

For the first time that morning Sir Montague's air of cheery calm seemed slightly ruffled. 'Yes, I should say so.'

'I have a witness, Sir Montague, that said they heard Monsieur Dupont making some kind of threat to you on the night Monsieur Lapin was attacked. I think you owe a great deal of money at the casino?' The inspector's tone had hardened.

'Obviously Jerard had some concerns. As I said, I've had a bit of a run of bad luck, but you know a chap is entitled to some credit. It was nothing worth worrying about.'

'You have then the means to settle your account for the outstanding amount?' the inspector persisted.

'Now see here, Inspector!' The volume of Sir Montague's voice had risen, attracting curious stares from the occupants of nearby tables. He seemed to realise this and lowered his voice again. 'My good man, I assure you that Monsieur Dupont has no need to worry about my ability to satisfy any creditors. In fact, I am on my way now to my bank.' Sir Montague subsided back in his seat still clearly annoyed by the conversation.

'*Eh bien*, thank you, Sir Montague. I am most delighted to hear it. You will be continuing with your stay here in Nice for a while longer?' Inspector Villier finished his notes and closed his book.

'Um, I think so, for a few more days at least.' Sir Montague picked up his newspaper as if eager to be off once more.

'Good, thank you for your time,' Inspector Villier said.

Sir Montague wished them all a good morning and tucking his paper back under his arm he strolled away down the terrace. Although Kitty thought he looked much less sanguine than when he had first set out that morning.

'Do you think that's true, Inspector?' Kitty asked. 'Has he the finances at his bank to pay his debts? Candace didn't seem to think he had any money.'

The inspector put away his book and his pen. 'Obviously, Madame Bryant, I shall be talking to Monsieur Real, the bank manager. No doubt we shall discover the truth lies somewhere in between those two statements.'

'It's almost lunchtime, will you join us for lunch, Inspector?' Matt asked after consulting his watch.

'Thank you, Captain Bryant, but no, I regret that I must get on. I have other people to speak to if I am to solve these murders. Thank you for the tea, it was most refreshing.' The inspector picked up his hat and rose from his seat. He nodded to them both before replacing his hat on his head and bidding them a good morning.

'That was all most interesting,' Kitty said thoughtfully as she watched the policeman depart. 'Who else has he got to interview I wonder?'

'The Duponts? The comte?' Matt suggested.

'It's quite a horrid feeling that perhaps one of the handful of people we have come to know here may be responsible for both of those deaths.' A shiver ran along Kitty's spine.

'The brigadier did warn us that this could become quite a tricky job,' Matt said.

'It also seems we are not able to leave even if we wished to at present, so we have to see it through. I hadn't thought we would seriously be considered as suspects,' Kitty said.

'No, that part is very uncomfortable. I don't think either of us wish to spend time in a French prison. We do really need to crack that code in the matchbook. Perhaps that trip to the casino again this evening might throw some light on it.' Matt seemed unusually thoughtful, and she wondered what her husband was thinking.

'Should we have mentioned our plan to go to the casino again tonight to the inspector do you think?' Kitty asked.

'He already appears to think we know far more than we actually do about these murders. No, I think we should just go and see what happens. If we learn anything that pertains to Federico or Monsieur Lapin's death, then we can pass that on. Our first obligation, however, is to complete the job we came here to do and that is to recover those documents.'

Mrs Delaware didn't make an appearance until later that afternoon. Kitty and Matt had spent the rest of their day reading and relaxing on the terrace, followed by a short excursion onto the sands. No further ideas had occurred to either of them about the meaning of the number in the matchbook.

Kitty had her eyes closed behind her sunglasses and her head tipped back on her chair enjoying the feel of the sun on her face when she became aware of someone at their table once more.

'Mrs Delaware, do come and join us. Here, have a seat.'

Kitty's eyes opened at the sound of Matt's greeting and the scraping of a chair being moved on the marble flags of the terrace. She sat herself more upright and tried to shake herself fully awake.

'Thank you, Matthew, I have been in my room for most of today with the most ghastly headache. I'm so worried about Candace and that man.' Mrs Delaware did appear unwell. She too was wearing dark glasses with circular lenses and her face was pale in the bright afternoon sunlight.

Matt summoned a waiter and ordered some iced lemon drinks.

'I'm sure Candace won't do anything rash. She does seem to be a very sensible young woman,' Kitty attempted to calm Mrs Delaware's fears.

'Ordinarily, Kitty, my dear, I would agree with you but I'm afraid this Fetherington man has turned her head. To throw away the prospects of a title and a fabulous estate in England for a penniless journalist.' Mrs Delaware shook her head mournfully. 'It's not what I had hoped for.'

The waiter deposited a chrome tray with a large jug of lemon and several crystal tumblers on the table.

'She may change her mind. It's early days yet and perhaps it may even turn out for the best. They may be better suited to each other you know.' Kitty poured them all a drink, taking care to disperse ice and mint sprigs equally into each glass.

'I wish I had your optimism, my dear, but Candace will be a very rich young woman and this Fetherington may be taking advantage of her.' Mrs Delaware pressed her fingertips against her temples.

Kitty refrained from pointing out that Sir Montague would have been taking advantage of Candace's wealth too if a marriage had come off.

'Do have a drink, Eunice, and try to put it from your mind for now,' Matt advised.

Mrs Delaware reluctantly accepted a glass and sipped obediently. 'I have no idea where anyone has gone. Candace, I assume is with that man. She left straight after breakfast without telling me where she was going. Poor Sir Montague must be nursing his broken heart elsewhere and even Luciano has been nowhere in sight today.'

'I believe Sir Montague had an appointment with his bank,' Matt murmured.

'Well, it's very bad form of all of them,' Mrs Delaware complained. 'Thank goodness you two are being so kind to me.'

Matt caught Kitty's gaze and she bit her lip trying not to smile at their companion's woebegone tone.

'May I ask what your plans are for this evening?' Eunice asked after another fortifying sip of lemon.

'Well, we had thought that after dinner we might actually return to the casino. After everything that happened the other evening, we never did get the chance to try our luck,' Matt said.

'The whole thing was so distressing that I hope that seeing it again might replace those bad memories. It keeps playing on my mind you see,' Kitty added.

Mrs Delaware immediately perked up. 'That does seem a splendid idea. I shall accompany you. Yes, it would be nice to have better memories. I'll have Luciano arrange cars again.'

'How very kind,' Kitty said. She hoped Matt knew what he was doing.

CHAPTER SEVENTEEN

Matt was unsurprised when the comte accompanied Mrs Delaware into the dining room that evening. He was much more surprised when Roland Fetherington joined the table with Candace on his arm. There seemed to be a polite hostility between the slightly down-at-heel journalist and Candace's mother, and he hoped the truce would hold. If not, then it promised to be an uncomfortable evening.

'Sir Montague will not be joining us for dinner this evening,' Mrs Delaware informed them with a pointed glance at Candace. 'Luciano has arranged for cars to take us to the casino after dinner.' She appeared to have forgiven the comte for his neglect earlier in the day. Although still a little wan, she had rallied from her despair of the afternoon to don a peacock-blue satin gown and sapphire and diamond dropper earrings.

Candace had the air of a cat that had successfully acquired the cream and smiled and sparkled at the rather less comfortable-looking Roland Fetherington. The comte's faultless good manners, however, helped to smooth the way and thankfully dinner passed successfully. Although Matt wondered where Luciano had spent the day.

It was decided that Mrs Delaware and the comte should travel to the casino in one car, with Candace and Roland accompanying Matt and Kitty in the second car.

'Have you been to the casino to play before, Mr Fetherington?' Kitty asked once they were on their way.

'No, it's not something I would usually do. I'm more accustomed to standing outside with Marc making notes of who is attending,' he said. 'I'm not really a gambling man.'

This comment seemed to meet with Candace's approval as she beamed at her beloved.

'Were you outside the casino the night Monsieur Lapin took the photograph of the man killed in the alley?' Matt asked.

'You know I've been wracking my brains all day trying to remember that evening. The one when Marc took that picture of the man in the alley. I'm fairly sure it was the night I was late getting there. There had been a problem at my lodgings, and I was delayed setting off for the casino. There were lots of people in that evening from the yachts in the harbour.' Roland frowned.

'It's a pity you didn't see him,' Kitty said.

'I for one am quite relieved you didn't.' Candace placed a white satin gloved hand on Roland's arm. 'You might have been assaulted too.'

'It will be strange going there tonight without Marc being there taking pictures.' Roland looked upset. 'He was a very kind man. He really helped me when I arrived here, you know, pointing people out to write about for my society column.'

'It may also help you too,' Kitty remarked in a sympathetic tone. 'Like laying a ghost of a terrible experience. That's what Matt and I thought it might do for us. It feels as if we have been dogged by tragedy ever since we arrived in Nice.'

* * *

The cars pulled to a halt outside the casino and once more the liveried doorman came to open the car doors and greet them. No sooner had they walked up the short flight of marble stairs than Helene Dupont appeared to welcome them in the foyer. She was as elegant as before, this time in a bright-yellow gown with a diamanté and marabou fur trim.

'My dears, welcome back to Casino Plessy. Luciano, Eunice.' She kissed the cheeks of the older couple. 'I'm so pleased you have all decided to return after everything that happened. Do come in and have a drink.' She led them through the busy gaming hall and into the private area where once more they were served with chilled glasses of champagne.

Jerard Dupont was at the bar deep in conversation with some German or Austrian guests. Matt noted that the man appeared to be as fluent in their language as he was in English. No doubt a skill that served him well in his line of business.

'My dear Luciano, and your lovely friends, welcome back.' Jerard broke off from his other guests and came to join his wife. He shook hands with the comte and Matt. 'We are delighted to see you, and, Monsieur Fetherington, you are joining us too this evening.' He looked a little doubtfully at Roland before extending his hand to him. Matt thought the man was probably assessing how much an impoverished journalist might add to the casino's coffers.

'We were saying on the way here that we hoped to replace the unfortunate memories of the other evening with more pleasant ones.' Kitty smiled at their host.

'I am delighted you are giving us another chance, *ma cher* madame.' Jerard bowed over Kitty's hand.

Matt clenched his teeth as he kept a pleasant smile fixed to his face when the Frenchman was slow to release his hold.

'That wretched policeman gave me the third degree this morning on the terrace, didn't he?' Candace looked to Kitty and

Matt for confirmation. 'I almost felt as if he was about to accuse me of hitting that poor man over the head.' She shuddered.

'Inspector Villier has a reputation for being very thorough. He is like a dog with a bone, once he has his teeth in something he is reluctant to let go.' Jerard Dupont smiled, then bared his teeth and aimed a playful growl in Candace's direction.

The girl jumped and tightened her grip on Roland Fetherington's arm.

'Unless he is distracted with another juicier bone, eh?' the comte suggested.

'Enough, my dear Jerard.' Helene Dupont placed her hand on her husband's arm. 'You are alarming Candace with such talk.'

'My apologies, *cher* mademoiselle.' Monsieur Dupont smiled genially at the girl. 'Come, enjoy your evening. Have a small bet on me.' He reached into the pocket of his evening jacket and handed round some white coloured counters.

'Yes, let's have no more talk of murder and unpleasantness. Inspector Villier also called upon us today, so I am certain by now he has talked with everyone. We have no more cause to think on such things.' Helene Dupont smiled regally at the group as if issuing a royal decree.

Matt wondered if that were true. He would have liked the opportunity to have listened in on the inspector's interview with the Duponts. They were certainly an interesting couple.

Madame Dupont invited them to return to the private area in an hour or so to partake of a light supper since they had already eaten dinner.

'Our way of making amends for any uncomfortable impression your last visit may have caused,' Helene assured them.

Mrs Delaware thanked their hostess profusely while the rest of the group's response was more muted. As they made their way out into the main hall of the casino, Helene Dupont called the comte back and Matt saw they had their heads close together.

He had no time to wonder what it might be about as the security guard had lifted the heavy red silk rope cordon for the group to pass through. The casino was once again buzzing with activity. A light film of bluish cigarette smoke hung in the air above the tables and jewels glittered on the gowns and around the necks of the well-heeled gamblers at the various tables.

Mrs Delaware immediately made a beeline for the card table. Candace and Roland Fetherington appeared to have settled on merely walking around to watch the various groups.

'Do you fancy a turn on the roulette table?' Matt asked as Kitty seemed more interested in that area of the casino.

'Why not? It has a number twenty-eight on it,' she murmured.

They headed towards the table, and he saw that Sir Montague was already in the casino. He could only assume he had arrived before them as it looked as if he was well established. Unlike the previous visit, however, it seemed that the run of luck was not going his way.

The pile of counters before him on the green baize was diminishing and there was no sign of the attractive young ladies who had been attached to his side before.

'Sir Montague, good evening, I didn't realise you were intending to visit tonight. You could have shared our car,' Kitty greeted him as a space opened close by.

'Kitty, Matthew, good evening. I wasn't aware you were coming here tonight.' Sir Montague glanced quickly at them before returning his attention to the wheel now slowly coming to a stop with the metal ball rolling into place.

The croupier swiftly raked in the losing counters before passing out the winners and requesting people to place their bets.

'No, it was something of a spur of the moment decision this afternoon,' Matt agreed.

He saw that Sir Montague was not amongst the winners.

'Perhaps you could show us how to play?' Kitty requested as Matt passed her some of the counters they had acquired the previous evening.

'Of course, dear lady, you may even bring me better luck,' Sir Montague responded gallantly, advising her to choose red or black to begin with until she was more confident to try different spreads.

Kitty placed a couple of counters on black and Sir Montague followed suit. 'I may as well give this a go, nothing else is working tonight it seems.' He gave a tight smile as the croupier span the wheel.

'It seems you are indeed a lucky omen, Kitty.' Sir Montague smiled as the ball settled on a black number and their winnings were slid towards them.

Matt watched as Kitty, aided by Sir Montague, played a few more times. Their partnership, whilst not making them rich, at least appeared to have slowed Sir Montague's run of ill fortune.

'If you are feeling very brave, my dear, or moved by a particular spirit, one can bet on single numbers. The return is obviously much better as the odds are greater,' Sir Montague informed her.

'Oh, what fun.' Kitty smiled at him. 'I must have a try at least once, or I shall not feel as if I've had the full experience.' She took the white counter Monsieur Dupont had given them and placed it on the number twenty-eight.

'Very bold, I shall join you.' Sir Montague added one of his lowest value counters on top of hers.

The wheel was spun once more sending the metal ball hurtling around, bouncing about the divisions between the numbers before finally stopping.

'Number twenty-eight! I won!' Kitty gasped and looked at Matt in surprise.

'I say, dear lady, you are indeed my lucky star this evening.' Sir Montague beamed at her as a pile of counters was sent their way.

'I really think I should stop now while I am ahead.' Kitty scooped up her winnings, passing them to Matt to stow away in his pocket.

Sir Montague looked disappointed at the prospect of her defection. 'I hope you have at least turned the tide for me tonight.'

'I hope so, too.' Kitty slipped away from the table with Matt beside her.

'He didn't react to you choosing that number,' Matt said in a low voice. 'I assume that was your plan?'

'Yes, I watched the croupier too and she also didn't blink at all.' Despite her unexpected win Kitty sounded disappointed.

'It's been a while now, so I suggest we avail ourselves of the Duponts' hospitality. We wouldn't wish to cause offence.' Matt placed his hand on his wife's back to guide her through the crowded room towards the private area.

He had a feeling that upsetting the Duponts at any time would be most unwise.

* * *

Kitty led the way back to the private area. The man at the entrance lifting the rope from the stanchion once more to give them access. It seemed Mrs Delaware was missing, and Kitty assumed she must still be at the card table.

'Madame, monsieur.' A young girl in a black-and-white maids uniform directed them towards a small table containing all manner of delicious-looking savoury snacks.

'Madame Bryant, Kitty dear, please try the caviar,' Helene Dupont suggested, wafting across the room to greet them.

Kitty meekly obeyed, taking one of the small crackers piled with the black delicacy onto her plate. She chose a few more items and wandered over to join Candace and Roland where they were seated on the black leather furniture. Matt remained talking to Madame Dupont about the food.

'How are you enjoying your evening?' Kitty asked as she took a seat on one of the sofas opposite Candace.

'It's very different seeing it from inside,' Roland replied. 'I can see how people get sucked in to returning night after night.'

'Have you tried the tables at all, Kitty?' Candace asked.

'Sir Montague is at the roulette wheel. He very kindly showed me what to do and we were quite fortunate with some of our spins,' Kitty said. She had a feeling that Sir Montague was one of those people who did come night after night.

She picked up the caviar and tried it. She had eaten caviar before, but it wasn't something she was especially fond of. Helene Dupont was right though, this did taste quite good.

'I see Mother hasn't come to join us.' Candace's voice was heavy with disapproval as she looked towards the entrance of the room. 'Once she gets on the card table, it is so difficult to dislodge her.'

Matt came to join them, taking his place next to Kitty. 'According to our hostess I believe the comte has gone to try and persuade her.'

There was a slight stir at the entrance to the room. A distinguished-looking older man with silver hair, neat beard and a monocle escorting a shorter plump woman entered and Helene and Jerard Dupont rushed to greet them.

'I presume they must be important,' Kitty said.

'The German ambassador to France and his wife. We met them before in Paris at an embassy party before the election,' Candace said.

The Duponts were clearly delighted to have such distinguished visitors and Kitty suspected that the repast they were now enjoying was probably primarily for the diplomat and his wife's benefit.

The comte entered and Kitty watched as he was introduced to the newcomers, bowing over the lady's hand, and greeting the ambassador. It was all extremely interesting. She watched covertly as the small group continued to converse.

After a few minutes, the group moved towards them, and Roland and Matt stood to greet them.

'May I present Herr and Frau Friesenbaum.' Jerard Dupont introduced the rest of the party to the German couple. 'Mademoiselle Delaware, I think you have met before?'

The couple exchanged pleasantries and greeted Candace warmly.

Mrs Delaware arrived in the room and came over to join the party.

'Now we are together, tomorrow is my darling Helene's birthday. I propose you all join us at our home for a celebratory dinner.' Jerard looked around the group.

'We should be delighted, of course,' the German couple accepted.

'How delightful, we shall come obviously.' Mrs Delaware clearly included Candace in that, and Kitty assumed she must also mean Roland as well since he was part of the group.

'That is most kind of you, of course Kitty and I would love to come,' Matt accepted the invitation on their behalf.

'Wonderful, wonderful. Shall we say drinks at seven at our house tomorrow evening? Villa du Mer, Twenty-Eight Rue de la Plage.' Jerard beamed happily at his guests.

CHAPTER EIGHTEEN

Kitty was glad she had swallowed her mouthful of champagne before Jerard announced the details of the dinner invitation. Surely the number of the Duponts' house couldn't be a coincidence, could it? The ambassador and his wife circulated around the room talking to some other guests, notably some of the German clients who had been with Jerard earlier in the evening.

'It's a good job Lucy loaned me some of her evening gowns.' Kitty looked at Matt. 'I had no idea that I would need so many.'

'Jerard and Helene's house is very lovely. It's out on the coast road a little out of town. Mother and I went there with Luciano for a supper party and cards when we first arrived in Nice.' Candace took a sip from her drink.

'Do you think that maybe I can get an interview with the ambassador?' Roland looked thoughtfully at the older couple who were currently talking with Jerard and Helene.

Kitty looked at Matt. She was aware that before he had left his government post to come to Devon he had encountered many embassy staff in a number of countries. She hoped that the ambassador was not one of the people he had met in his previous role.

The ambassador had not seemed to recognise him when Jerard Dupont had performed his introductions earlier, but one could never be too certain.

'Roland, darling, Mother will definitely be most upset if you start to quiz other dinner guests. Especially when you need to try and win her over,' Candace pointed out.

'Very well, I'll just have to try and come up with a new angle on these murders instead.' Roland looked a little sulky at having his plan thwarted.

'Have you sold stories about the murders to the newspapers?' Kitty asked.

'Rather! Got quite a lot of interest from one of the French nationals, a couple of the English papers and an Italian paper.' Roland perked back up again. 'The whole mystery man angle played out really well. I think that was how Inspector Villier finally managed to discover who the chappie in the alley was. They printed his picture alongside my article.'

Kitty had wondered how the police had worked out Federico's real identity so swiftly. 'That's amazing,' she responded politely.

'It would be marvellous if Roland could get a permanent staff job with one of the papers from this.' Candace smiled fondly at the journalist.

The evening wound down and the cars were sent for once more. Sir Montague was still at the roulette table when they made their way back to the foyer and bade farewell to the Duponts.

'We shall see you all tomorrow evening.' Helene stood beside her husband as the doorman opened the car door for them to get inside.

'We shall look forward to it,' Matt assured her as he followed Kitty onto the back seat of the Rolls Royce.

Kitty longed to discuss the coincidence of the Duponts' house number with Matt, but Candace and Roland were sharing their car, and she wasn't sure if the chauffeur was monitoring their conversation.

Instead, they discussed what they should take as a gift for Helene for her birthday and Candace told them more about the Duponts' villa.

Once back at the hotel they declined Roland and Candace's suggestion of a nightcap before retiring and made good their escape back to their room.

'That was very unexpected, wasn't it?' Kitty said as she prepared for bed.

'The number of the Duponts' house, or the arrival of the German ambassador?' Matt asked with a smile.

Kitty tapped him lightly on his arm. 'Both, but I must admit I have had the number twenty-eight on my brain ever since we discovered it in that wretched matchbook.'

'Yes, I was taken aback when Jerard gave out the address, I must admit.' Matt sounded thoughtful.

'You didn't know the German ambassador, did you? I was a little worried that you might have met him before,' Kitty said.

Matt shook his head. 'No, I understand from my connections at Whitehall that many of the embassy staff in the key countries are all new these days.'

Kitty slipped into bed and sat up, hugging her knees as she waited for Matt to join her. 'Now we have to buy a suitable birthday gift for Helene Dupont too. We can hardly turn up empty-handed.'

'I suppose flowers are always a good option,' Matt suggested. 'I don't think either ours or the brigadier's budget would run to jewellery.'

Kitty grinned at the idea of the brigadier's expression if they were to present him with an invoice for the cost of a diamond bracelet. 'You're probably right. Helene Dupont has some very expensive jewels already.'

Matt joined her in the bed, the springs of the mattress creaking slightly as he settled down, hands behind his head. He stared thoughtfully at the ceiling.

'The Duponts' house sounded quite isolated according to what Candace was telling us in the car.'

Kitty lay down and turned to look at him. 'Yes, she said it stood on its own up a private road a little off the main coast road. Do you think Federico went there?'

'If so, why? He was making arrangements with the brigadier's department to hand over the documents to us,' Matt said.

'Was Federico a double agent perhaps?' Kitty frowned.

'I didn't get that impression from the brigadier's briefing before we left. There had to be a reason for his visit to the casino though.' Matt glanced at Kitty.

'Perhaps when he arrived here, he thought himself unsuspected? He could have been doing the usual social round, you know to avoid suspicion. As we've been doing,' Kitty suggested.

'Then something happened that tipped him off that all wasn't well. That was when he sent the telegram to the brigadier.' Matt adjusted his position, moving his arms to make himself more comfortable.

'Hmm, I can't see that he would have hidden the papers at the home of the man who was looking to get hold of them. Do you think the ambassador is here to try and collect them?' It had been on Kitty's mind that the prestigious client Luciano and Sir Montague had mentioned at the chateau could have been the German.

'It's very likely. A diplomatic bag would be the ideal way to get them out of the country and presumably the information in the papers would be of use to their government,' Matt said.

'What do you think we may find at the villa then?' Kitty asked.

'Perhaps some evidence that Federico was there? That there is some connection between him and the Duponts? That matchbook has to be telling us something.' Matt yawned his reply and clicked off the lamp.

Kitty decided it was all too complicated for now. Tomorrow evening's trip to the villa was really their last throw of the dice to find the documents. After that she wasn't sure what else they could try.

* * *

Immediately after breakfast the next day they made their way into the town. They headed to a prestigious flower shop that had been recommended by the receptionist at the hotel.

'We could have just placed the order by telephone,' Matt grumbled as they studied the array of blooms in the shaded area of the shop.

There was indeed a splendid choice; lilies, roses, mimosa and a great many artfully arranged displays. The air was heavy with the damp perfume of the flowers.

'We could, but I have no idea how the costs of flowers here compare to home or what might be considered acceptable to reflect Helene and Jerard's generosity towards us,' Kitty reproved him as she examined the flowers.

Her caution proved right as it seemed a display of an appropriate size was rather more expensive than Matt had anticipated. Kitty hoped the brigadier would approve the expense on their return home. She was starting to think that diamonds might have been the cheaper option after all.

With the flowers chosen and delivery arranged they ventured back into the mid-morning warmth of the street.

'Shall we stop off for a coffee on our way back to the hotel?'

Matt suggested as they strolled along, looking in the shop windows as they walked.

'Why not? I must admit it would be nice to do something relaxing, and with just the two of us,' Kitty agreed. Apart from their trip out to the cathedral and to the view point they seemed to have spent all their time either at the hotel or the casino.

She had to say too, that she would not ordinarily have chosen to spend her time with the companions that seemed to have attached themselves to her and Matt. Especially after what she had overheard between the comte and Sir Montague.

It struck her as they made their way towards a small café bar that had a couple of tables under the shade of some gaily striped umbrellas that none of their new acquaintances were particularly trustworthy.

The Duponts clearly had their fingers in many pies and were middlemen in some sort of deal to do with the missing papers. The comte and Sir Montague appeared to have been working together to secure the documents. Roland Fetherington might be using his position as a journalist for cover. He had followed Matt back from Bar Twenty-Eight the other evening and he could have killed Monsieur Lapin.

Even Candace and her mother were not above suspicion. They seemed to have visited a lot of embassies and to have many connections. They knew the German ambassador. Was Mrs Delaware working with the comte? Or maybe she and Candace were using the men to acquire the papers for some purpose of their own?

It seemed too that Federico himself was not the straightforward person she had assumed from the brigadier's briefing. He could have been playing a dangerous double game which had eventually caused his demise. Kitty took her seat at the table outside the café, her mind still whirring with all the possibilities.

Matt ordered coffees and pastries from the plump, white apron-clad proprietor who appeared to take their order.

'Are you all right, old thing? Not worrying about tonight, are you?' Matt asked once the man had disappeared back inside the café.

'No, I was just thinking about everything that's happened and what we should look out for at the villa,' Kitty said.

She was a little concerned about the evening ahead. Clearly Helene Dupont made a big deal of her birthday and with the German ambassador and his wife attending it promised to be a grand affair. Her one consolation was that they were unlikely to come to any harm with so many distinguished guests in attendance.

'All we can do is play along and keep our eyes and ears open.' Matt patted her hand. 'If there is something there, then I'm sure we'll find it.'

The waiter returned and deposited a cafetière of coffee and a tall metal jug of steamed milk on the table. Kitty's stomach gave a low rumble of approval at the sight of the delicate cream-filled pastries which accompanied their drinks.

After a mid-morning snack and a cup of coffee Kitty started to relax, enjoying taking in the sights and sounds of Nice.

'Isn't that Sir Montague?' She spotted a smartly dressed familiar figure exiting the stone steps of what she assumed must be his bank. He had his walking cane and his newspaper as usual furled under his arm.

Matt looked up from where he was studying the crossword in his own copy of the paper. 'Yes, I wonder if he was depositing winnings or trying for more credit? He certainly seems to visit his bank quite often,' he mused.

Kitty watched with interest as Sir Montague paused to adjust the position of the paper under his arm. He seemed to take a furtive glance around him as he did so, before setting off along the street away from where Kitty and Matt were seated.

She noticed a young boy aged about ten in worn clothing appear as if from nowhere and set off after Sir Montague.

Another man, seemingly at a signal from the boy, peeled himself away from where he had been leaning casually against a wall and also headed in the same direction.

Their actions set up an uneasy feeling in the pit of Kitty's stomach.

'Matt, I think that Sir Montague may be in trouble.' She nodded towards the man following Sir Montague who was about to disappear from view. 'There's an urchin there too.'

'Stay here.' Matt moved quickly from his seat, abandoning his crossword to walk swiftly after the men.

Kitty watched anxiously as Matt vanished from her sight. If the café bill had been paid, she would have gone after them. Instead, she was forced to remain in her seat trying to appear calm and composed.

After what seemed like an age, she saw Matt returning, with Sir Montague at his side. Matt had a grim expression on his face and appeared to be nursing his right fist. Sir Montague looked slightly dishevelled and was leaning heavily on his cane. His paper was missing and there was a dirty mark across the leg of his cream flannel trousers.

'Are you both all right?' Kitty jumped up from her seat in alarm as they drew closer.

She could see now that Sir Montague appeared to have a swollen lip and a cut on his left cheekbone.

'Dashed villain jumped me as I turned off the main street. If your husband hadn't turned up when he did...' Sir Montague tailed off as Kitty pulled up an extra chair for him to join them.

'Matt, are you all right?' Kitty asked in concern as her husband too sat down rather heavily on the seat he had vacated only a few minutes earlier.

'Your husband is a hero, Mrs Bryant,' Sir Montague said.

The café proprietor, seeing the new arrival, bustled outside. He clicked his tongue in concern at Sir Montague's dishevelled appearance. Kitty ordered a round of brandies for all of them.

'The bounder had a knife.' Sir Montague pulled out his handkerchief and dabbed carefully at the cut on his cheek.

Kitty gasped. 'You could both have been killed. Did he steal anything from you?' she asked.

Sir Montague placed his soiled handkerchief on the table and patted down his pockets. 'No, fortunately your husband arrived in the nick of time just as he was threatening me.'

The café proprietor deposited the brandies on the table. Sir Montague's hand trembled slightly as he picked his glass up.

'What happened exactly?' Kitty asked her husband.

'The man you saw following Sir Montague waited until he turned from the main strip. The boy whistled when the coast was clear and then the man rushed forward with a knife in his hand. They hadn't seen me as I'd hung back a bit to keep an eye on them. The lad darted forward to trip Sir Montague as the man with the knife got to him,' Matt explained.

'I thought I was done for. That wretched boy knocked me off balance, then the cad was standing over me with the knife when your husband launched himself on his back. Thankfully he managed to knock the blade away, giving me time to get to my feet,' Sir Montague chipped in. 'The boy fled as I retrieved the knife, by then your husband was knocking seven bells out of the chappie.'

'Where is the man now?' Kitty asked, horrified by this description of events.

'He scarpered as soon as he could break free from your husband,' Sir Montague said.

'Yes, unfortunately, he broke free and got away,' Matt confirmed.

'I saw him follow you when you left the bank.' Kitty wondered if Sir Montague had been targeted at random. It had seemed to her, however, that the assailant had been waiting especially for Sir Montague. The presence of the urchin seemed to confirm her theory.

'Well, he would have been disappointed if he had taken my wallet.' Sir Montague drained the rest of his brandy. His voice sounded steadier now he was recovering from the attack. 'I rather fear I shall have to cut short my stay here soon and return to London.'

'Oh dear.' Kitty assumed that Sir Montague probably had creditors pressing him back in England as well as the ones in France.

'Still, I may as well enjoy the remainder of my stay. I presume you will be attending the party tonight at the villa for Helene Dupont's birthday?' Sir Montague asked as he brushed some dirt from the handle of his walking cane. He checked the silver handle, wincing slightly at the dent on the tip.

'Indeed. You will be attending too?' Matt asked.

'I wouldn't miss it for the world. The Dupont parties are renowned locally. I shall see you both later today then. Thank you once again for your assistance.' Sir Montague rose from his seat and tipped his slightly battered panama hat to Kitty and shook hands with Matt before striding away. This time keeping firmly to the main street.

CHAPTER NINETEEN

Matt watched Sir Montague depart. 'I'd say I arrived in the nick of time.'

'He was deliberately targeted, wasn't he? That wasn't a random assault?' Kitty asked. She took a sip of her brandy. The incident had shaken her, and she wondered if the man with the knife had been the one who had killed Federico. The assault could have taken place in just the same way, only there had been no Matt to come to his rescue.

'Indeed. No, I only caught a bit of what was said when the man jumped him, but I heard the words money owed.' Matt looked at his wife.

'I assume that Sir Montague may owe money to others in Nice as well as the casino.' Kitty was unsurprised by this, given what they knew of Sir Montague's finances. 'I notice he made no mention of calling the police.'

The corners of Matt's mouth lifted in a brief smile. 'I have a feeling that Sir Montague would very much rather the police were left out of this. Interesting that he has received an invitation for this evening's party.'

'Well, perhaps if the ambassador were expecting to receive

the papers, then Monsieur Dupont may believe that Sir Montague or the comte are still capable of delivering,' Kitty said thoughtfully.

'Or he has to find a way to save face and perhaps delay a little in the hope that they *can* still deliver,' Matt said. He was not looking forward to the evening, although he had not said as much to Kitty.

The isolated location of the villa troubled him and their reliance on cars being arranged for them meant they would be unable to leave quickly if problems arose. He flexed the fingers on his right hand. His knuckles felt bruised, although he had managed to land a couple of good punches on Sir Montague's assailant.

'Is your hand injured?' Kitty asked. She had clearly noticed his movements. 'Shall I request some ice?' She glanced around as if looking for the café proprietor.

'No, please don't bother. I'm sure it will be fine,' Matt assured her. He didn't want her to worry.

They finished their drinks and called for the bill, leaving the proprietor a generous tip. Kitty took Matt's arm as they started their leisurely stroll back to the hotel.

'I wonder if Inspector Villier has asked Sir Montague to remain in Nice?' Kitty mused.

'Like his request to us, you mean?' Matt said. 'It is only a request. He has no real power to keep any of us here, you know, unless he arrests or charges us for an offence.'

'I suppose so.' Kitty's expression was troubled. 'Unless, of course, he does really suspect us. I mean I can see his point of view. Stumbling over one dead body is bad enough but to then find another victim, you can hardly blame him for being suspicious. I must admit I'm quite relieved Sir Montague didn't suggest contacting the police. Can you imagine the inspector's face if we were involved in another crime?'

Matt could see her point. He wished there was some way

they could discuss the situation with the brigadier or Kitty's uncle. He could only hope the postcard Kitty had sent might have reached Enderley by now. Usually, the postal service was quite efficient, but he had a feeling that anything they sent might be prone to delay or interception.

* * *

Kitty didn't feel much like lunch when they returned to the hotel. The pastries they had eaten earlier had been quite filling. Also, since it had sounded as if dinner that evening was to be a grand affair, they decided that a late afternoon tea might instead prove to be a more sensible option.

The seams on a couple of her borrowed gowns had become a little tight and Kitty suspected it was all the sitting around she had been doing. Lucy was slightly slimmer than she was anyway, and the dresses had been snug to begin with. Apart from a few days when they had walked, much of their time had been spent idling on the terrace and eating delicious food.

She had no wish to damage any of her cousin's dresses. She guessed they were much more expensive than the ones that she owned. Which brought her back to the thorny question of what to wear for Helene Dupont's birthday dinner. She had one dress that she had not yet worn but it would mean wearing her highest pair of heels. Fortunately, the blisters on her feet that she had acquired on arrival were almost healed.

However, if they were to get the chance to go sneaking about the villa, she wanted to be certain she wasn't going to turn an ankle or give herself away by clopping over marble tiles like a cart horse. She wished Alice were there so she could discuss her dilemma. Matt would simply laugh if she raised such concerns with him. *It was all right for men*, she decided crossly. They never had to consider such things.

The hotel was busy when they returned and at first Kitty

thought they would be unable to find a space to sit on the terrace. Candace Delaware, however, had a table in the shade of a large umbrella and waved them over as they entered the grounds. She smiled as she set aside the nail file she was using on her fingernails.

'You must tell me everything. I ran into Monty about an hour ago in the lobby. He told me he had been assaulted in the town by a man with a knife and that Matt had come to his rescue.' Candace's kohl-rimmed eyes were wide with excitement. 'Is it true? He did look a little battered and you know how smartly he dresses usually.'

'I'm afraid it is true.' Matt sank down on a vacant chair and removed his hat, placing it down on the table.

'Oh my goodness, I hope no one tells Mother, she'll never let me out again,' Candace said. 'That was terribly brave of you, Captain Bryant. I mean with the man having a knife and everything. I saw poor old Monty had a cut on his cheek.'

'I suspect Sir Montague has overstated my role in his rescue,' Matt replied, looking slightly uncomfortable at Candace's enthusiasm.

'Well, if Roland gets to know about it, I expect he will write a piece for his editor. You could be famous,' Candace said.

'I had much rather remain anonymous.' Matt sounded alarmed at the prospect of his name being splashed about the newspapers yet again.

Kitty couldn't help but feel that if that were to happen it would put the tin lid on their failed mission to remain low-key and unobtrusive while they acquired the documents. Not to mention what Inspector Villier would think if he read it.

'Where is Roland today?' Kitty asked.

'I'm not supposed to say really, but he's been following Inspector Villier about town. He wants to be first on scene when the inspector makes his arrests for the murders. Can you imagine? What a scoop that would be,' Candace said.

'I didn't realise the inspector was so close to solving the case? That is good news,' Kitty said. It would be interesting to know who the inspector believed was responsible for the murders.

'I don't know exactly if he has worked it all out yet, but Roland clearly feels he must be onto something.' Candace picked up her file once more and started to examine her cuticles with a critical eye.

'Are you looking forward to the birthday party tonight?' Matt asked.

'Oh yes, much more now that Roland has been invited too.' Candace smiled happily as she applied herself to shaping her thumbnail.

'Sir Montague said he had been invited.' Kitty wondered if Candace felt at all awkward about flaunting her boyfriend in front of the man her mother had chosen for her.

'Yes, he told me when I saw him. I expect lots of people will be there. I believe the mayor will be in attendance.' Candace seemed to have no such concerns. 'Mother has gone for some new beauty treatment in town. She tried to get me to go with her. It's supposed to rejuvenate one's skin.'

'I was trying to decide what to wear tonight,' Kitty said, ignoring the slight quirk of Matt's eyebrow at the introduction of such a feminine topic.

Candace's expression lit up. 'Oh, everyone will be in their best tonight. I have the most marvellous white-silk dress that I picked up in Paris.'

Kitty resigned herself to wearing the uncomfortable shoes with the higher heel.

Later in their room as they were dressing for the party, Kitty was assisting Matt with his bow tie when he started to tease her about the afternoon's conversation.

'You were not contemplating asking Candace for the address of her mother's beauty advisor, were you?' he asked.

Kitty's nimble fingers stilled from where she was straightening his collar. 'Why? Do you think I could use a little beauty treatment?'

Matt grinned at her, the dimple flashing in his cheek. 'Now you are just fishing for compliments, my dear Mrs Bryant. You know perfectly well that you are quite lovely enough just as you are.'

Kitty blushed and grinned. 'Very well, since you are being so charming, I shall let you off.'

'Seriously, darling, you look absolutely spiffing.' Matt smiled at her as she turned away to drop her lipstick and compact into her silver evening purse.

She hoped her dress would pass muster. She also hoped that sneaking about the villa didn't involve too much bending and stretching. The bias-cut of her deep-red satin gown was not intended for anything more strenuous than cocktails and waltzing.

Their transport for the evening had been arranged once more by the comte. Candace and Roland Fetherington were travelling with Mrs Delaware and Luciano. Kitty and Matt were sharing their motor with Sir Montague.

The butterflies in Kitty's stomach as the black Rolls Royce rolled away from the hotel felt the size of bats. Matt had opened the window next to him as usual and Kitty was glad of the light, refreshing breeze on her face.

'Have you visited the villa before, Sir Montague?' Kitty asked. She was sure she had heard him say that he had but thought a little conversation might distract her.

'Yes, I've been fortunate enough to visit a couple of times. Luciano introduced me to them just after I arrived in Nice. It's a super place, very large,' Sir Montague said.

The cut on his cheek seemed to have closed and there was a

smudge of blue-green bruising surrounding it. It gave him a somewhat piratical air.

It took twenty minutes or so before they were clear of the town and following the road along the coast to the villa. Presently they turned off to head inland up a narrow dirt track road between the pine trees.

Suddenly up ahead in the space between the trees, Kitty saw a bright white house with several motor cars all parked outside. The faint sounds of music drifted into the car.

'Here we are, my dear,' Sir Montague announced as the driver pulled the car to a halt next to the vehicle that had transported the rest of their party. The chauffeur jumped out and came around to open the door and assisted Kitty out. Matt came to join her, discreetly tipping the driver while Sir Montague looked around him.

A flight of three shallow, curved marble steps led to a double wooden arch-topped entrance door which stood open. A large man in a black dinner suit stood at the door, taking names and greeting guests.

Kitty took hold of Matt's arm, and they followed Sir Montague up the steps and inside the villa. The sound of the piano grew louder and mixed with the buzz of chatter and the faint scent of cigarette smoke and lilies. The large square marble-tiled foyer was filled almost to capacity with extravagant flower arrangements.

Helene came forward to greet them. Clad in a gold sheath dress and a gold Egyptian-style necklace studded with emeralds, there was no doubt about who was the star of the party.

'Welcome, thank you so much for the beautiful arrangement. I do so adore flowers. I am so lucky to have such generous and kind friends. Come through to the terrace and we'll get you drinks.' Helene led the way through a large, elegant drawing room where the pianist was situated at a grand piano. Her heels clicked on the tiled floor as they continued to the terrace which appeared to run all around the back of the house.

Kitty couldn't help gasping at the vista which opened up before them as they stepped out onto the terrace. The villa was perfectly positioned on the hillside to overlook the trees below and give a wide view over the sparkling blue sea.

The sun was already beginning its descent and Kitty guessed the terrace would afford stunning views of the sunset.

'How very lovely,' she said to Helene, who smiled with satisfaction at Kitty's response.

'It is rather special, isn't it?' Helene agreed. 'Now, you must have a drink.' She summoned a white-jacketed young waiter bearing a silver tray of champagne goblets.

Kitty and Matt dutifully took a glass each, while their hostess went to greet some other new arrivals. Mrs Delaware and the comte were already busily conversing with the German ambassador and his wife. Sir Montague was greeting another couple of people who he obviously knew, and Candace and Roland were with Monsieur Dupont and some other guests.

After saying hello to some of the other people present, Kitty and Matt drifted to a quieter corner of the terrace to sip their drinks and admire the view.

'I hadn't realised it would be so busy this evening,' Kitty remarked as she looked out at the sea.

'No, it seems that Helene has invited everyone who is anyone, and us.' Matt smiled at her.

'Yes, I see even the mayor is here as Candace promised.' Kitty inclined her head towards a very self-important looking gentleman with a splendid moustache wearing a sash over his dinner suit.

Kitty wished the uneasy feeling in the pit of her stomach would settle down. Even with so many guests and respectable people in attendance at the villa she couldn't shake off the feeling that something was not right. Quite how they were going to get the opportunity to look around the house she wasn't sure.

The white-jacketed waiters started to circulate with hors d'oeuvres of bite-sized portions of caviar and other delicacies. The sound of chatter and laughter grew louder, and Kitty and Matt were drawn into conversation with some of the other guests, until Monsieur Dupont announced that it was time for dinner.

The dining room was as large and magnificent as the rest of the house. Silver candelabra glittered on the pristine white cloths and the silver cutlery and crystal glasses sparkled from the light of the candles. The marble walls were lined with what Kitty could tell were expensive modern works of art.

Floral displays in delicate pinks and purples ran along the length of the vast table as everyone took their places, which were marked by elegant white cards bearing their names. Kitty was relieved to find herself flanked by Matt and Roland Fetherington. The comte and Mrs Delaware were seated immediately opposite.

More champagne was poured and before the first course was served, Monsieur Dupont proposed a toast to the birthday girl. Helene beamed at her guests as they raised their glasses to her health and happiness, before the French onion soup was served.

'This is a splendid bash, eh?' Roland said as he placed his spoon down in his empty bowl.

'Yes, the Duponts certainly seem to move in the highest society,' Kitty agreed.

'Candace told me about Sir Montague's run-in with an assailant today in the town. I wonder if it could have been the same one who killed that Benedetto chappie.' Roland looked at Sir Montague who was talking to the mayor's wife.

'Oh dear, I hadn't thought of that. I don't know. It all happened so quickly. I'm just glad neither Sir Montague nor

Matt were seriously injured.' It had, of course, already crossed Kitty's mind that the man who attacked Sir Montague could have killed Federico but she wasn't about to admit that to Roland.

The assailant's interaction with the young urchin and the organised nature of the attack spoke of something that they had carried out before together.

'Candace mentioned that you had been shadowing Inspector Villier. She said you thought an arrest might be made soon,' Kitty said as the waiters collected up the empty soup dishes.

'Ah, yes, um, I want to be first with the scoop when he does make the arrest for the murders. I've obviously done a piece on the attack today,' Roland said.

'You didn't mention Matt and I in it, did you?' Kitty asked in alarm. She really wanted to avoid drawing the inspector's attention to their names.

'No, I linked it all to the growing tide of crime in the town. I'd rather hoped to get a quote about it from the mayor, but Candace is insisting I leave it for this evening.' Roland cast a sad glance in the direction of the mayor who was seated beside the ambassador's wife.

'Well, perhaps tonight is not the time nor place.' Kitty privately agreed with Candace.

A plate with a delicate fillet of sole was placed before them decorated with edible flowers and herbs. Kitty sniffed appreciatively. The Duponts had certainly employed a very good chef.

'Do you know who the inspector suspects?' Kitty asked as they tucked into the fish. She was interested to discover if the police were close to discovering who was behind Federico and Monsieur Lapin's deaths. And if so, who might be in the frame.

'He seems to have been here, there and everywhere. Talking to Monsieur Lapin's neighbours, the casino staff and poking about at a derelict villa on the outskirts of town,' Roland said.

'Gracious, he has been busy,' Kitty said. It sounded as if Inspector Villier had found Federico's hideout.

'I should hope so too, it's quite disgraceful that no one has been caught yet.' Mrs Delaware appeared to have caught the tail end of their conversation.

'I agree, Eunice, my dear, and now you say our friend Sir Montague has been attacked?' The comte had clearly been paying more attention to what Roland and Kitty had been saying than she had thought.

'Yes, a failed robbery one assumes, as I gather he had just left the bank,' Roland confirmed.

'Murders and robbery. That is it. Candace, I forbid you to go out into town alone.' Mrs Delaware glared at her daughter who was seated on the other side of Roland.

'For heaven's sake, Mother,' Candace protested wearily.

'Mr Fetherington, since she will not pay attention to me perhaps you can persuade her,' Mrs Delaware appealed to the journalist.

'My view of places is coloured by my experiences of the worst things that happen. I'm sure Candace will be quite safe as she only ventures in the main streets and in respectable areas,' Roland attempted to placate Mrs Delaware.

Eunice did not seem impressed by his argument. 'Well, if an arrest is not made soon then we are leaving Nice. I have a hankering for more travelling any way,' she declared.

'But, Eunice, darling, the weather here is so delightful, and we have such good society. I am certain the inspector will capture his man soon,' the comte said soothingly.

'I don't see how if he is spending his time messing around ancient houses.' Mrs Delaware too had obviously heard what Roland had said about the derelict villa.

Kitty shivered. Had the police discovered that they had already been there? Was there a clue there that she and Matt had missed?

'I'm sure he must have his reasons for doing that,' Matt said, before taking a sip of champagne.

'What's your theory on these murders, Captain Bryant?' Roland asked. 'Do you think this spy story that's going around the town is true?'

Kitty was aware that the comte and Mrs Delaware had both focused their attention on her husband.

'I don't know. Inspector Villier seems to believe it possible, and we are not too far from the border with Italy here. Of course, too, there are yachts coming in and out all the time,' Matt responded with a slight shrug.

'Hoodlums, that's what it is. Robbery and theft, one hears about these things all the time. I read it in the newspapers.' Mrs Delaware's hand strayed to touch her pearl collar.

'And the unfortunate death of Marc Lapin, my colleague?' Roland asked.

'He obviously saw someone about to be robbed or assaulted. He was clearly in the wrong place at the wrong time,' Mrs Delaware declared.

'You may be right, my dear,' the comte agreed. 'Perhaps we are all reading far too much significance into recent events.'

The subject was dropped and conversation during the rest of dinner took a different tack. When it was time for dessert a chrome and marble trolley was wheeled in with a huge cake ablaze with candles.

The birthday songs were sung in both French and English before Madame Dupont blew out her candles and the cake was taken to one side and portioned up for dessert. Coffee followed out on the terrace and in the large drawing room that they had passed through earlier in the evening.

The last orange sliver of the sun was just sliding below the horizon when Kitty stepped back out into the cooler evening air. The pianist had finished, and music was now being provided from the gramophone player. Some couples were dancing and once again the volume of chatter had risen.

Matt placed his arm around her waist and Kitty lay her head on his shoulder as the sea and the sky turned to gold, and orange.

'We need to try and take a look around,' Kitty murmured.

'I agree, now is a good time while everyone is moving about.' Matt's breath was cool against her ear.

'Where shall we try first?' she asked.

'I thought there was a door in the hall where we came in, near the ladies' cloakroom, that could be Jerard's study,' Matt said.

'I'll go and try there.'

'Very well, hurry and be careful, I'll keep watch.'

Kitty moved away from her husband and surveyed the room. Jerard's study was the obvious place to try but could she get there unobserved without arousing suspicion?

CHAPTER TWENTY

Kitty took her time as she made her way back through the drawing room. The last thing she wished to do was to draw attention to herself. She paused to exchange pleasantries with a couple of guests and to take another glass of champagne from one of the waiters.

Her hope was that the large gentleman who had been manning the doors when they had arrived would have moved from his station now that the party was well underway. She noticed that Helene Dupont was engaged in conversation with the ambassador and his wife as she sauntered out into the hall.

At least she could always claim she was looking for the cloakroom if anyone saw her wandering around the ground floor. The large square hall appeared deserted, and the doorman had gone from his post. Kitty breathed a small sigh of relief and looked more closely at her surroundings.

A stylish metal and marble staircase rose from the rear of the hall leading to the upper floor of the villa. Large potted palms flanked either side of the stairs. There was a door to the dining room where they had enjoyed dinner earlier, a door to the drawing room, one to the gentlemen's guest cloakroom, one to the ladies' guest cloakroom and another door that Matt had surmised might be a study.

Kitty wandered as quietly as she could across the marble floor admiring the expensive modernist paintings that hung on the walls as she moved. Everyone else appeared to be outside on the terrace or in the drawing room and she had the space to herself.

She stopped outside the mystery oak-panelled door next to the ladies' cloakroom and listened for a moment. She had no wish to try the door and discover Monsieur Dupont on the other side. Everything was quiet so far as she could tell. She glanced back towards the drawing room and saw that Matt was loitering near the open entrance. He gave a discreet nod indicating the coast was clear.

Kitty grasped the round brass door handle and twisted. She was unsurprised but not a little vexed to discover it was locked. She glanced back at Matt and gave a little shake of her head to let him know she couldn't open it. She had guessed it would probably be locked but it had been worth a try.

Helene Dupont came into view and Kitty hastily moved to the door of the ladies' cloakroom and entered. The room proved to be a spacious one, with a coat rail running along the wall just inside the door. The maid on their arrival had taken the ladies' stoles and wraps, hanging them inside the room.

Beyond the rail, the room opened out into a comfortable and luxuriously appointed powder room with twin pink sinks shaped like shells set in a marble counter. There were a couple of small deep-pink velvet upholstered shell-shaped chairs and large gold-framed mirrors above the sinks reflecting the gold-plated taps.

It was clearly a very feminine space and Kitty could see now why the ladies had been directed to this area and the gentlemen to another cloakroom near to the drawing room. The Duponts had obviously designed their home to be used for entertaining large parties and had planned the public area of the house in much the same way as the casino.

There were two more doors in the room leading to the lavatories. On hearing the outer door to the cloakroom open and the sound of female voices, Kitty darted inside one of the lavatories and closed the door.

The clicking of heels on tile stopped and she heard the rustling sounds of taffeta and silk in the area near the sinks and chairs. Kitty waited for a moment intending to flush the chain and emerge from the lavatory at an appropriate time.

'So, my dear Helene, I do hope our friend the ambassador is not too unhappy that he hasn't received the parcel he was expecting just yet?'

Kitty froze as she recognised Eunice Delaware's voice. The inference in her words was clear.

'It was a little awkward, but Jerard has explained that we hope it is merely a temporary hiccup,' Helene said.

'I'm so relieved to hear that, my dear. We have such hopes of Germany. I was concerned when that Fetherington boy said the police had discovered the villa,' Eunice replied.

'It is of no consequence, we had already checked there,' Helene responded. 'Please do not distress yourself, *mon cher ami*, we are all working to the same end, and I have no doubt that we shall succeed.'

'And the English couple?' Eunice asked. 'They must have been sent by London.'

Kitty's heart pounded as she realised Eunice must mean herself and Matt.

'So long as we keep an eye on them, we feel they pose no real threat. They clearly have not discovered anything useful.' Helene's voice sounded fainter, and Kitty heard the sound of heels on tile retreating.

'Let us hope you are right,' Eunice said with a tinkling laugh.

Bile rose in Kitty's stomach making her feel sick. She hoped the two women had merely entered the room to refresh their lipstick and to talk privately. If either one decided to try the lavatory doors, then she would be placed in a very perilous situation. With luck the women were getting ready to return to the drawing room.

She listened intently and heard the door of the cloakroom open once more and more female voices greeted Helene and Eunice. There was a general amount of chatter, before someone entered the lavatory next to the one she was hiding in.

Kitty leaned against the wall of the cubicle, the marble tiling cool against the bare skin of her back. She decided to wait it out. Hopefully no one would realise that her cubicle had been occupied before the group had entered. The toilet flushed and after several more minutes of taps running and chatter in French and English the room grew quiet as the women departed.

After waiting for another minute, she risked unlocking the door and peeking out. To her relief, the room was now empty. She refreshed her own lipstick and fluffed up her blonde curls and headed back out into the hall.

She really needed to let Matt know what she had just overheard. The conversation had confirmed that the Duponts weren't in possession of the documents, and they had already known about the house Federico had been using before Kitty and Matt had visited.

It had also revealed that Eunice Delaware was also involved with the espionage and hoped to get the plans to the Germans. Although Kitty wasn't sure if Eunice knew of Luciano and Sir Montague's quest to recover the papers. The American woman certainly seemed close to the comte, and, of course, he was very friendly with the Duponts. It would also explain why Eunice encouraged Sir Montague to hang around.

* * *

Matt too had been unsurprised that Kitty had discovered the door to Monsieur Dupont's study was locked. With so many guests in his house it would have been extremely careless of him to have left it open. Still, it had been worth a try, although like Kitty he hadn't expected to discover much even if it had been open. Jerard Dupont didn't strike him as being a careless man.

Helene Dupont and Eunice Delaware had passed him to go out into the hall and he hoped Kitty had managed to either avoid them or place herself in such a way that they would not be surprised to encounter her.

In Kitty's absence, Matt found himself being drawn into a conversation with Monsieur Dupont, the comte and the mayor.

'Of course, this level of violence is most unusual. I have taken Inspector Villier to task and I expect results from his investigations very soon.' The mayor blew out his cheeks as if to add to his stature. 'Captain Bryant, the comte tells me that you and your wife were the ones who discovered the first victim?'

'Yes, sir, it was most distressing. We hadn't long arrived in Nice,' Matt said.

'A disgraceful state of affairs. Then that business with Monsieur Lapin at your casino, Jerard.' The mayor looked most disgruntled. 'Villier seems to have this theory about espionage. Load of rubbish, I say. I've heard there is a gang here from Marseille. I'll warrant they are behind all this. Drugs probably. That first man, what was his name? Benedetto, he was probably one of them.'

'You are not inclined to believe the inspector's spy theory then, sir?' Matt asked.

'Bah, the good Villier, I think he spends too much time watching the films at the cinema.' The mayor chuckled at his own joke and the others smiled politely, humouring the man.

'Of course, with the elections having taken place so recently and all this unrest elsewhere, it is unsettling.'

'Of course, but it is the way of the world. Things will settle down soon enough, I'm sure. Let us hope the inspector solves the cases quickly,' Jerard said as he took a glass of champagne from one of the passing waiters.

'If he rounds up these villains from Marseille then I am certain this will be an end to it all.' The mayor also accepted another glass.

Matt risked a discreet peek at his watch. He wondered what could be keeping Kitty. She'd been gone for a little while now and he was starting to become concerned. He was about to make his excuses so that he could go and look for her when he saw her slip back into the room.

He saw her smile brightly at a few of the other guests before accepting another drink and making her way out to the terrace. Now he had seen she was unharmed from her snooping adventure he focused his attention back on the conversation with his companions.

'Luciano has told me that you and Madame Bryant are hoteliers in England? How are our hotels comparing with your English ones? Favourably, I hope?' the mayor asked.

'Yes, monsieur, it's most interesting to see the differences in the English way of doing things compared to the French,' Matt said.

'You have not always been in the hotel business though, Captain Bryant?' Jerard Dupont's eyes gleamed shrewdly.

'No, sir, as you have probably realised, I was in the army for quite some time before meeting Kitty.' Matt took a sip of his champagne.

'Then perhaps you are the one we should ask about this espionage theory of the inspector's?' Luciano gave a hearty laugh. 'Especially since you have been so unfortunate to be on scene both times.'

The mayor goggled at Matt. 'Both times? You found Marc Lapin as well?'

'We heard Miss Delaware call for help. We happened to be closest to the scene at the time.' Matt gave a slight shrug. 'Although we were all close at hand.' He gave the comte a bland smile.

He wasn't sure what game the comte and Dupont were attempting to play but he was determined not to be sucked in.

The mayor shook his head at Matt and Kitty's misfortune. 'I hope you do not have such crimes in England where your hotel is situated.'

'I think in any town which has a harbour and where people come and go, there will be incidents from time to time,' Matt said.

'That is very true, so long as you do not hold it against us. Our reputation must be protected.' The mayor nudged him jovially, seemingly reassured by Matt's reply.

He excused himself and made his way through the room outside onto the terrace to look for Kitty. It was dark now with just the light from the open windows and doors spilling out onto the flagstones. A few moths fluttered past drawn by the brightness, and the pine scent of the surrounding forest seemed stronger.

The music was quieter and the air had cooled. He could hear the sound of the cicadas all around the villa as he looked for Kitty. Everyone else appeared to have gone inside since the sun had set. Kitty stood alone at the far end of the terrace looking out at the stars above the sea. She had a glass in her hand and seemed lost in thought.

'Penny for them,' he asked quietly as he approached.

'Sorry, darling, I was miles away. I needed to get outside for a bit of peace for a few minutes,' she explained as she set her glass down on the broad sun-warmed stone of the balustrade.

'Is everything all right? I saw you couldn't get into the study,' he asked. 'Where did you go?'

Kitty crossed her arms and rubbed the bare skin on the tops of her arms as if suddenly chilled. 'I overheard a conversation while I was hiding in the ladies' cloakroom.' She told him of the conversation between Helene and Eunice.

'So Eunice Delaware is after the documents too.' He responded by telling her of the strange conversation he had just had.

'I really don't like how all this is going.' Kitty looked up at him and he could tell she was afraid.

'I think we have done all we can here.' Matt took her in his arms and kissed the top of her head. 'Let's sleep on it tonight when we return to the hotel. If nothing new strikes us tomorrow, then I think we should look at leaving and going back to England.'

'What about the inspector?' Kitty asked. 'He asked us to remain in Nice.'

'If it would make you feel better, we can talk to him before we leave. We don't need to slink away like thieves in the night.'

'You're right, I just hate feeling like such a failure. I think it's because it's late and everything is playing on my mind.' She smiled up at him.

'Come back inside, we had better do our best to be good party guests until it's time for the cars to be brought around.'

* * *

The remainder of the night seemed to pass by in a blur. Kitty's jaw ached from smiling by the time the cars were sent for, and everyone was busy collecting stoles and coats ready to depart. Sir Montague was to share their ride back to the hotel once more it seemed.

Kitty was relieved she didn't have to spend time with Mrs

Delaware and the comte. Not that she trusted Sir Montague much either. She knew he was involved in the attempts to retrieve the papers. In fact, she decided as she wrapped Lucy's white fur stole around her shoulders, she didn't like or trust any of them.

If they did decide to leave tomorrow, one of the blessings would be that she wouldn't have to see any of them ever again.

Sir Montague looked a little worse for wear as he wove his way somewhat unsteadily to the car and Kitty was unsurprised when the chauffeur requested that 'Monsieur might prefer to travel in the front of the car.' She presumed this was so that he was less likely to disgrace himself on the way back into Nice. He had clearly been taking advantage of the champagne.

They followed the other stream of cars pulling away from the villa to progress down the unlit mountain road and on towards the wider coastal route. Kitty snuggled up under her borrowed stole, the night air circulating through the car was much cooler now than when they had set off.

'Dashed good evening, eh?' Sir Montague slurred from the front seat, swivelling his neck around to look at them.

'The Duponts are certainly very generous hosts,' Matt replied politely.

'Jolly generous,' Sir Montague mumbled, turning his head to look out through the windscreen once more.

The car turned onto the main road and Kitty was relieved to see the lights of Nice glimmering ahead in the distance. Sir Montague slumped into silence until they pulled to a stop outside the hotel.

The chauffeur stepped out to open the door for Kitty and to assist her from the car. Sir Montague made no attempt to exit even when his door was opened. The chauffeur had to shake his shoulder and prompt him into leaving.

'Here already, eh? Whoops-a-daisy, one, two, three.' Sir

Montague launched himself forwards almost landing on his face on the pavement.

Matt tipped the chauffeur, and the man touched his peaked cap and wished them a good evening before driving away. Kitty took her husband's arm, and they said goodnight to Sir Montague as he staggered off inside the hotel.

CHAPTER TWENTY-ONE

Despite their late return to the hotel Kitty woke early the following morning. Something that had been said last night was niggling at the back of her mind and she couldn't quite think what it was.

Matt was still sleeping peacefully as she dressed quickly and went downstairs in search of an early morning cup of tea. The hotel was quiet with only a few other early rising guests pottering about the reception area. It had always been one of her favourite times of day at the Dolphin. A few minutes of peace before the working day began in earnest.

She requested a pot of tea and took a seat on one of the charming rattan chairs beside a potted palm in the corner of the lobby. Perhaps once fortified with tea she might be able to recall whatever it was that had disturbed her sleep and caused her to rise so early.

The waiter delivered her tea, and she requested it be charged to their room. They could settle their bill afterwards if they did decide to leave later in the day. Kitty settled back in her seat as she waited for her tea to steep in the small chrome pot, before pouring it through the strainer into the cup.

She watched the receptionist setting out the delivery of daily newspapers, putting aside those pre-ordered by various guests and neatly stacking the others ready for sale. It was soothing and oddly reassuring watching someone else undertake the kinds of tasks she herself had done for years at the Dolphin Hotel.

A guest entered the lobby and requested his key from the receptionist. Kitty waited until the man had moved away from the desk before venturing over to the desk.

'Pardon, monsieur, but I was hoping my friend Lady Mersham might have arrived yesterday? She said she had requested room twenty-eight?' Kitty held her breath after asking her question. It had to be worth a try.

'*Ah non*, madame, I think your friend is mistaken. That room is taken by Monsieur Bell. He arrived two days ago *avec* his family,' the receptionist assured her.

'How foolish of me, I must have misheard either the date or the room,' Kitty said, thanking her lucky stars that there didn't seem to be a real Lady Mersham staying in the hotel. Otherwise, she might have had some awkward explaining to do.

She returned to her seat and poured her tea. At least that had ruled out another possible meaning of the cryptic number on the matchbook. She opened her bag and took the matchbook out once more, flicking it open to examine it again.

The numbers were faint but clear, they had not misread them. They had to mean something, but what? Kitty tried to put herself in Federico's place. He had been frightened for his life. In disguise to try to escape. He had hidden the documents somewhere safe knowing the brigadier would send an agent to collect them.

He had obviously not wished them to fall into the wrong hands since he had sent a message to the brigadier, and he was expecting someone to arrive imminently. Kitty frowned; he had been concerned that his mission had somehow been betrayed, possibly by someone in the chain of command leading to the brigadier. Hence the cryptic telegram.

She sipped her tea, relishing the warm drink. So, he'd stashed the documents and left a clue to their whereabouts in the most secret way he could devise. No doubt he had hoped or expected that if something happened to him whoever was due to pick the papers up would work out the message.

If she were a proper agent, not just a hotelier turned private investigator, what would the matchbook tell her? The striking strip showed no indication of being used yet three matches were gone. Had they been removed just to create the space for Federico to write the numbers?

Excitement started to build as she stared at the matchbook. Why three matches, why not two or four? Had the clue been staring them in the face all this time? That was what had niggled her from last night. Sir Montague leaving the car and saying one, two, three.

Three. Suppose it was three hundred and twenty-eight? Or two hundred and eighty-three? That would change things, wouldn't it? A surge of hope washed over her. Perhaps there might be something they could investigate after all. It might even be a telephone number.

She set her cup back on its saucer and went back to the receptionist.

'*Pardon*, monsieur, but do you have a telephone directory that I could look at?' Kitty had no idea how she would find a random number in a directory but at least she could see how the numbers were structured. She had no idea if French numbers were three digits in the same way English ones were.

The receptionist raised an eyebrow but reached beneath the counter to hand her a small book. 'If you could return it as soon as possible, madame.'

'Oh, of course, thank you so much.' Kitty scurried back to her seat and started to look through the directory.

As she had expected it was divided into trade and personal numbers. Each section set out alphabetically. The personal or private section was disappointingly slim, and the numbers were far longer than their English counterparts.

She blew out a sigh of frustration and returned the book to the slightly nonplussed receptionist.

'You desire to make a call, madame?' he asked as she thanked him for the use of the directory.

'*Non, merci.*' Kitty resumed her seat once more and drained the last of the tea into her cup. Perhaps the extra strength might give her a boost.

A shadow loomed over her. 'Good morning, Kitty, you are up and about early this morning?'

'Good morning.' Kitty looked up to see the comte standing next to her. 'Matt is still sleeping so I thought I would come down and get some tea. Would you care to join me?' She made the offer out of politeness hoping he would decline.

'Thank you, that would be most delightful.' The comte stepped away to ask for more tea from the desk before returning to sit opposite her. 'Ha, I see you have one of Jerard's matchbooks.' The comte smiled indulgently at her as he picked up the closed book.

Kitty's heart thumped in her chest as she prayed he wouldn't examine it more closely. She should have put it away while he was at the desk.

'Yes, a small souvenir of our time here. I have a little collection of them at home, it's all rather foolish really.' She smiled brightly and waited for him to return it to her.

'Not at all, dear lady, it sounds a most pleasant hobby, and one would never be short of a light.' He passed the matchbook back to her.

Relieved, Kitty tucked it away safely inside her handbag. 'That's very true.'

'Did you and your husband enjoy Helene's party last night?'

he asked as a replacement tray of tea was put before them and the old tray taken away.

'Yes, the Duponts are very good hosts, and the house is quite lovely. It was very kind of them to invite us,' Kitty said. 'How do you know them?'

She decided to try to discover more about the comte's friendship with the casino owners.

'I met Jerard several years ago, his family have a vineyard not far from here and I was asked to look at the possible value of a portrait the family owned. He and Helene were looking to raise capital at that point to build the casino. It was after the war, you understand, and he thought there was an opportunity. We have been friends ever since.' The comte poured himself some tea. Kitty shook her head when he offered to pour her another cup.

'It was clearly a good business choice on Monsieur Dupont's behalf. The casino seems to be very well established,' Kitty said.

'Yes, Jerard is a good businessman and, of course, Helene plays her part too.' Luciano added sugar to his cup and stirred.

'Speaking of having a business to run, Matt and I were thinking of leaving today,' Kitty said as the comte sipped his tea.

'Surely not, my dear lady. Can your hotel not manage without you a while longer? You have scarcely been here for anytime at all,' Luciano responded gallantly.

Kitty noted though that his gaze was shrewd and appraising despite his charming words.

'My uncle was most generous to send us on this holiday, but I suppose all good things must come to an end. Our business really can't spare us for too much longer.' Kitty tried to look regretful.

'I suppose so, although I know that Eunice and Candace will certainly miss your company when you leave. Perhaps when you are in England we could come and look you up?' he suggested.

Kitty privately thought she could think of nothing worse, but instead forced herself to look pleased and agreed that it would be lovely to see them again in England.

'Our plans are not yet fixed but I think if we don't leave today then we shall definitely go tomorrow,' Kitty said.

'Shall you go by air or by train?' the comte asked.

'We arrived by air, which my uncle had arranged for us. I'm not sure how we shall return. I'd quite like to take the train to Paris and fly from there as it would allow us to see more of France.'

Somehow, she thought train tickets were more likely to fit the brigadier's budget, especially as it seemed they would be going home empty-handed.

'That is true, and it would no doubt be less expensive and quicker than hiring a private car,' the comte agreed.

'I should like to see something of the countryside on the way back. It has been a very interesting holiday, not the kind of thing we are used to at all,' Kitty said as she started to gather her things ready to make her excuses to return to her room.

'Yes, I suppose that is very true. One fortunately does not fall over murdered people all the time in one's everyday life, thank goodness. At least after such a bad start, and despite the unfortunate Monsieur Lapin, your holiday improved,' the comte said.

'Indeed, that was so horrible and shocking.' Kitty shuddered. She wasn't sure if Luciano was testing her in some way. Did he know she and Matt were private investigators?

'I hope you and your delightful husband will change your minds and decide to extend your holiday for a little longer,' the comte remarked, helping himself to more tea.

'Perhaps, but I really expect it will depend on what travel arrangements we can make for our return home. I should go and see if Matt is awake and ready for breakfast. Perhaps we shall see you later?' Kitty rose and picked up her bag.

The comte stood politely. 'I hope so, Madame Bryant.'

* * *

Matt woke to find himself alone in the room. He sat up in bed and squinted at the time on Kitty's leather-cased bedside travel alarm clock. It was still quite early, and he wondered where Kitty had gone. He glanced around the room but could see no sign of a note, although he noticed her favourite straw handbag was missing.

He guessed she must have woken up and had taken herself off downstairs somewhere in the hotel. She had always been in the habit of waking early ever since he had known her. She had no doubt gone on a hunt for tea. Matt shaved and dressed ready for the day before heading downstairs to look for Kitty.

The newspapers had arrived in the lobby, so he stopped to purchase one from the reception desk.

'Ah, Captain Bryant, I have message for you from England. I was about to take it to your wife.' The receptionist handed him a folded piece of hotel stationery.

Postcard arrived safely. All well here. Tell Kitty not to fret over Mother's present. Your affectionate Uncle E.

It seemed Kitty's message had been received and understood. The implications were clear from the response that they were not to endanger themselves in an attempt to retrieve the papers.

'Good morning, Captain Bryant, up and about nice and early I see. Your charming wife not with you?' Mrs Delaware was dressed for a morning in town judging by her smart pale-blue coloured linen dress and short-sleeved jacket.

'Kitty rose before me, she often does. I expect she's about here somewhere scouting up a pot of tea.' Matt slipped the message into his pocket before folding his paper and tucking it under his arm.

'Wasn't it a marvellous party last night at the Duponts? The German ambassador is such a fascinating man to talk to, don't you think?' Mrs Delaware asked.

'Most interesting.' Matt had scarcely exchanged more than a few sentences with the man. He didn't especially wish to talk to him.

'What are your plans for today?' Eunice persisted.

'I'm really not certain. Kitty and I were talking about possibly leaving today. It all depends on if we can arrange flights and trains. Kitty is keen to see more of France on our way back to Paris.' Matt spotted Kitty talking to the comte in a far corner behind a large fronded potted palm.

'Oh dear, can we not persuade you to stay longer?' Mrs Delaware pouted. 'It has been so delightful to have other company during our stay here.'

'I shall see how Kitty feels, she is missing home and our pets. Also, we do have a business to run.' Matt saw Kitty stand and gather her bag. 'Ah, there she is now, I expect she will be ready for breakfast.' He excused himself politely from the American woman and walked across to meet Kitty at the midway point of the lobby.

'I was just coming to find you.' He offered his arm to his wife. 'We have had a message from home. Shall we go in for breakfast and you can take a look?'

Kitty took his arm, and they walked through together into the dining room where a waiter showed them to a table for two. They gave their order for breakfast and waited for the waiter to leave. Matt passed the piece of paper to Kitty and she read it quickly before placing it in her bag.

'That would seem to give us the green light to leave,' Kitty said.

'I agree. I saw you talking to the comte,' Matt said.

'And you to Eunice Delaware.' Kitty smiled at her husband, a gleam of mischief in her blue-grey eyes.

'*Touché*.' Matt smiled back. 'She was fishing about our plans for the day. I said we may go home.'

'I said the same thing to the comte.'

The waiter returned with their coffee, fruit juice, toast and eggs.

Kitty ignored the drinks and set about buttering her toast. 'What did Eunice say when you said we might be going?'

'She wanted us to stay. What about the comte?' Matt drank his orange juice and helped himself to coffee.

'Much the same. I expect they will either think we have found the papers, or are giving up the hunt. Either way I suspect they will be watching our every move until we are out of Nice.' Kitty gave an involuntary shiver.

'I think that they have been doing that already. What do you think? Shall we try to leave today? We seem to have received permission,' Matt asked as he lopped the top off his boiled egg with a knife.

'I was wracking my brains in the lobby when the comte came to join me. I thought perhaps we had focused on the number written in the matchbook and hadn't thought about the missing matches.' Kitty glanced around to ensure there was no one within earshot.

Matt frowned, unsure of what she meant. 'I'm not with you, old thing.'

'There were three gone from the matchbook and no marks to show they had been struck so I thought perhaps the number was significant.' Kitty must have seen his confusion.

He took a sip of coffee. 'I see, yes, that would make a difference.' He nodded slowly, his mind racing through the possibilities.

'My initial thought was a room number or a telephone number, but I drew a blank on both of those.' Kitty looked downcast as she added strawberry jam to her toast.

'Those would have been both of my thoughts too,' Matt consoled her.

'Are there any avenues left to explore here, do you think? Or should we just cut our losses?' Kitty asked before she popped the last bit of her toast into her mouth.

'I must admit I can't think of anything else at the moment. I wish we could have discovered more about who may have killed Federico and attacked Monsieur Lapin, but I'm increasingly minded to believe that it was orchestrated by someone we have come to know during our stay here.' He paused and drank some of his coffee. 'I think the inspector will do his best to get to the bottom of it all.'

Kitty looked vaguely dissatisfied by his answer and he knew that she would have loved to have solved the mystery of the murders, even if they couldn't find where the documents had been hidden.

'I suppose so. I think we underestimated how difficult and dangerous accepting this job would be.' Kitty sighed as she spoke.

'We were warned in advance, but yes, you're right. I think it has proved much more complicated than we thought,' Matt agreed.

'Then shall we make arrangements to leave?' Kitty asked as she patted the corners of her mouth with the linen napkin.

'I'll telephone the airline in Paris, then get the receptionist to arrange for train tickets.' Matt reached across the table and patted Kitty's hand. He understood her disappointment. 'Chin up, darling. We've done our best.'

CHAPTER TWENTY-TWO

Kitty couldn't help but feel despondent, as they finished breakfast. She hated feeling that they had failed in their mission to retrieve the papers. She also felt somehow guilty that they didn't know for certain who had arranged for Federico's murder and been responsible for the death of Monsieur Lapin.

At least the message they had just received from England hadn't hinted at any sign of recrimination or disappointment. It was just so frustrating to have to leave with so many unanswered questions.

Matt went to the reception desk to make their travel arrangements and she set off towards the stairs ready to go and start their packing.

'I say, Mrs Bryant, Kitty, Mother says you are leaving today?' Candace stopped her near the foot of the stairs.

'Yes, I'm afraid so. Matt is making the arrangements at the desk now. It all depends if we can get a flight from Paris and organise our train,' Kitty said.

'Oh, that's such a shame. We shall miss your company. I hope you have a safe journey home though.' Candace looked disappointed.

Roland Fetherington sauntered up to join the conversation.

'Kitty just told me she and Matt may be leaving today,' Candace informed him.

'If we can sort out trains and a flight from Paris,' Kitty said.

'Candace's mother will miss you both, I think she's enjoyed having company, eh, Candy?' he looked at his girlfriend.

'She has. Rather selfishly from our point of view it's also been a huge boon to us having someone else to entertain her. You must let us have your address back in England before you go,' Candace suggested.

'Of course,' Kitty agreed. Privately she had no intention of staying in touch with Mrs Delaware or her daughter. Not that Candace appeared to have been involved in her mother's scheming, but it seemed that none of them could be trusted.

She said her farewells and escaped up to her room to start packing their belongings. She had managed to get all of Matt's things put away and was halfway through her own things when Matt came to join her.

'That's all sorted. We can collect our train tickets from the booth at the station. The flight leaves from Paris tomorrow morning early so I've also booked a hotel there for tonight,' Matt said as he entered the room.

'That sounds splendid. How long have we got until the train? I still have half a trunk to pack.' Kitty wished her friend Alice was there to assist her. Alice would have laughed to see how dreadful Kitty's packing skills were. She'd had come to her rescue on more than one occasion.

She hoped Lucy had managed to convince her friend to go to Enderley at least for a few days. It had been awful to see how sad she had been for the last few weeks, although she had tried to put a brave face on things.

'The train leaves just after midday. The taxi is booked to collect us at eleven so we shall have plenty of time. At least two hours,' Matt assured her.

'What about Inspector Villier? Should we tell him we are leaving?' Kitty asked. She felt bad that the inspector had instructed them to remain in Nice until his inquiries were complete, but they really had nothing more that they could tell him.

Matt ran his hand through his hair and turned from where he had been standing by the open window looking out at the sea view. 'Will it make you feel better if we do?' he asked.

Kitty paused from where she was carefully rolling up her stockings. 'I just feel as if it's the right thing to do, and if he cannot stop us from going then, well, why not? Like you said yesterday, we shouldn't need to slink away as if we are guilty of something.'

'Very well, I'll go back downstairs and telephone him,' he offered.

'Thank you.' Kitty was relieved. It simply went against everything she believed in to have gone without letting the police know.

Matt was gone for some time, and she had finished all of the packing by the time he returned to the room.

'I left a message for him at the police station to let him know our plans. They said the inspector was at the town hall. I expect the mayor probably wanted an update on the murders. You know what he was saying last night about them. I must admit I feel a little sorry for the inspector. Then just as I was coming away from the desk, I ran into Sir Montague.'

'I take it you also told him we were going today?' Kitty said as she checked all the drawers once more to make sure she hadn't missed anything.

'Yes, he wished us a safe passage home. He looked rather worse for wear this morning, I have to say.' Matt smiled as he spoke.

'I'm not surprised. He did rather tie one on last night.' Kitty clicked her tongue in disapproval as she locked her dressing case.

'Are we all set?' Matt looked at the mound of luggage.

'Yes, I think so.' Kitty took another look around the room. 'I keep wondering about that matchbook. It's niggling me that we didn't work it out.'

'Perhaps when we are back the brigadier can get another one of his agents to work on it. Someone more familiar with Nice or who knew Federico may have better luck,' Matt suggested.

The hotel porter was summoned, and their luggage taken downstairs to await the taxi. Kitty took a few minutes to write a thank you note to the Duponts for their hospitality which she dropped in the post box in reception. She had no desire to be thought rude, even by people she didn't care for. Her grandmother would never forgive her if she felt Kitty skipped any of the social niceties.

There was no sign of any of the people they had spent time with when the taxi arrived. That at least was something to be thankful for. With any luck they had seen the last of the Delaware party. In no time at all their luggage was stowed away and they set off on the short distance through the town to the station.

Once they reached the station, a porter was summoned with a trolley and he was delegated to take charge of their luggage until the train arrived. Matt collected their tickets from the office.

'We have a little time before the train is due.' He looked up at the large black and white clock hanging over the platform. 'Do you wish to get something from the stall? Some sweets for the journey, perhaps?' he suggested.

Kitty brightened at the mention of sweets and the thought that there might even be an English magazine at the stand which she could buy. She took Matt's arm and they walked towards the small well-stocked stall.

As they walked along the busy platform, something caught her eye and made her halt in her tracks. 'Matt, I just had a thought. Look what's over there.' She tightened her grip on the sleeve of his jacket.

'The left luggage lockers.' He looked at her. 'Do you think?'

'We have a few minutes before the train, what harm can it do to check?' Kitty urged.

'We haven't a ticket or a key for them.' Matt frowned then smiled at her. 'But you're right, yes, let's see what we can do.'

They changed direction and headed in the direction of the booth and rows of lockers at the rear of the platform behind the waiting room area.

Kitty waited eagerly as Matt made enquiries in French at the left luggage booth. It sounded to her as if he were giving the middle-aged lady manning the booth some kind of heartfelt sob story.

Whatever he said to her seemed to work and the lady somewhat begrudgingly eventually produced a key.

'Come on, Kitty, we shall have to be quick. Our train is due any minute and we need to get back to the porter.' Matt headed for the bank of grey, metal lockers. 'This is for 328. I thought it more likely than 238 as logically you would notice the missing matches first.'

Kitty scanned the metal locker doors for the number, her excitement building as she looked. 'Down here.'

Matt moved swiftly to insert the key into the lock.

'Hurry, the train will be here any time now,' Kitty urged.

Matt turned the key and opened the door of the locker.

Kitty peered over his shoulder, eager to see what was inside. 'There's a canvas bag.'

Matt pulled the small, dull-green bag out and took a quick peek inside. Out on the platform edge Kitty heard the crunch of the train wheels on the track and the squeak of brakes followed by the hiss of steam.

'Matt, the train!' she warned.

He quickly stuffed the bag inside her straw handbag and they ran to return the locker key to the lady in the booth, before hurrying to their porter who had begun to load their luggage onto the train.

Matt opened the carriage door and assisted Kitty up the step into the carriage where their seats had been reserved. He followed after her, pulling the carriage door shut behind him once he was certain the luggage had all been placed on board.

Kitty settled herself in her seat and peered out anxiously through the carriage window scanning the platform to check they had not been seen taking the bag from the locker. As she looked, she thought she saw a young boy who appeared very like the urchin who had been in town when Sir Montague had been attacked.

All along the length of the train there was the slamming of carriage doors, and she could hear the sound of steam compressing in the engine ready for the train to depart. Matt sat beside her, the warm weight of his thigh pressing against her leg as he too looked out through the carriage window.

'That boy, over there. Can you see him? The one standing beside the luggage trolleys.' Kitty indicated to where the lad stood next to a large wicker-lidded basket. 'He looks like the one who was in league with Sir Montague's attacker.'

Her pulse raced as she waited for the guard to blow his whistle and raise his flag so they could be on their way. The sight of the boy had made her anxious. Suppose they had been seen at the lockers? She looked around for the man Matt had fought with when he had rescued Sir Montague.

To her relief she saw no sign of him. However, she noticed two gendarmes enter the station and look about the platform. Had they come to prevent her and Matt from leaving? The boy melted away at his first sight of the gendarmes, disappearing into the crowd like a wisp of smoke.

'Can you see anyone else?' Matt asked.

'Only the police.' Kitty felt sick with anxiety.

There was the sound of the whistle and the loud hiss of steam as a plume of smoke went past the closed window of the carriage.

'I agree with you – that young lad looked familiar. Be on your guard. It looks as if we may have been followed here.' Matt took the canvas bag from Kitty's handbag and hid it as far back as he could underneath the train seat.

'Are the papers we were sent to collect in there?' Kitty asked. She hadn't been able to glimpse the contents when Matt had taken a brief peek when he had peered inside the bag outside the lockers.

'There are papers of some sort. Whether it is what we are after, or just some old lady's knitting patterns, I'm not certain and until we are safely back in London I daren't look more closely.' Matt's jaw was set in a firm line as he resumed his seat. As he moved next to her again, she felt something hard and metallic against her hip.

'You have your gun with you.' It was a statement rather than a question. Matt always took his gun with him when they travelled. Usually it was hidden in a secret compartment at the bottom of his trunk. It was a hangover from his former life as both a soldier and as an agent working for the brigadier's department in Whitehall.

She wasn't sure if she felt safer knowing he had it concealed about his person, or more concerned that he thought it might be needed.

'If we were followed to the station, then there may well be someone on board this train who wishes us ill,' Matt said.

Kitty nodded. She knew what he meant. It could be anyone from the knife carrying thug who had attacked Sir Montague, or even someone they knew from the hotel. Virtually everyone had enquired about their plans and how they had intended to travel.

Then there had been the sudden arrival of the gendarmes just before the train had pulled out. Would they be stopped at the next station and escorted from the train? If the papers were found in their possession, then was that going to cause a diplomatic incident? The brigadier had been very clear that they could expect little support from the embassy should such an event occur.

Their luggage had been stowed in a space along the corridor that led into their carriage. She could see no way of accessing their trunk in order to try and hide the papers from the locker.

When she had looked at the train timetable, she had discovered that this train was an express and only made a few stops between Nice and Paris. If anyone were to try and confront them, they would have to wait and board at one of those, or they would have to walk from one of the other carriages down to where they were seated.

She could only hope that the boy she had seen at the station had not had time to alert an accomplice to board the train. Matt stood and moved position to sit opposite her so that he was facing anyone who might come through the door from the corridor.

Kitty's heart raced in time with the chunkity-chunk of the wheels on the track. All they could do was hope and pray they had managed to make good their escape. Now it felt as if they were on a race to return to London in safety.

* * *

Matt took up his post opposite Kitty so that he could see who was moving around in the short corridor outside their carriage where the luggage was stowed. His view through the etched glass panel at the top of the door was limited but he thought it was better than having his back to the door.

He could see from Kitty's face that she was scared. Her gaze was fixed on the scenery outside the window, and she had her hands resting on her lap as if to stop them from trembling. Spotting the urchin at the station had clearly shaken her and he wondered if someone else connected with the boy had boarded the train.

He tensed as someone entered the corridor. However, the man merely stopped to lower the window using the leather strap and proceeded to light a cigarette. Whoever it was stood and smoked before throwing the butt from the window of the moving train and raising the window once more, before returning to his carriage.

Matt relaxed slightly, still keeping his hand within easy reach of his gun. The train whistle sounded as the track curved and they were plunged into darkness as they entered a tunnel.

Seconds felt like hours in the darkness. There was the sound of a clunk almost like something falling. Tension coiled in Matt's stomach and his hand crept even closer to where his gun was concealed beneath his jacket.

The train emerged from the tunnel and Matt found himself face to face with Comte Luciano Malfiore who had one arm around Kitty, holding her still, and his other hand holding a gun trained on Matt.

CHAPTER TWENTY-THREE

'I would suggest, Captain Bryant, that you give to me the papers you have retrieved from the locker at Nice Station. In that way your delightful wife, and yourself, will be unharmed,' the comte said.

The comte was seated close to Kitty on the bench seat holding her securely in his grasp.

'I'm sorry, Luciano, but what makes you think we have any such things. We merely collected a bag of Kitty's from the left luggage.' Matt kept his tone calm despite his inner panic.

'We shall arrive at our next stop in about ten minutes time. Give me the papers and I shall leave the train. You will not see me again and you can continue your journey without interruption,' the comte said and narrowed his eyes.

'I don't know what you mean, old boy.' Matt held his nerve and hoped he was doing the right thing. He was determined to force the other man to at least confess who he was working for and if he had any part in Federico and Monsieur Lapin's deaths.

The comte tightened his grip on Kitty forcing a squeak of surprise from her. 'The time for playing games is over. I can assure you that I have no problem with ending both you and your wife to get what I want.'

'Just like you did with Federico Benedetto and Monsieur Lapin?' Kitty asked.

'Benedetto was a mistake, those idiots Jerard hired were supposed to capture him not kill him.' Luciano's eyes glittered.

'But then once he was dead you had no way of finding whatever it was you wanted,' Kitty countered.

The comte continued to watch Matt although he answered Kitty.

'We knew he had the goods and that he would have sent a message back to England for another agent to collect them, as he had been found out. When none of the people we had been expecting arrived, we knew that it had to be someone else outside his department.'

'Why did you assume it was us?' Matt asked.

'You found Benedetto. You also seemed to take stumbling across a murder remarkably calmly. Then when we shadowed you, you went to the villa where Benedetto had been hiding. You had a key to the padlock,' the comte said.

'Then it was you with the binoculars that morning? The one watching us from the hillside?' Kitty said.

'There were several interested parties watching you.' A grim smile lifted the corners of the comte's mouth. 'Those documents are sought after.'

'Why were you working with Sir Montague? I overheard you talking, the day we went to the castle,' Kitty asked.

'That idiot was in debt to Jerard. It was Jerard's idea that a fellow Englishman might discover information that you wouldn't give to me. It was a stupid idea; he was more of a liability than an asset.' The comte's tone was contemptuous and dismissive.

'Was that why he was attacked? You wanted to get rid of him?' Matt asked.

There was a movement in the corridor behind the comte. He wondered if anyone else was behind the closed door to the corridor.

'He drinks too much, and his nerve is gone. He suspected that I had been responsible for Lapin's death. At any time, he could crack and give the whole game away.' The comte edged slightly more forward on his seat, dragging Kitty with him.

'And were you the one who killed Lapin?' Matt asked. 'Were you the one who went into the gardens to hit him over the head with that rock? Why?'

'He had pictures of your friend Benedetto taken with me outside the casino. I had followed him from Italy, over the border, waiting for an opportunity to discover where he had hidden those documents.' The comte smiled grimly once more. 'Villier is like a dog with a rabbit. If he had seen those pictures, he would have latched onto me as a suspect and would not have let go. I had to deal with both Lapin and his photographs.'

'And Monsieur Dupont, he was aware of all of this? He was the middleman brokering a deal with the German ambassador as the buyer for the documents?' Kitty asked.

Matt could only admire his wife's calm tone considering the danger they were facing. Outside the carriage, the dark-coated figure in the corridor had crept closer and Matt guessed whoever it was had their ear to the door listening. Was the man outside friend or foe? But if the man was with the comte, why did he not enter the carriage?

The train had to be drawing closer now to the stop and he guessed Luciano could not afford to be caught. He was likely to kill them both with or without the documents he so desperately wanted.

'Jerard and Helene have many connections. They know a lot of people in Nice and beyond who are in very high places,' the comte said.

'What is in it for you? Money? It doesn't sound as if you

have any interest in returning the documents to your government. You are betraying your country for a handful of silver.' Matt was aware that his comment and the contemptuous note in his voice was likely to anger the man, but time was running out. His heart pounded as he waited for the answer.

The line of Luciano's mouth hardened. 'I do not expect you to understand, Captain Bryant. I do this *for* my country. Some of us have seen a glimpse of the future, of partnerships between nations and a greater glory.' His eyes had now taken on a fanatical gleam.

'And Eunice Delaware? Does she share this grand vision? Or is she simply being used to bankroll all of this?' Kitty winced as the comte tightened his hold on her still farther.

Matt instinctively moved forward in his seat to protect her, but the comte levelled his gun.

'Stay right where you are, and keep your hands where I can see them,' he warned, looking at Matt. 'Mrs Delaware is committed to our ideals. She too has visited Germany and seen the future.'

Matt was forced to remain where he was, unable to get to his own weapon. Not that it would help at present as the comte was in the stronger position. It was agony seeing Kitty in such danger.

'I am not sure your government would believe you,' Matt said.

'Enough! Where are the papers? Mrs Bryant, open your bag,' Luciano demanded.

Kitty picked up her large straw bag embroidered with dark-blue flowers and opened it as requested.

'Tip the contents out onto the seat,' the comte ordered.

Kitty did as she was told. Her small black-leather purse, a silver powder compact, a lipstick, a comb, a handkerchief and the novel she was reading tumbled out onto the upholstery.

'Where are the papers?' A pulse ticked near the corner of

the comte's mouth once he realised the bag they had retrieved from the station locker was missing.

Kitty's gaze met Matt's and she gave a faint shake of her head. The silence in the carriage seemed to stretch before the comte scowled. His handsome face darkening with fury.

'Very well, perhaps you need some persuasion. Mrs Bryant, open the carriage door, some fresh air may help you to make up your mind.' Luciano held on tightly to Kitty. He pushed her along the seat forcing her towards the door that would open onto the track and the embankment they were travelling along.

The movement scattered the contents of Kitty's handbag off the seat and onto the floor of the carriage to roll about their feet.

'Open the door, or I shall shoot your husband.' The comte moved his finger fractionally on the trigger and Kitty was forced to comply. Matt's pulse jumped with fear for his wife and himself at the peril they were in.

She fumbled with the leather strap of the latch until the carriage door flew open to be whipped back against the side of the train. A breeze blew in, flicking the pages of Kitty's book with smoke-scented air where it lay next to her feet.

'Now, give me the papers, or Mrs Bryant will be leaving the train early,' Luciano snarled.

He shoved Kitty further along the seat, while still keeping his gun firmly trained on Matt. Kitty desperately dug her heels down against the floor of the carriage.

Matt knew that the comte would kill them both, even if they handed him the documents he so desperately wanted. Right now though, the papers were the only bargaining chip he possessed. That and the unknown identity of the lurking figure in the corridor.

'Let Kitty go, and I'll tell you where they are,' Matt offered, trying not to let his desperation show in his tone.

'I don't think so. You are in no position to set the terms. Where are they?' Luciano's voice rose and he pushed Kitty even closer to the opening where the carriage door was now banging back and forth against the side of the carriage with the motion of the engine.

He saw Kitty's gaze flick upwards towards the emergency stop pull over the top of the door, but he knew that neither of them could reach it to halt the train. At least not without getting themselves shot in the process.

'The bag is under your seat.' Matt took the gamble and hoped. Either Luciano would believe him or would think he was bluffing. He saw Kitty dig her nails into the upholstery of the train seat bracing herself to prevent Luciano from pushing her from the train.

'Get it,' the comte ordered. 'And remember I can and will shoot you or dispose of your wife if you try anything stupid.'

Matt cautiously moved forward in his seat; at some point he would need to take his eyes off the comte. Luciano was seated on top of the bag, and he needed to reach forward in order to get hold of it.

Luciano moved his legs as he realised where the papers had been placed to allow Matt to stretch down from his seat and grope on the floor for the bag. As he shifted his gaze to look for the documents, he heard Kitty scream. He felt a sharp blow on the back of his neck and everything went black.

* * *

Kitty braced herself, fearing that once Matt had retrieved the documents Luciano would simply push her from the moving train. She had visions of tumbling through the open carriage door out and into the scrubby bushes that grew alongside the train track. Or of falling beneath the moving wheels.

Luciano shifted slightly allowing Matt to bend forward to reach for the bag. As Matt lowered his head and pulled the bag out the comte hit him hard at the base of his neck. Kitty's scream was swallowed by the train whistle as her husband slumped forward from his seat onto the floor. Her favourite lipstick rolled past her feet and tumbled out of the train through the open door.

Kitty thought her heart would stop. Was Matt dead? The comte briefly slackened his hold on her to move his arm to grasp the canvas parcel from the floor of the carriage before it could slide out of the open door to be lost along with her lipstick.

Kitty seized her chance to wriggle free of Luciano, hitting the arm holding the gun as hard as she could in an attempt to force the weapon from his hand. She was desperate to get to Matt. The man retaliated immediately, bringing his elbow back to hit her forcefully in her ribs, knocking the breath from her.

'Oof!' Kitty almost doubled over as pain seared through her.

The comte had hold of the bag and his expression was triumphant as he turned on Kitty. His gun was now pointed toward her. Matt was still and unmoving on the floor of the carriage. Without giving herself time to think of the consequences she drew back her foot and kicked the comte hard on his shin.

Angered by the pain, he advanced upon her with a roar of rage. 'You'll pay for that!'

He swung at her with the gun as if intending to hit her in the same way he had hit Matt. She ducked and moved herself away from the open gap. As she sidestepped to the far wall the door leading to the corridor burst open and another man entered the carriage.

The mystery man launched himself on the comte, grabbing the arm holding the gun. Kitty cowered back in the corner as the two men tussled. She longed to check on Matt as he lay on the floor while above him the two men fought for the gun. The force with which the comte had hit him meant she had no idea if he were alive or dead. Her heart was beating so hard she thought it would fly out of her chest. She could only pray Matt was simply unconscious.

'This is the police, surrender your weapon!'

The police? Kitty suddenly realised it was Inspector Villier who was tussling with the comte. With his dark hat and coat she hadn't recognised him. She assumed that he had boarded the train at Nice. The comte continued to resist and there was a loud bang as the gun was fired. Kitty covered her eyes and ears momentarily with her hands, afraid to see what had happened.

She peered out between her spread fingers to see that the gun had now been knocked clear from the comte's grasp to lie on the floor of the carriage. The two men continued to trade blows as the comte fought to break free of the inspector. His intention was obviously to retrieve the gun.

The train swayed as she tried to see if she could get her hands on the gun. Inspector Villier caught the weapon with the side of his foot sending it skidding across the floor of the carriage. It vanished from sight for a moment. She looked frantically for any sign of the weapon.

The movement of the carriage and the scuffling of the men made it difficult to see where the gun had gone. At first Kitty thought it had followed her lipstick onto the tracks. She had to find it. All their lives depended on it. If the comte got to it first, then who knows what he was capable of doing. Then she spotted it. It lay just beyond her reach where it had slid to a halt close to the open door.

The train whistle sounded again, and the carriage lurched once more, tilting slightly and sending the gun spinning nearer to Kitty. She dived forward to grab hold of it, her fingers shaking as they closed around the white pearlescent handle.

She straightened up, leaning against the side of the carriage for support as she raised the gun.

'Stop! I have the gun!' She pointed it at the men trying to sound commanding and hoping she wouldn't be forced to use it.

She had never really liked guns, even when Lucy had persuaded her to go on a pheasant shoot once.

As she spoke the inspector shook himself free of the comte's grasp and punched out, landing a blow squarely on Luciano's chin.

Before Kitty could say or do anything more, the comte staggered backwards from the force of the strike. He wobbled towards the opening in the side of the carriage. His back foot hit the sill of the doorframe as the train lurched once more.

It seemed to Kitty as if he were suspended for a moment, his hands scrabbling at air to try and catch hold of something to prevent the fall. She was horrified, sure she must be imagining it. Inspector Villier swiftly moved to try and catch his opponent, but it was too late. He went tumbling through the gap and from the train.

Inspector Villier staggered back and collapsed down heavily onto one of the seats.

'*Mon dieu*, I did not expect...'

Kitty wasn't sure if he was speaking to her or to himself. The whole thing had happened so quickly it had felt almost as if they were in some scene from a horrific film. The pace of the train started to slow, and Kitty guessed they must be approaching the town.

She set down the gun and dropped to her knees beside Matt, stroking his hair and feeling for his pulse to reassure herself that he was alive.

"Matt? Please God, Matt?"

Much to her relief, she heard him groan. His eyelids fluttered open as if sensing her presence.

'Kitty?'

'It's all right, darling. I'm here. The inspector is here. We are both safe,' she assured him. She looked up at Inspector Villier who appeared dazed and bloodied on the seat. 'Inspector? Are you all right?'

'I shall be, Madame Bryant. You are unhurt?' the inspector asked.

'A little bruised and battered but we shall live, thanks to your bravery,' she assured him. Relief rushed through her body, and she sagged against the side of the seat for support.

Matt stirred, moving his hand to rub the base of his neck. 'Bounder caught me unawares.' He attempted to sit up with Kitty supporting him.

Kitty realised the bag containing the papers had fallen to the carriage floor during the scuffle and now lay next to the crushed remains of her powder compact. She picked the silver compact up and surveyed it ruefully. It had obviously been trodden on during the fight and the lid was dented. The small ruby-coloured stone from the centre of the lid had vanished.

Matt levered himself up from the floor and onto a seat opposite the inspector as Kitty collected up the rest of her belongings, including the documents, and restored them to her bag. She took her seat next to Matt. The train continued to slow, and the whistle sounded once more as the station came into view.

'What happened to the comte?' Matt asked as he continued to rub his neck.

Kitty glanced towards the still open door and Matt closed his eyes.

'I shall send men to search the side of the track when we stop,' Inspector Villier said. 'Captain Bryant, do you require a doctor?'

'No, thank you, Inspector. I have a hard head and I shall be all right, I'm sure,' he assured the policeman.

'*Eh bien.* Do you wish to continue your journey to Paris?' Inspector Villier looked at them.

'Yes, we have a hotel booked and a flight for tomorrow. If you need our statements, we can do them for you before we leave France,' Kitty said as the train came to a juddering halt at the station. There was a whoosh of steam and a screech of brakes accompanied by voices.

The inspector nodded. 'Very well. Give me your address in Paris and I can arrange for your report to be collected before you depart. I think I heard enough of the comte's confession to attribute the murder of Monsieur Lapin and also that of Signor Benedetto to him. I would prefer to know nothing of any papers, you understand me.' He looked meaningfully at them.

There was a shout outside the train and a railway employee came to the open door of the carriage, a horrified look on his face. He had obviously seen the open door as the train had pulled up to the platform.

His rapid-fire French halted when the inspector produced his identity card and stepped out of the carriage, taking the comte's gun with him. Kitty hastily scribbled the name of their hotel on a fragment of paper torn from the back of her novel and handed it to him.

'*Merci, au revoir*, Madame Bryant, Captain Bryant and *bon chance*.' The inspector closed the carriage door.

CHAPTER TWENTY-FOUR

Kitty was relieved that no one else came to join them in their carriage for the remainder of the journey into Paris. She was concerned that Matt should have seen a doctor, but he assured her that he was fine and that the aspirin she had procured from the staff in the restaurant car were working.

She hoped that the train company would not be too annoyed about the bullet hole in the ceiling of the carriage. The bullet had fortunately lodged itself in the roof lining and not gone right the way through to the outside. She was still shaking from the after-effects of the attack and her ribs were sore from where she had been assaulted.

Just seeing the hole surrounded by scorch marks above their heads made her shiver as she realised how lucky they had been. It could have been her and not the comte who had been sent tumbling from the train. She placed the canvas package inside her dressing case, squashing it in and locking the case with her key. It had to be safer there than in her jaunty straw holiday handbag.

She was also extremely grateful that Inspector Villier had allowed them to continue their journey. He would have been within his rights to ask them to get off the train. She suspected that he wished to avoid becoming embroiled in some kind of diplomatic incident and she wondered if the comte's demise would be attributed to an accident or suicide.

Then there would be no need to mention either herself or Matt or the cause of the struggle. The inspector might choose to say the comte was resisting arrest for the murder of Monsieur Lapin. He had clearly signalled to them as he had taken his leave that he wished to know nothing of anything that might cause a diplomatic problem.

Matt was half-sitting, half-lying across the bench seat of the carriage with his head resting on her lap. His eyes were closed. Her ribs ached, and she suspected she would have some nice bruises on her arms from where the comte had grabbed her. They were both rather the worse for wear and the sooner they were back in London the better.

When they arrived at the station in Paris, Matt roused himself and procured them a porter for their cases and a taxi to their hotel. Even though she longed to be home, she was glad their flight wasn't until the following day as it would give them both the chance to recover.

'How are you feeling now, Matt?' she asked anxiously once they were alone inside the privacy of their hotel bedroom.

'I must admit I've felt better,' he grimaced and rubbed the nape of his neck. 'That was a narrow squeak, old thing.' He gave her a wan smile.

'I know. I must admit I'm feeling rather knocked about myself.' Kitty returned his smile. 'Shall we be terribly spoiled and order room service for our dinner? We have a very nice table and chairs here.'

Their room was surprisingly spacious for a Parisian hotel and was more like a suite. The gold striped wallpaper and dark-gold tasselled drapery around the window added a luxurious touch.

'Why not? I'll go downstairs and request a menu in a moment,' Matt agreed.

'Do you think it safe to let the brigadier know we are in Paris and on our way back home?' Kitty asked. 'Obviously without mentioning the papers, or should we wait until we are back in London and just deliver them to his office?'

'I think we need to just wait and get to London first. Where did you put the documents?' Matt asked.

'I locked them in my vanity box. I checked and everything is in Italian so I assume they must be what we were sent to retrieve,' Kitty said.

'Good. We aren't out of the woods yet, I'm afraid. I fear news of the comte's accident will travel back to Nice quickly and it's possible that someone may still attempt to get their hands on those papers.' Matt frowned as he spoke.

'That's true. I suppose it's even possible for someone to fly here from Nice.' The thought made Kitty quite downcast. She had just begun to feel better about the whole mission.

'I shall be much happier once we are in London, and happier still when we are back at Enderley.' Matt kissed the top of her head. 'It's not much longer, now though, darling. You've been simply marvellous through all of this.'

* * *

Matt's head was still aching when he woke the following day. He could have cursed himself for not expecting the comte to have attacked when he did. At least he was still alive to tell the tale, however, so that was something. Thankfully, a good night's rest had helped enormously, and he was hopeful that by the time they touched down in London he would feel much better.

After breakfast he and Kitty had written out their statements for the inspector. They had left out any mention of the documents, merely stating that the comte had entered their carriage and attacked them. They had included his confession to the attack on Monsieur Lapin and of being involved in the assault on Sir Montague and Federico Benedetto's murder.

Matt had agreed with Kitty that it would be wise to avoid all possible mention of anything which might cause a problem for either the inspector or the mayor, who would undoubtedly be anxious for both of the murder cases to be closed.

Their transport to the airfield was booked and he would be very relieved to be safely back in London with the documents delivered to the brigadier. This case had been far more complicated and dangerous than he had anticipated. Despite having carried out work like this in the past, he had forgotten how much he disliked it and the challenges it presented.

It had only been the brigadier's appeal to his patriotism, and the involvement of Kitty's uncle, that had helped to persuade him to take it on. He felt even more regretful that he had not tried harder to dissuade the brigadier about having Kitty accompany him. It was one thing to place himself in danger, but quite another to involve his wife.

The argument that a married couple would arouse less suspicion had been a good one. Or they had thought so at the time, but it had come at a price, and he had hated seeing Kitty in so much danger on the train. She had handled it well, but it didn't make him feel much better about the whole affair.

Kitty was just fastening the last strap on their trunk when there was a tap at the door.

'There, that's the last one,' she said.

'Just in time.'

Matt went to open the door, expecting it to be the hotel's portering service to take their luggage to the lobby ready for the taxi.

Instead, he was confronted by the elegant and familiar figure of Eunice Delaware, pointing a gun directly at his chest.

'You had better let me inside, Captain Bryant, or Kitty will be a widow.'

Taken by surprise he had little choice but to stand aside and allow the American woman to enter. His heart sank when he realised that she sounded as if she meant business. Kitty straightened up from where she had been kneeling to deal with the luggage, a startled expression on her face when she first saw Eunice, and then the gun.

'I'm sure you can both guess why I'm here,' Eunice said firmly, keeping the weapon trained on Matt.

'I can only presume that the news of the comte's unfortunate accident has reached Nice.' Matt wished he had kept his own gun under his jacket. The American woman was something of an unknown quantity. Could they take the risk that she was bluffing? He could see panic in Kitty's eyes although she was trying not to show it.

Eunice gave an unladylike snort. 'We all know that was no accident. Now, I've got no time to waste, hand over the documents.'

'I'm afraid they have already gone,' Kitty said. 'You're too late. The police were here earlier and collected them.'

Matt could only admire Kitty's quick thinking. If Mrs Delaware had been watching, then she would indeed have seen a uniformed gendarme collect a package containing papers from their suite. It had, of course, contained their statements on the comte's attack, but Eunice wouldn't know that.

'You're lying. I don't believe you.' Mrs Delaware's eyes narrowed as she attempted to decide if Kitty was telling the truth.

'I'm afraid you have had a wasted journey. The police will no doubt even now be returning them to the Italian embassy. They seemed most anxious to avoid any kind of diplomatic incident,' Kitty said.

Matt held his breath for a moment before saying, 'The porters will also be arriving here at any minute to take our luggage downstairs.' He looked towards the door of the room. Hopefully, help was on the way in the form of the innocent bellhop.

'No, I don't believe you. Either of you. It's a lie. You have to have the papers. I need them.' The gun wavered in Eunice's hand as she glanced first at Matt and then at Kitty.

Matt debated with himself briefly, trying to judge if it would be safe to make a grab for the gun. He couldn't afford Kitty getting shot.

'It's quite true. You may as well turn around and leave now. Candace must wonder where you are. I can only presume she is ignorant about all of this?' Kitty said.

'Leave Candace out of it. She is with that Fetherington boy, back in Nice.' Eunice's voice wobbled. Matt released a silent breath at the first crack in the woman's resolve.

'She would be mortified if she discovered you were here now, doing this.' Kitty's tone was softer now.

A lone tear escaped and ran down Mrs Delaware's cheek. 'I'm doing it for Candace. It's for all of us, for a brighter future.' She tightened her grip on the handle of the gun.

Matt watched her carefully, hoping her nerves wouldn't cause her to pull the trigger. His shoulders ached with tension.

'How is any of this helping Candace?' Kitty asked. 'She is in love with Roland, she intends to marry him. Mr Fetherington is a bright young man, with your support and Candace's drive he could do well. This political brouhaha isn't worth it.' Kitty's voice was soft and persuasive.

Matt could see the indecision in the woman's gaze. Like Kitty he suspected Mrs Delaware's heart was not fully in her ill-thought-out scheme. She must have heard of Luciano's demise and taken the first flight out of Nice to Paris.

'Go back to Nice, to your daughter. Help her plan her wedding,' Matt added his voice to Kitty's. 'We can forget this ever happened.'

There was a faint rumbling sound out in the corridor and Matt guessed the porter was on his way to their room.

'The bellhop is on his way,' Kitty said. 'Please, Eunice, put the gun away in your handbag and go. There is nothing more you can do here.'

The rumble of the luggage trolley grew closer. Matt waited, poised in case the woman decided to continue holding them hostage.

Eunice wavered as if undecided about what to do, before finally opening her large tan-leather handbag and dropping the gun inside. The rap on the door came just as she fastened the clasp on top of the bag.

'Come in,' Matt called to the porter, once he was certain that Mrs Delaware had abandoned her plan.

The American woman pushed her way past the young uniformed porter as he opened the door, leaving him standing with a surprised expression on his freckled face. Matt scarcely had time to blow out a sigh of relief before the trolley was loaded.

Matt took Kitty in his arms and she released a small sob into his shoulder.

'Come on, darling, let's get out of here.' Matt kissed her tenderly.

Kitty dried her eyes and picked up her vanity box and handbag. Within minutes they were in the taxi on their way to the airfield.

'I really thought that perhaps that was it when Eunice arrived,' Kitty said as the taxi approached the airport building.

'Me too. It was expected that someone might have one last throw of the dice but unexpected that it would be Eunice, if you know what I mean,' Matt agreed. He hoped that would be the last of it and they could finally get out of France without any further problems.

* * *

Kitty was still shaken from the encounter with Mrs Delaware as they boarded the flight. The plane was full, and she couldn't help glancing nervously around checking to make sure there were no more nasty surprises in store. She kept her small vanity case on her lap, unwilling to allow it out of her sight.

She had not expected to be able to persuade Eunice to give up her plan. When she had appeared holding the gun Kitty had been convinced their luck had finally run out. Getting the woman to abandon her plan had done much to improve her confidence.

The flight was mercifully uneventful and in very little time they were back in a dreary-looking London. Matt ordered a car and at Kitty's persuasion they decided to call in at the brigadier's offices in Whitehall, before going on to the hotel. Kitty just wanted shot of the documents before anything else could happen. The driver dropped them off in the street outside the building and continued on to their hotel with their luggage.

A fine drizzle set in as they crossed the street and walked towards the entrance of the building. Unlike the sunny weather in Nice, London was grey and damp. Matt gave their name to the female receptionist. They took their seats on a couple of hard mahogany wooden chairs in the reception area beneath a picture of the king while they waited for someone to collect them.

Kitty was tired now, and her ribs ached from the attack by the comte yesterday. She wondered if Mrs Delaware had gone straight back to Nice, or if she would remain in Paris to try and discover if the documents had been returned to the Italians.

'Captain Bryant, Mrs Bryant? Please follow me, Brigadier Remmington-Blythe is expecting you.' A pleasant-faced young man in a grey suit led them along a corridor and up in a brass-caged elevator to the third floor of the building.

Kitty looked around her curiously as they made their way through the long corridor to the brigadier's inner sanctum. They passed numerous blank wooden doors with brass name plates and a room which appeared to be set aside for typists. Rows of young women all tapping away furiously at their machines.

They walked past the clatter of the typewriters, their heels sounding on the solid floors of the building until they halted outside a door. Their escort knocked smartly on the polished wood and a familiar voice boomed from inside, 'Come!'

The young man opened the door and Kitty followed Matt into the brigadier's office. The office was large and square, all the walls were filled with wooden filing cabinets and above them were hung photographs of what appeared to be various army regiments. The brigadier stood to greet them, extending his hand to Matt first, then Kitty.

'Matthew, my boy, and Kitty, do come and sit down. I'm glad you made it back safely.' He indicated a pair of chairs in front of his large utilitarian desk.

While they were seating themselves, the brigadier opened another door leading from his office into what was presumably his secretary's room.

'Tea for three,' he bellowed at whoever was seated in there, and closed the door. Kitty tried to see through the frosted-glass panel in the top of the door.

'Now then.' The brigadier took his place behind his desk and looked expectantly at them. 'I received the postcard you sent to your uncle, Kitty. Smart work, my dear.' He smiled approvingly at her.

'Thank you, sir. We're very sorry about what happened to Federico,' Kitty said as she took out a key from her purse and opened her small shagreen vanity box.

'Yes, well that wasn't your fault. Other forces were at play there, I'm afraid. You did the best you could,' said the brigadier.

'Well, we do have something here of interest for you,' said

Kitty. She pulled out the canvas bag containing the precious bundle of documents and placed it on the desk in front of the brigadier. His silver bushy eyebrows rose dramatically at the sight of the parcel.

'We haven't properly looked inside the bag, sir, but there seems to be papers written in Italian, so we assume that these are what we were asked to obtain,' Kitty said.

The brigadier pulled the bag towards him and opened it, taking out the documents. He leafed through them, his sharp eyes scanning each page. Kitty could see that as well as the typewritten papers there were drawings and sketches of what seemed to be maps and directions.

Eventually, the brigadier looked up. 'Yes, these are the documents. They were produced for the Italian cabinet for a briefing outlining the strength of their forces, the stations they are based at and a number of other very significant figures and calculations. All of which are enormously helpful. Thank you, my dear.'

There was a knock again on the door with the frosted glass and their escort from earlier entered bearing a loaded wooden tea tray, which he set down carefully on the brigadier's desk. The brigadier moved the bag and papers aside to make more room.

Once tea had been poured, biscuits dispensed, and the secretary dispatched, the brigadier looked at Matt. 'I was very concerned when I received your card. We did our best, discreetly of course, to try and establish what was happening. So now, my boy, a full report if you please.'

Matt dutifully obliged giving his employer all the details of everyone who had been involved.

'It's a dashed shame about that Lapin chap. Poor fellow just got caught up in it all.' The brigadier stroked his moustache, clearly concerned that an innocent man had died.

Matt continued his report, going on to inform the brigadier

of the German ambassador's presence at the Duponts' villa and that they believed he was to be the intended recipient of the papers that now lay on the desk before them.

Kitty quietly sipped her tea as she listened to Matt's concise recitation of events. The brigadier appeared unsurprised by the news of the German ambassador's involvement.

'Yes, I think they are as interested as we are in the Italian's intentions given their own increases in military strength. The business of the Rhineland doesn't bode well,' the brigadier said as he reached for another biscuit.

Then Matt went on to detail the events on their journey back to Paris.

'Good heavens, Mrs Bryant, are you all right?' the brigadier asked in some alarm when Matt detailed how the comte had been attempting to force her from the moving train.

'Yes, sir, thank you. Although I think we both still feel rather battered by it all.' Kitty glanced at her husband, slightly amused that the brigadier was less perturbed that he had been knocked unconscious by the comte.

'And this man, Comte Luciano Malfiore, presumably died in the fall from the train?' the brigadier asked.

'We believe so, sir.' Kitty told him of Eunice Delaware's attempt to obtain the documents from them at their hotel in Paris. 'She said news of the comte's death had reached them in Nice.'

'I expect there will be notices in the French and Italian papers,' the brigadier said.

'I would imagine that to be the case. He was quite a well-known and well-connected man. Inspector Villier would be able to confirm the matter obviously.' Matt placed his now empty cup and saucer back on the tray.

'It sounds as if this mission was much more dangerous and difficult than we envisaged.' The brigadier sighed heavily and looked at Kitty. 'I apologise for that, my dear. Both of you have shown a great deal of courage and initiative to get these papers out of France. I cannot begin to tell you how valuable they are to us.'

'Thank you. We shall, of course, send our expenses and invoices to you as arranged. Would you like our report in writing?' Matt asked.

The brigadier's eyebrows beetled together. 'Hmm, send your invoices and so on but best not put anything official about what happened during the operation on paper. You've debriefed to me and that is sufficient. I still have concerns about the department so I'm keen to keep you and Mrs Bryant out of the frame.'

'Very well, sir,' Matt agreed.

Kitty could only assume that both she and Matt were useful to the brigadier since they were not official employees of the department. That gave him a certain amount of freedom if there were tasks that couldn't be officially attached to Whitehall. Much like the one they had just carried out.

Not that she, or she suspected Matt, was in any hurry to undertake such a job again for quite some time.

Their tea finished, the brigadier summoned his secretary once more to lead them out of the building and back onto the busy street outside. Kitty rested her gloved hand on Matt's arm as he took her vanity box from her to carry it.

'I'm so glad that's all over.' She looked up at him as they strolled towards a nearby taxi rank.

'You and me both,' Matt agreed.

'We had better go and claim our luggage and check in to the hotel. A nice hot bath seems most tempting right now.' Kitty squinted up at the gloomy, grey London sky.

'Then your wish is my command.' Matt smiled and hailed one of the cabs at the rank.

CHAPTER TWENTY-FIVE

The following day saw them back in Devon, safely ensconced at Enderley Hall in time for afternoon tea. Bertie was, as always, delighted to have them back. His plumed tail wagging in a non-stop welcome as he happily stole cake crumbs from under the tea table.

'I'm glad to see you both back safely.' Her uncle kissed her warmly on both cheeks and shook hands with Matt.

'Yes, we were all dreadfully worried, especially when your postcard arrived saying you had been mixed up in a murder again,' her aunt said.

Kitty's cousin Lucy, who had been feeding her own dog, Muffy, a few treats from the tea table, exchanged a smile with Kitty.

'Mother, darling, you know Kitty can't help it. She and Matt are like a magnet for murders.'

'Lucy, darling, please, not at the tea table.' Kitty's aunt frowned at her unrepentant daughter.

'Well, I'm sure it was all jolly exciting,' Rupert, Lucy's husband, said as he helped himself to scones.

'Yes, and I'm frightfully miffed that you can't tell us all the juicy details,' Lucy grumbled.

'Now, then, you know that Kitty and Matthew are bound under the Official Secrets Act to keep silent,' Kitty's uncle joined in on his wife's reprimand.

'I still think it's too bad. I think I might have been quite good as a spy.' Lucy patted the top of Muffy's head. 'What do you think, Rupert?'

Her husband grinned at his wife. 'I don't think so, darling. You are far too fond of being comfortable to do all the things that Kitty gets up to.'

Lucy sighed and reached across to squeeze Kitty's arm. 'I'm afraid he is probably right. You are jolly brave. You and Matt.'

Kitty smiled and thanked her cousin. She didn't think she was particularly brave. Given the things that had happened she thought anyone might well have reacted the same way. It all came down to survival when your life and the life of someone you loved was threatened.

She looked at her cousin as Lucy smiled up at Rupert. Lucy's hand was placed protectively across her abdomen and Kitty's breath hitched a little in her throat. She hoped her cousin was right and that they were going to have an addition to their family.

'Alice will be joining us shortly. She's been such a help to me since she arrived,' Lucy said.

Kitty was pleased to hear this and she hoped Alice was feeling in better spirits now she had been away from Dartmouth for a few days.

'Oh, I'm so glad. I can't wait to see her,' Kitty said.

Matt was engaged in conversation with her uncle discussing the outcome of Italy's occupation of Ethiopia. The last few days in France had been hard and frightening at times but she knew she would have felt worse had she not been with Matt.

If she were in Lucy's shoes, expecting a child, then all of

that would have to stop. Her role in the business would increasingly be confined to typing letters, answering the telephone and balancing the accounts.

In short it would be almost the same as if she had not given up her duties at the Dolphin. The weight of what she would lose seemed suddenly to weigh heavily on her shoulders. Could she be content as just a wife and mother? Was that what she wanted? What Matt wanted? Was it really so awful that she simply couldn't picture herself pushing a pram along the quayside at Dartmouth?

They had agreed that they would simply wait and see what happened. If a baby were to come their way, then all well and good, but they wouldn't actively seek professional help if this didn't occur. To Kitty it had seemed as if Matt was as on the fence about having a family as she was.

Yet now, looking at Lucy and Rupert, she couldn't help feeling a tiny pang of longing. A baby that looked like a mixture of her and Matt. His bright blue eyes and a dimpled cheek and her blonde hair.

'The trouble with you, Kitty, is you want to have your cake and eat it,' Mrs Craven's, her grandmother's friend's, often quoted words of admonishment floated through her head.

Bertie nuzzled his nose into her hand as if sensing her thoughts. She patted his fuzzy head. Dogs, she decided, were infinitely less problematic than babies. Perhaps if she were expecting, she would feel differently about things.

Matt, as if sensing she was watching him, turned and smiled at her. Kitty's spirits lifted. No matter what the future held for her so long as Matt was at her side, they would be all right, she was sure of it. Baby or no baby.

'I expect you will be glad to get back home after all of your adventures,' her aunt's voice broke into her thoughts.

'Yes, I think we will. Not that we don't love it here, of course,' she hastened to reassure the older woman.

'I know, but there is nothing quite like one's own home, is there?' her aunt said as she adroitly moved the last of the biscuits from out of Muffy's reach.

'Very true,' Kitty agreed.

Alice slipped into the room and Kitty rose to embrace her friend. She scanned Alice's thin face anxiously hoping to see her looking brighter than when she had left her.

'I'm right glad as you'm back. We were all worried when you sent that card,' Alice rebuked her as she took one of the small chairs near to Kitty.

'Well, here we are, safe and sound.' Kitty smiled at her friend. 'How are you now?'

Alice blushed. 'I've been helping Miss Lucy with one or two jobs as she needed doing. And, well, while I've been here, we got to talking.' She halted and looked at Lucy as if for encouragement.

'Oh yes, what's going on?' Kitty asked, looking at her cousin.

'Tell her your plans, Alice,' Lucy urged, her eyes sparkling.

'Well.' Alice paused and took a deep breath before plunging on. 'I'm going to leave the Dolphin.'

Kitty froze for a moment, not sure she had heard her correctly. 'Leave the Dolphin? Darling, what will you do? Don't tell me you are leaving Dartmouth too?' she asked.

Lucy giggled. 'Not quite. Alice and I have had our heads together while you were gone.'

'What's happening?' Matt caught the end of the conversation and looked enquiringly at them all.

'You know I've always been good at sewing, doing alterations and making dresses and things?' Alice's cheeks were now as red as the strawberry jam on Kitty's scone.

'Yes, you are quite brilliant,' Kitty agreed.

'I'm thinking of setting myself up in business. Finding a little place as a workshop and doing just that kind of thing,'

Alice explained. 'You know as things didn't work out as I'd hoped with, well, you know.' Her hands fluttered.

Kitty nodded. She noticed Matt stayed silent on this matter since she was aware that he perhaps knew more of Robert Potter's side of things than she or even Alice did.

'I think it's inspired. Miss Alice Miller, seamstress.' Kitty clapped her hands together. 'You will certainly get lots of work from me. My dresses are always too long.'

Alice looked relieved by Kitty's enthusiasm. 'You and Captain Bryant will help me look for suitable premises? Our Dolly will help with my bookkeeping, but I think I shall need a hand to find a place and sort out a lease.'

'It'll be our pleasure. The least we can do after everything you've done for us,' Matt assured her.

Kitty smiled gratefully at her husband. It seemed that the winds of change were certainly starting to blow, even in their small corner of the world. A shiver ran through her and she wondered what else was to come for the future. But at least they could enjoy one more lovely afternoon at Enderley, surrounded by their family and friends.

A LETTER FROM HELENA DIXON

Dear reader,

I want to say a huge thank you for choosing to read *Murder on the French Riviera*. If you enjoyed it and would like to keep up to date with all my latest releases, just sign up at the following link. Your email address will never be shared, and you can unsubscribe at any time. There is also a free story – *The Mysterious Guest*, starring Kitty's friend, Alice.

www.bookouture.com/helena-dixon

The Negresco Hotel is a well-known fixture in Nice. These days it is just as gorgeous as it was when Kitty and Matt visited and is full of works of art. I have tweaked a few little elements of the hotel to make it work for the story but you can still visit all of the places in the book today. Bar Twenty-Eight, however, is entirely fictional! I do hope you loved *Murder on the French Riviera* and, if you did, I would be very grateful if you could write a review. I'd love to hear what you think, and it makes such a difference helping new readers to discover one of my books for the first time. You can get in touch on social media or through my website.

Thanks,

Helena

KEEP IN TOUCH WITH HELENA

www.nelldixon.com

ACKNOWLEDGEMENTS

My thanks as always to my lovely Tuesday zoomers who are so fabulous and supportive. During the course of writing this book we lost Lynn, our funny, brilliant friend. She provided so much information about Nice to help me write this book and make it come to life. Lynn was one of life's wonderful people. She loved music, pink, flamingos, scurrilous jokes and bad puns. All of us are determined to Live Like Lynn from now on. My thanks also go to the incredible Maisie and team Kitty at Bookouture and my brilliant agent, Kate Nash.

PUBLISHING TEAM

Turning a manuscript into a book requires the efforts of many people. The publishing team at Bookouture would like to acknowledge everyone who contributed to this publication.

Audio
Alba Proko
Sinead O'Connor
Melissa Tran

Commercial
Lauren Morrissette
Hannah Richmond
Imogen Allport

Cover design
Debbie Clement

Data and analysis
Mark Alder
Mohamed Bussuri

Editorial
Maisie Lawrence
Ria Clare

Copyeditor
Jane Eastgate

Proofreader
Shirley Khan

Marketing
Alex Crow
Melanie Price
Occy Carr
Cíara Rosney
Martyna Młynarska

Operations and distribution
Marina Valles
Stephanie Straub

Production
Hannah Snetsinger
Mandy Kullar
Jen Shannon

Publicity
Kim Nash
Noelle Holten
Jess Readett
Sarah Hardy

Rights and contracts
Peta Nightingale
Richard King
Saidah Graham

Made in the USA
Las Vegas, NV
10 August 2024